JUDE'S GENTLE GIANTS

Written by Les Graham

Copyright © 2014 by Les Graham

ISBN # 978-0-9904775-0-1

Library of Congress Control Number: 2014914414

Published by:
>BRITCHIN BOOKS from Colfax Publishing
>616 270th Ave NW Suite G
>New London, MN 56273

Printed by:
>Lakeside Press
>PO Box 1075
>Willmar, MN 56201 USA
>(320) 235-5849

Table of Contents

Acknowledgements

I was amazed at the work and time needed by others to get this novel up and running. My wife Kathy, after many 'Kathy can you check this' still calls me her husband. I'm very blessed to have her. Thank you Kathy!

My children, Kale, Ben, Rebecca and their spouses were asked many times for input and counsel. I thank them for their love, patience, support and believing in this endeavor. Ben came up with the titles of both books.

My very first editor, Rachel Westby, took the very RAW first draft, waded through it and still kept her sanity! She gave me moral support and did a great job. Thank you Rachel!

My second editor, April Kummrow, added many thoughtful suggestions. She was very thorough and professional. Thank you April!

Mark and Marie Peterson were the final editors and led me through some significant changes while keeping the story true. Their insight was very important and even though I had doubts at times, thank you for sticking to your guns!

Also, my sister Mona was one of my many test readers and gave me some great input. She also listened to me ramble on the phone about how excited I was with the project.

Lakeside Press designed the awesome cover and designed the layout of the inside of the book. Their team was easy to work with and treated the project like it was their own. Thank you for your professionalism!

Mike Bregel the illustrator worked under a very short time period to meet my deadline. His patience was greatly appreciated when I needed a few sketches revised. The illustrations add so much to the book. Thank you, Mike!

Thank you also to Mark Peterson Photography www.markpetersonphoto.com for taking the cover photo and to Chris Nye www.nyeswebdesign.com for designing my website.

Most important, I thank God for ALL He provides and for trusting me with this story. With God's help, I was able to write this story and persevere.

God Bless you all!
Les Graham

Endorsements

"Growing up on a farm in Minnesota, it was easy to identify with this story. Full of adventure, emotion and a sincere Christian message. Graham writes with a real understanding of his subject. I'm looking forward to the sequel."

Roger Schmidt
Good News Book Store

"I truly fell in love with the characters in this warm, wholesome depiction with Biblical reference of a Christian family aspiring to live as God intended. It actually encouraged me to examine my own life as I became part of the family. Very difficult to put down, and looking forward to his next book."

Mona Tomaszewski

"Integrity comes wholesomely through in this homespun, true to life novel. Family love, and sure discipline, hard work, and dedication are values so aptly portrayed in the storylines. Anyone of us can fondly identify with the hero Jude and villains Greg and Judy. I became part of the story as teenage Jude went through many trials, horse raising and training, and maintained his eloquent faith in the Lord. Each aspect of a Godly life is portrayed in this fetching novel."

David W. Helmstetter

"This story is a heartwarming journey of youthful adventure, laughs, danger, and the unpredictable twists and turns of life. This book is ideal for young men, who will undoubtedly enjoy Jude's rat hunting, hockey playing, and horse rearing, however it appeals to a wide audience ranging from children to adults. There is truly something for everyone in this enjoyable and touching novel."

April Kummrow
High School Success Coordinator

"Les' book was an excellent surprise that could intrigue even a non-reader. Because the characters seemed so real, I felt along with them and was engaged in the story. What a fantastic book that glorifies God! Give this book a try; you won't be disappointed."

Emily Molemaar
Teacher

Chapter 1
"Thinking Back"

It was another round of tests that had me cooped up in the St. Cloud hospital. God is not a big fan of self pity, but that particular day I had a hard time not feeling sorry for Jude Bonner. I tried praying, reading, playing solitaire but I could not stay focused on any of them. I was having an old fashioned pity party as I gazed out the window of my hospital room.

The sky was a deep blue and not a cloud in sight. Just as a nurse opened my door, I thought I caught a glimpse of something floating in the air. As she took my vitals she stood between the window and me and blocked any chance for me to figure out what I had seen. As soon as she left, I looked out the window again. I saw another one, a thistle seed, dancing through the air in slow motion. A little smile came across my face as I watched it fade away into the sky. Thistle seeds travel with the air currents in the fall, and fall is my favorite time of the year.

It's funny how God works at times. That thistle seed took me back to my high schools days. I didn't know it at the time, but those high schools days were pretty simple compared to now. Sure I was ridiculed for my faith in Jesus Christ. Keeping my grades up did not come easy for me, and I had a lot of chores to do at home. To top it off, I developed a growing obsession with a Percheron draft mare named Molly.

As I watched more thistle seeds float by, I thought back to what God did with that obsession. Yes, God answered my high school prayers, the joy it brought me, along with all of the hard work and challenges. I lay there thinking back to the wins and losses of coming of age.

Chapter 2
"School Days"

It was a Friday afternoon, and there I was sitting in school, where I was supposed to be paying attention, yet as I gazed out the window, God's creation was calling me. It was a fall day in 2005 I would not soon forget. The air was crisp, the trees had their red, orange and yellow leaves. This was my favorite time of the year. I was watching thistle seeds drift by and leaves falling from the trees when suddenly a slimy spit wad hit me right in the ear. As I looked around, Harold Posey and Perry Carper were trying not to laugh. Harold and Perry were my best friends. I checked to see if the coast was clear and shot one back at Harold but missed.

I went into stealth mode and had Perry all lined up when Mrs. Norman called my name. "Jude Bonner, you may come to the front of the class!" Now how did she see me? Mrs. Norman was our senior high English teacher who demanded respect and actually deserved it. She had taught for many years and still had a lot of compassion for each and every student. Why, I bet she would teach without pay. I quietly walked to the front, as everyone else laughed.

"Now, students, settle down. Mr. Bonner has a special talent to share with us!" When she said this, it meant she was going to humiliate a student in front of his friends. For some reason this had a profound effect on your behavior! One either performed her request or had to visit the office of Mr. Haas, the principal, and believe me, that was an easy decision.

"Well, Mr. Bonner, I think the class would like to hear a song. Isn't that right students?"

A chorus of voices answered back. "Yes, we would, Mrs. Norman." While Mrs. Norman thought of a song, I turned twelve shades of red.

"How about 'I'm a Little Teapot'? What do you think class? Wouldn't that be nice?" She had the words for several songs in her desk drawer. While she looked for the song, Harold and Perry started chanting, "Jude, Jude, Jude!"

She looked up over the top of her glasses. "Mr. Posey and Mr. Carper, maybe we should make it a trio."

"Mrs. Norman, with all due respect, I think Jude would be highly offended by sharing this grand stage!" Harold quipped.

I was trying my best to give Harold and Perry a menacing look, but all I could do was smile as they sat there untouched. Mrs. Norman gave me the sheet music for "I'm a Little Teapot."

"Okay," she directed me, "now face the class and sing loudly. Remember, if they don't like it, you get to do another song."

Have you ever tried singing when pretty much everyone in the room is hoping you'll fail? My throat felt like I had a lump of hot coal in it. I raised my head up and quickly scanned the class and caught the eyes of Greg Shants and Judy Clemons. Greg and Judy were classmates that I really had a hard time respecting, to put it kindly. They were just plain, nasty people, always looking for a fight. God has a plan for everybody, even Greg and Judy, I just wasn't sure why God had them in my life all the time.

I felt naked as a baby standing up there. I said a little prayer and started singing. The first couple of words sounded like a baby pig squealing, but I gained my confidence and made a strong finish. The class cheered as I hustled back to my chair.

I was just sitting down and starting to get my dignity back, when I heard Mrs. Norman say, "Mr. Bonner, who said you could return to your chair?" Using me as an example was her way of keeping control of the situation. I headed back to the front of the room.

"Okay class it's up to you, did Mr. Bonner sing well enough or do we need another song?"

As soon as Mrs. Norman asked, Judy screamed out. "That was horrible, he didn't try hard at all! Make him sing again."

Of course Greg chimed right in. "Yes, that was super weak, he was off key the whole time."

"Okay class raise your hands if Jude needs to sing again."

The bell was ringing for the end of class as I watched four hands come up: Judy, Greg, Perry and Harold. I gave Perry and Harold a dirty look and didn't even bother with Greg and Judy.

"Mr. Bonner it looks like you passed, however, you will stay after class. The rest of you are excused." I was thankful as sometimes the class would force you to sing a second time.

"Jude, I trust you've learned from your solo today," Mrs. Norman said. "I have a lot of hope for you as you are usually a pleasure to have in class. My, Greg and Judy sure seem to be out to get you!"

"You're not kidding, Mrs. Norman, I've tried to get along with them but it only gets worse. Someday, I should let them have it!"

"I'm sure God will deal with that some day if you let him. Now you get home and have a fun weekend. And with a voice as good as yours, I want to hear you do the National Anthem at a sporting event soon!" I was just out the door when Mrs. Norman said, "Jude, maybe you would like to sing 'I'm a Little Teapot' for the homecoming dance."

"I'll think about it, but I'm sure I'll have laryngitis that weekend. Thanks Mrs. Norman."

Harold and Perry were waiting outside the door. They tried not to laugh but couldn't hold it back as we gave out high fives. "Dude, I feel real bad that you had to go through that," Harold said as we walked towards the bus. "You're lucky she didn't have you sing it twice! Dude, I just don't understand what made you start shooting spit wads at Perry and me! Perry and I were trying to get a legit education and you're slinging spit wads our way."

"Yeah, right, Harold!" I pushed his shoulder with my free hand. "This is my bus, see you later. Maybe we can get together Saturday night and go rat hunting or something. As soon as I get home, I'm going to Quin Olson's place."

As I got on the bus, Harold followed me and yelled to the other kids that I had a song for them. I chased Harold away and slunk down in my seat with everyone staring at me. Before the bus left I sat there thinking about my two friends, Harold and Perry. What a crew! Harold was like six foot four, husky and very vocal. Perry was skinny as a rail and non vocal. Not that he was shy, he just didn't talk much.

I rode the bus home from school with my mind hooked on an idea! The bus door opened, and, like a marble out of a sling shot,

I sprinted to the house.

"Mom, I'm home! You got anything to eat?" As always, she knew what kind of hunger a sixteen-year-old works up when he's fretting over his dreams! She had my usual graham crackers and milk waiting. I was about ready to dig in, when Mom asked the age-old question, "Did you wash your hands?" I guess that's one reason why God made mothers: to keep the soap companies in business.

As she sat down with me, she asked, "Jude, so tell me about school today?"

"It was fine, Mom, but I'm in a hurry to get over to Mr. Olson's to see how Molly is doing."

"Now, Jude, are you sure you're not a bother to Mr. Olson? Remember, you have your own chores to do, and your dad's taking me on a date tonight! And, besides, are you ever going to get that Molly creature off your mind?"

"But, Mom, she's so beautiful and graceful! Someday I'm gonna own one just like her."

As I soaked my last bunch of graham crackers, I got dreaming again with the thinking fever about Molly, and my crackers fell in the milk. It's terrible what a thinking man has to go through!

"Jude Bonner, get your fingers out of that milk!" Mom yelled. "Are you going to wait for your sister to go with you to Quin's place?"

"Mom, do I have to?"

"Oh, I guess not. She's going to Julie's to stay overnight."

With that I wiped my mouth on my sleeve, and off I went! Mom hated it when I used my sleeve so she chased me out the door, but not without asking for a hug before sending me on my way.

I was pretty lucky to have parents like Mom and Dad. They showed sis and me lots of love and let us know they loved each other. We lived on a dairy farm near Belgrade, Minnesota. Belgrade is a small town in central Minnesota with a population of around seven hundred. Our home farm was a beautiful place dad's grandfather settled when he came over from Scotland in the 1880s. Our yard was full of burr oak trees, and to the west was a pine wind break Grampa had planted. We milked fifty Holstein cows, raised a few pigs, and even had some Barred Rock laying hens. Oh, and I almost forgot Old Fuzz! Fuzz was our wirehaired fox terrier dog. She was my best friend and tough as a two-dollar steak.

Quin Olson was our neighbor to the east and always had been since I could remember. He was a Minnesota bachelor, and both his parents had passed away in the 1970s.

Quin was a good man, a hard worker, and had one of the best dairy herds in the county. He was older than Dad, so Dad would look to him at times for advice. We always had him over for family gatherings and holidays. Mom would try to make pie when he was over, and there would always be one extra piece that she would send home with him. We would give him heck as he walked out the door with our piece of pie. The next day I'd ask him if he had eaten it. "Why certainly. Yep, I ate it when I got home," Quin would always say.

Fuzz's real name was Sunday because that's the day she was born. I called her Fuzz because she was a scruffy wirehaired fox terrier. She was the runt of the litter. Dad always said to take the runt because they have to fight harder for a nursing spot so they'll be a scrapper for life. That theory sure proved true with old Fuzz. She was the toughest dog I'd ever seen! She came a running out from under the porch wagging her stubby little tail and rolled over so I could scratch her belly. "Fuzz, how you doing? If I'm not careful I'll end up spoiling you! Come on, let's head over to see Molly." She and I were like Siamese twins, inseparable. Besides, I had to cross our pasture to get to Mr. Olson's place, and she could keep our Holstein bull in line. As we walked along in the pasture, several red tail hawks screamed as they soared through the clear blue sky.

"It's October, Fuzz, and the hawks are starting to migrate. You know, if you weren't so scruffy looking, they just might come after you." As we crossed the fence, Herbie our Holstein bull let out a low bellow, the kind that sends a chill up the spine! Dad always said never to trust a Holstein bull because they think you're after their girlfriends, the cows. I took a few more steps and Fuzz started growling. I looked around and Herbie was heading our way and I mean right now! I was too far from the fence to make a run for it so I turned and faced him while slowly stepping backwards. He trotted up with his massive head swinging from side to side and stopped about twenty feet away. He looked back towards the cows and took a few more steps in our direction. I looked down at Fuzz and she was on red alert with ears erect and her beady little eyes locked on his every move. He pawed at the ground with his front legs as he grunted at us. I wasn't sure what to do? If I sent Fuzz after him that could really set him off, and so far he didn't seem all that upset. I kept sneaking back while I still faced him. He threw more dirt and spun in a circle and kicked in the air and headed our way. He was only ten feet away when I sent Fuzz. "Sic'em Fuzz!" Fuzz dove into action immediately! Herbie stopped right in his tracks as Fuzz went right at his head barking like crazy. She was darting in and out as Herbie started backing up. He would swing that massive head at her and she would just duck. "Get, him Fuzz!" It was comical to see a fifteen pound mutt backing up eighteen hundred pounds of Holstein bull. It wasn't long and Fuzz had Herbie running back to his female friends.

I turned back and headed east again and soon Fuzz caught up with me. I reached down and picked her up. "Fuzz, you need to pick on someone your own size next time." She was licking me in the face. "Quit it, Fuzz, you scroungy mutt!" I rubbed her ears as I carried her against my chest.

We made it to the other side and into our alfalfa field. It was just a quarter mile to get to Mr. Olson's. I could hardly wait. It's kind of strange if you think about it, that at each end of our alfalfa field was power. Molly at one end and Herbie at the other end, kind of like good versus evil.

"Fuzz, look at all these gopher mounds! You and I better start trapping again." Dad paid Fuzz and me twenty-five cents for each gopher we caught and the township chipped in another dollar. This was fair income if we stuck with it. Dad always said if you wanted something out of life you had to work for it. Fuzz got pretty good at locating fresh mounds to set traps. Her little tail got going a mile a minute when she found a hot gopher mound. We would set a trap and by the next day we usually had one. Dad certainly appreciated it because the mounds were very tough on the haying equipment. We even caught an albino gopher one year. I put it in our freezer to save it for a taxidermist. Mom was fixing supper once and brought a bag in from the freezer, and you should have heard her when she saw it was my gopher! That episode cost me some explaining and a week of doing dishes.

As we ran through the alfalfa, I thought of all the time spent in this field. You can never forget the smell of freshly cut hay. A few days after cutting the hay, it is dry and ready to bale. Loading the bales and stacking them in the barn is hard work, but sort of fun in a way, maybe because it is so necessary to a dairy farm.

Dad prided himself in baling at just the right time. If you bale too early, the hay is too green and it will get moldy and dusty. Bale too late and all the leaves fall off the stems of the alfalfa. This is the field where I really learned to work hard. Either keep up stacking bales or slow the whole process down. Dad was fair, but he expected my best. One day we baled two thousand bales, so far a family best. Dad started me on the hay rack when I was fourteen years old. When I got older and stronger, I was up in the hay loft. That move can separate the men from the boys! One time we baled up a skunk and oh boy that brought tears to the eyes. The hay loft in June has to be the hottest place I've ever been. Gramps always said it was hotter than the devil's tavern! Gramps also thought that every kid, even the city kids, should have to bale hay or pick rocks. It was good training for them, like training a pair of horses.

Chapter 3

"Mr. Olson and the Offer"

Molly trotted past the fence, nostrils flaring, hooves pounding, and flicking mud behind with each step. I stood and watched in awe as she made several rounds in the corral. The muscles rippled beneath her shiny black coat, her mane trailing like milk weed seeds blowing in the fall breeze. With each step her hoof bottoms pointed straight up towards the sky. She floated by me as if on air! She held her head high, knowing she had an audience. Like me, Molly could smell fall in the air. Fall meant no more pesky horse flies or deer flies and she was celebrating! I called to her, and she came over to me and put her nostrils next to my mouth. I blew in her nose and she whinnied. Mr. Olson taught me this and most horses love it. She took off for another round, spinning and kicking the air and farting for the first couple steps. As she passed me, the ground shook as each hoof met the ground. She was alive. You could see the gleam in her eyes and her ears searching for every sound she could possibly take in.

I whistled and she hesitantly came back my way. She wasn't sure if she was done with her performance. "Molly, you big showoff, you act like we came over just to see you!" I talked to her in a quiet voice and she rested her massive head on my shoulder. Molly was a two-thousand-pound Percheron draft horse mare. She was nine years old, pure black, with a white snip on her forehead. She was a gentle giant.

Her ancestors long ago were called "War Horses." They were bred in LaPerche, France for carrying the heavy armor to protect the horse and knight. The armor with man weighed around 500 pounds. When these horses were replaced in war by the use of gun powder, they were used for farming and hauling freight. In 1839 they were imported to the United States of America.

Mr. Olson's great grandfather started with a team of Percheron mares in 1880. Ever since then, there has always been a team of Percherons on the Olson farm. Molly's mate for hitching was a Percheron gelding named Ladd. He was pretty laid back, well broke, and matched well in size with Molly, but did not have the charisma that Molly possessed.

As I stood there talking to Molly, Mr. Olson came over and said, "How you doing Jude?"

"Oh, I'm doing fine. I hope you're doing well also."

"Sure am, but as often as you are over here petting Molly, I'm surprised you haven't rubbed all her hair off!"

"I sure do like her and I hope you don't mind me being over here."

"Well you know you're welcome anytime Jude. How are your parents doing?"

"They're fine as always. They are going on a date tonight so I don't have a lot of time."

"Jude, you and that dog never miss a beat do ya, but I reckon that's the way it should be."

"Mr. Olson, can I brush and curry her?"

"I don't see why not, but old Ladd is going to get jealous if you don't favor him a little too."

"Okay, Mr. Olson, I'll do both of them. I guess that's only fair." I ran to the tack room and grabbed the brush and curry comb. Horses love to be curried. A curry comb is made up of stiff metal bands with serrations to dig into their hides. I started currying Ladd only to have Molly pull the brush from my back pocket and nudge me in the back. She was always seeking attention.

"Molly, you old nag, if you don't leave me alone I'll send you to the glue factory!" Back in the olden days many horses were sent there when they could no longer pull their weight.

Mr. Olson put his shoulder under Molly's neck and his arm

over her bridge of her nose and said in his soft voice, "Now don't you go shipping my Molly off to no glue factory because you'd end up killing two horses in one!"

"Oh, Molly you know I would never do that, but I guess you're big enough for two horses."

"That's not what I meant, Jude. Yah see she's with foal. I would think a fine horseman like you would have noticed she's putting on weight."

"Are you serious, Mr. Olson?"

"Why certainly! Do you think I would tell a lie in front of Molly and Ladd?"

"That's great, Mr. Olson! Why didn't you tell me sooner?"

"Well, Molly and I had an agreement to keep it top secret till fall. Never know if she might lose the foal in the summer heat."

"Molly, you old nag, you're going to be a mama." I gave her a big hug and blew in her nose again. She took off for a spin like she owned the world. As Molly was showing off some more, Mr. Olson continued talking.

"Jude, I was thinking that I could use some help this fall and winter with chores. You wouldn't know of some kid that would be interested in helping an old man out, would you?"

Mr. Olson knew dang well I was the kid he was referring to, but he was playing me for a lazy city kid.

"Now this kid would have to work hard and take responsibility, but I don't reckon you'd know anyone like that?"

"Well, Mr. Olson, I could probably find someone to fit the bill, but the pay would have to be mighty high to work with an old fart like you!"

"Why you little rascal." Mr. Olson grabbed me in fun and shook me up a little.

"If you are interested in that offer be sure to let me know, but talk it over with your parents first."

"I will, but I better get home and do my chores before Dad skins me alive!"

"Now, don't you think you should ask what type of pay I'm offering so you can tell your parents?"

"Mr. Olson, I know you will be more than fair so I'm not too worried."

"Well, you know, times are tough and I hate to part with my cash, so you don't suppose you'd consider finding room for Molly's foal in your barn and consider that paid in full?"

At first I thought he was just kidding me, but then I looked him in the eye and realized he was serious!

"But I suppose you really couldn't handle a well bred foal. It might get in the way of computer games or something."

"Mr. Olson, I sure would like to try. This is a dream come true!"

"Jude, you know I was ribbing you about not being good enough to raise a foal. You're a pretty good kid. That's something you should thank your parents for. So, that's my offer. Whatever comes out that old nag of a mare is yours for helping with chores this winter. You think it over and let me know the next time you're over."

"I will, Mr. Olson. This is too good to be true. Thank you very much! What do you think she's going to have?"

"God only knows at this time. Now you better get home before your Dad blames me and Molly for kidnapping!"

I ran over to Molly and gave her one last hug. "Now Molly, you be careful. You're taking care of a foal in that big belly! See ya later Mr. Olson and thanks so much."

"Fuzz, did you hear that? We'll soon be in the horse business!" I ran home thinking of how to present this opportunity to Mom and Dad.

"Fuzz, we have to deliver this type of information in a certain way so they understand the importance of it. I'll have to convince them that we need a foal, how much it will help with chores, and that I'll pay for all the shots, vet bills, and hoof trimmings.

"What do you think? Does that sound like a good plan?" I was so intent on planning that I tripped over a huge gopher mound and did a face plant into the ground. I got up, checked to see if anyone was looking, spit the dirt out of my mouth, and noticed I tore my pants.

"Now look what I did Fuzz. You're supposed to be watching out for me a little better than that. Now Mom's got some mending to do, right when I'm bringing this important proposition to them. What poor timing! I guess I can change my pants and hide these for a while until after I ask them." So that was the plan. I'd sneak in the back way so Mom and Dad wouldn't see me.

By the time I figured this all out I was home, so Fuzz and I went in the back way and there were Mom and Dad standing right there to greet me! They were supposed to be in the barn.

"Hi Mom, hi Dad. I thought you'd be in the barn!"

"Jude Bonner, my goodness what happened to your trousers? Did that Molly horse bite you or something? And look at your face, it's all grass stained!" Mom laughed.

"Me and Fuzz kind of fell over a gopher mound."

Dad looked stern. "Remember, I have a very important date with a very pretty woman tonight so you've got chores."

"I know Dad, but what time do you think you two will get home?" I looked at them. "I need to discuss something with you and Mom real bad!"

"It might be pretty late, but if you would like we can check on you when we get home to see if you're still awake."

"Don't you worry Dad, I'll be awake! You have a good time with that pretty woman and we'll talk when you get home!"

I changed my clothes and headed to the barn. Dad was just starting to let me do chores on my own. Fuzz was with me like always. She could keep Herbie in line and she helped get stubborn cows into their stalls. Milking went fine until I got to number twenty-eight. She was the meanest cow this side of the Mississippi. Dad said she teaches a person what life is like at times, kicking when you're not ready! Well, I was pondering about the foal, in somewhat of a daze, when she let a foot fly! She hit me like a sledge hammer with her left back foot, right on my thigh. Oh my gosh, the pain! It's amazing how quickly you wake up and focus on your duties when you get hit with that cloven foot. It seems like old number twenty-eight took a lesson from Mrs. Norman's school of punishment!

Dad always says, "You have to pay for your education!" I limped through the rest of milking wondering how big the bruise would be. After milking, Fuzz and I did calf chores. We were finished and on the way back to the house when I noticed I'd left the gate open to the sow pen. All three sows were out. I must have left the gate open when I was feeding them. This was the last thing I needed to deal with! I stood there wondering how to get them back in. I thought for awhile and came up with an idea that might work.

"Fuzz, sic 'em!" That was Fuzz's cue to round up the sows. Without her it would be pretty tough since they were in our standing corn field. "Fuzz go get them old sows." Fuzz got all excited and started smelling the ground and took off for the corn field. I was dead quiet hoping for that sweet sound of Fuzz chasing pigs back home. I started pacing back and fourth, waiting, and soon I heard a sow squealing bloody murder! Fuzz was unbelievable. She had all three sows heading back at the same time, they were sounding like a screaming freight train headed downhill! The two Durocs showed up first with the Hampshire following close behind and old Fuzz hanging on her jowls like a giant tick! They shot into that pen faster than greased lightning. Old Fuzz let go and I closed the gate! That was a sight I'll never forget. That Hampshire had a look of terror in her eyes with Fuzz hanging from her left cheek.

I knelt down by old Fuzz and rubbed her ears to thank her. "You know Fuzz, you're pretty special. You do all the work and all you ask for is an ear rubbing! Fuzz, don't you think you were a little rough on that old sow? How about I get rough with you?" I grabbed her by the mouth and shook, that's her signal to play fight. "I'm not that old sow." With that, we play fought for a while until she got a little too rough. "Now settle down, Fuzz. My hands aren't as thick as that Hampshire's hide!" A hog's hide is so thick it really doesn't hurt them when Fuzz grabs them, but it sure gets their attention. With that done I double checked the other gates and reviewed my chores. I couldn't afford any other mishaps because this was the night I had to ask Mom and Dad about Molly's foal!

Chapter 4
"The Sales Pitch"

When I got to the house I fed Fuzz and checked her water. "You sure deserve dinner tonight after that sow herding episode." I scratched her ears as she dove into her supper. "Fuzz, we've got a very important case to present to Mom and Dad tonight. How do you think we should go about it?" Fuzz just sat there and looked at me with her beady little eyes, then licked my hand. "Well, old girl, I think I'll start by talking with Harold. You get some rest now and remember no sneaking up into bed with me tonight. We have to be on our best behavior."

I fixed myself a couple of peanut butter, cheese, and mayonnaise sandwiches. This had become one of my favorite sandwiches since Gramps gave me one after working all day. I thought he was crazy, but when you're a growing boy and that's the only thing to eat, what else do you do?

I couldn't wait to tell the good news so I called Harold. "Harold you'll never guess what Quin Olson said tonight when I was over there!"

"I know he said we could go rat hunting, but we've done that before so what's the big deal?"

"No it's much bigger than that! You've got to help me do some planning. Molly's in foal!"

"Well, Pal," he said with a little sarcasm in his voice, "what's that got to do with you and me planning?"

"Please listen. Mr. Olson told me I can have the foal for

helping him with chores this winter! But I have to ask my parents, so we need to plan a good way of presenting this to Mom and Dad so they say yes!"

"Why didn't you say that sooner? Are they home right now?"

"Nope, that's why we can talk. Dad took Mom on a date tonight."

"You're right, Jude, this is pretty important stuff. When I need a favor I always make sure my room is clean and help Mom in the kitchen by picking up after myself."

"That's good thinking Harold, but I'd better get going. I'll call you about rat hunting tomorrow."

"Yeah Pal, don't forget to brush your teeth and wash behind them ears. Remember, mothers can spot dirt on a flea but they can't say no to a clean kid!"

"Thanks, see you later."

I was pondering what to do next when it hit me that in all my excitement, I hadn't talked to God about this. I knelt right there. "God, I'm sorry for not thinking of you sooner. I sure do thank you for today, especially the part at Mr. Olson's place, and if you can help me with this foal thing I'd be mighty thankful, amen!"

The phone started ringing and I thought it was Harold calling me back to say he had a different idea for me. It turned out to be Mr. Olson.

"Jude, is that you?"

"Yes Mr. Olson."

"Well I was thinking of hitching Molly and Ladd tomorrow to spread a few loads of manure, maybe you could help?"

"I'll check with my parents when they get back home and let you know in the morning. Thanks for the offer. I'll maybe see ya tomorrow."

"Why certainly, that's fine Jude. Remember you've got chores to do for your parents first. Goodbye."

One of Mr. Olson's favorite sayings was "Why certainly." That was his way of saying yes.

I went into action right away; first I cleaned my room, then the dishes, and I even took the garbage out to the barn gutter. The whole time my mind was figuring how to bring my proposal to Mom and Dad. Then I'd start dreaming of a foal on our place! I thought I was ready for them to get home when I realized Mom always scrubbed the floors on Saturdays. I went to the utility room and looked for the broom and dust pan to sweep the floor.

I found the soap that she used to scrub, read the label, and mixed up a solution. I started scrubbing on my hands and knees. Man, this was not a lot of fun! I was about halfway done when old Fuzz decided to help me. She snuck up to me and put her head under my arm and started licking my face!

"Now Fuzz, how's a man to get work done with a mutt like you licking him in the face?" All I could do was laugh and the more I laughed the more excited she got. I finally had to send her outside. I finished the floors and put the bucket in the utility room where Mom could see it when she got home. Maybe this way she would notice I had done the floors.

It was getting later and later. I thought they would never get home. I went to my room and decided to write down the positive and negative things that could happen if we had Molly's foal. Dad taught me to write things down when you have a tough decision to make so you can see it from both sides of the fence. Well, you can guess I didn't have a whole lot of negatives but I had plenty of positives. With the list to show Mom and Dad, they would know I did my homework.

I was getting pretty tired. I think scrubbing the floors had worn me out. I was fighting sleep big time so I decided to climb in bed soon. I brushed my teeth, took a shower, even cleaned behind my ears a second time, and knelt by my bed for my evening prayers. When I knelt I could sure feel the pain from number twenty-eight. I should have put some ice on it.

"Lord, you are an awesome God and I thank you for today. I ask you to bless Mom and Dad's time together as they are out on the town this evening. And I thank you for my parents. And Lord, thank you for Mr. Olson. He is such a neat man. And Lord, again I'd like your guidance in this foal situation. Maybe you could help Mom and Dad to see the need for a horse like I do. I pray this through your son Jesus Christ, amen."

With that I climbed into bed only to realize that, now that fall was in the air, I needed another blanket. Now there is nothing worse than getting back out after you're in bed, so I lay there procrastinating about getting up to get the blanket. Just then I heard the back door open. Mom and Dad were home. I was saved since Mom could get the blanket when she came up to my room.

I yelled down, "Mom, Dad, can you come up so we can talk? Please bring another blanket on your way up."

Mom replied, "My feet are aching, Honey. We'll just be going to bed if you don't mind."

"Mom! That ain't fair! Remember we were going to talk when you guys got home!"

"Just hold your britches on, we'll be right up! Give me time to get that blanket you so desperately need. Do you want anything else, Sir Jude Bonner?"

"Yes, but you've got to come up before I tell you."

Well, they finally made it up the stairs. I'd thought they were moving in slow motion. Mom threw the blanket over me and even brought me a glass of milk. Now that they were right here I got a little nervous about asking, so I decided to bring it up gradual like.

"Dad, how was that date you had tonight? Was she able to keep her hands off you?"

Mom responded in her special tone of voice, "Jude Bonner mind your manners!"

"Jude, who do you think we ran into at the restaurant tonight?" Dad asked, "Would you believe it was someone that said you can sing a mean teapot song?"

I assumed Dad was talking about Mrs. Norman, but I decided to play dumb.

"Gee whiz, Dad, I wouldn't have any idea," I said with a smirk.

"Well Mrs. Norman said some boy had to sing in front of class today and that he had a pretty good voice. We thought you might know who it was?"

"Oh my, I never saw that boy before, but he was a good singer and also well behaved."

With that Dad grabbed me and dragged me halfway out of bed. He knew Mrs. Norman was talking about me so it was time to rough me up a little for playing mind games with him. There I was hanging half out of bed with Mom seeing my undies! I didn't have a chance. Dad had the strength of two men and they say he never lost at arm wrestling. When he started to give me a grinder, all I could do was beg for mercy!

"Now Jude, who was that boy that sang today?" Dad was grinning but he gripped me all the harder as he asked!

There I was fighting for my dignity and laughing at the same time!

"Dad, quit it. I give up! I'll tell you if you let me go!"

Dad let go, but I had no intention of a total surrender. I crawled back under the safety of the covers as quick as I could.

"That's how you play, is it? Are you going to fight like a man, or are you going to hide behind those sheets like a little girl?"

That was all I could take. I whipped those covers back, stood on the bed, and jumped at Dad! If he wanted to fight I was going to fight him, undies and all! Dad caught me in mid air, spun me around like a rag doll and back on the bed I went. Before I could get up, Dad held me down and threatened me with a snuggy.

"If I don't get an answer these undies start going up!" Dad hollered.

"Okay, okay, I give up."

"Say Uncle!"

"Uncle, Uncle!" I laid on the bed gasping for air. "That talented young man was yours truly."

"That's better, son. For a while I thought I might have to get physical," Dad joked.

"Gee, Dad, if I wasn't in my undies I might have had to hurt you," I said as I started to laugh. Dad and I got along pretty well. He wasn't mad about the singing episode; he just used it to get a wrestling match out of me.

"Bud and Jude Bonner," Mom said, "I declare I'm not sure if you two will ever grow up."

"Now Mother, you know I have to whoop him every so often to keep him in line."

Mom said, "Jude, whatever you've got to say must be pretty important 'cause I noticed the floors were mopped!"

"What did you guys do tonight?" I changed the subject because I didn't want to go spilling the beans too early.

Dad smiled. "It's like this, when you're married to the prettiest woman in the county you can't help but have a good time."

Mom just looked at Dad. You could see the gleam in their eyes. They were in love.

Mom said, "Now quit changing the subject, Jude Bonner. Your room is clean, the kitchen is picked up, so what's on that 16 year old mind?" Mom was just kidding. She wasn't mad, but isn't it amazing how moms see right through you and your motives?

"Ya see, Mr. Olson offered me a job this winter helping him with chores."

"That's pretty nice of him to do that, but I don't see why we're having this big meeting over you helping Mr. Olson. You know your mother and I would have no problem with that. Now close your eyes and get to bed. We have some work to get done tomorrow."

"But Dad, Mr. Olson told me to talk to you guys about what he's offering to pay me."

"Jude you know he's always been fair with pay before, so why would you question it now?" Mom asked. "I hope you were polite to him."

I couldn't hold it in any longer so I blurted out, "Molly's pregnant!" I thought they would put two and two together, but they just stood there with the "deer in the headlights look."

"Mr. Olson offered me the foal that will be born next spring. I would be in the horse business with Molly's foal!"

Dad rubbed his forehead as he looked at mother. "Son, that's a mighty fine offer, but a horse can be a pretty expensive adventure."

"I made a list of the good reasons and bad reasons for accepting his offer and I have them right here."

"It's getting late." Mom said as she yawned, "We're glad you did the extra house chores and made the list but this is something we can't decide tonight. Let's pray about it and let your dad and I talk it over. We can continue this talk in the morning, honey."

We all prayed together, said our good nights, and off to bed they went. I laid there just dreaming, wondering how Mom and Dad took the news. I went over the whole bedroom talk trying to decide if things were going like I'd hoped. I set my alarm so I could help Dad with chores in the morning. I heard something coming my way and sure enough it was Fuzz, sneaking up to my bed. She knew to come quietly so Mom and Dad wouldn't hear her. They pretended not to let her up in my bed but they really didn't care that much.

"Fuzz, you old rascal, get up here and make yourself at home." I think this was the longest night I ever had to endure. First I couldn't sleep, and then came dreams of a foal in my arms, and I was training the foal...

Chapter 5
"The Answer"

When that old alarm went off it sure was tempting to stay in bed. I laid there for a few minutes as an owl called from the west grove. I said my prayers, got up and went to the barn. Of course Fuzz was right behind me.

"Morning Dad. Sorry I'm a little late. I didn't sleep all that well."

"You don't reckon it's related to any hunk of horse flesh, do ya?" Dad chided.

"No, Dad, I'm sure that had nothing to do with it."

"Why don't you go do outside chores while I finish milking? Don't forget to check the calves for scours."

"Did you and Mom talk about Mr. Olson's offer?"

"Oh, a little. The sooner you get chores done the sooner we can go in and talk with Mom."

"Okay. Make sure you pay attention to twenty-eight by the way. She got me pretty good with her left foot last night. Why don't we send her to the packing house?"

"Well, son, she's a good milker, she's pregnant, and you can learn a lot from her. Some day you will run into people like her, and you can't just ship them off to the packing house."

"I can't imagine any person that mean, Dad, but anyway, I'm going outside for chores."

"Remember Jude, Mom's got waffles when we're done."

Saturday morning waffles had become a family ritual. Mom would even make a few extra for Fuzz. Fuzz thought she owned the place, watching every move we made until she got her waffles. Mom would give them to her, always pretending that Fuzz was a lot of trouble, but deep down Mom loved Fuzz as much as the rest of us. With breakfast over, I was getting pretty nervous. So far, neither Ma nor Pa mentioned anything about the foal!

"Bud, Jude, I'm going to town to pick up Rebecca. Is there anything you guys need?" Mom asked.

"Well, young lady, we could use some teat ointment from the elevator and a couple pairs of winter chore gloves. Oh, and I almost forgot to make a list for some supplies from the lumber yard," Dad said.

Mom asked, "Do I need to take the pickup or the car?"

"That all depends on the horseman over there," Dad explained, nodding in my direction.

My ears perked up. "What list Dad? What do we need at the lumberyard?" I asked.

"If you're going to be in the horse business you've got to have a place to keep that foal."

"What, are you guys saying I can accept Mr. Olson's offer?"

"We thought you might have forgotten about it son, but your Mom and I talked it over last night and thought it should happen."

"Mom, Dad, thank you so much, it will be so much fun! I don't know if I can wait!"

Dad said, "Now remember, you have to keep your school work up this fall and winter or the deal's off. Do you understand what we are saying?"

"Sure do, Dad. I'll work extra hard. This is too good to be true. Can I go over to Mr. Olson's to tell him the good news?"

"Now just back up a little Jude. I think you better make that list for the lumberyard stuff first so we can get to making a stall for that critter before it's too cold."

"Where are we building the stall Dad?"

"I was thinking to put her in a lean type structure off the main barn by the manure spreader. That way you could fence in the south side and give her some room to roam." Dad's idea sounded perfect to me.

"Mom, thanks for the breakfast! I've got to get to work. Dad,

I'll clean the barn and spread the manure, and then we can make that list of lumber for Mom to get."

Fuzz and I headed out to the barn. I was floating on air. Just imagine, a foal on this place!

I stopped to pray, "God, thank you for this day. Please help me to stay focused on my responsibilities and oh, I almost forgot, thanks for all you give me."

I ran the barn cleaner while scraping the aisle after letting the cows out. Herbie let out one of his bellows and started checking cows for heat. I spread the manure in the alfalfa field while Fuzz ran beside me. I'm sure she thinks I couldn't do it without her. As wheels of the tractor went over some bumps, I was reminded of the gopher mounds. When I finished spreading the load, Fuzz and I set a jag of traps.

Now that I was done with those chores, Fuzz and I met Dad in the milk house. "Fuzz and I got the barn clean and the traps set. Can we figure what supplies we need for the horse stall now?"

"Sure, get a tape measure and paper so we can make the list."

We went to the south side of the barn and started figuring. I couldn't wait to start pounding nails. I think Dad could sense that I was chomping at the bit.

"What do you think we should use for lumber, Jude? And do you want tin on the sides or wood, and how much money do you have in your gopher fund?" Dad asked.

These questions were all things Dad knew, but he was getting me to think for myself. I hadn't given any thought to expense so he caught me off guard.

I felt a little foolish, all my dreams were about a foal. Now Dad was bringing reality into the equation. "If we put tin on the sides we'll have to keep the livestock away so they don't damage it. But I suppose wood could get a little expensive."

"How are you going to stop that critter from chewing everything? I like horses but they sure can chew things up."

"I know you can treat the wood so they aren't supposed to like chewing it."

"That costs money, son. Now think what else can be used that they won't chew." He saw I was stumped so he gave me a hint. "What do they have over at Grady's sawmill?"

"Gee Dad, why didn't I think of that? We could use oak instead of pine and maybe some slab wood for siding. Even a draft horse won't chew white oak."

"Now you're thinking, son. We're not after a palace. After lunch we'll run over there to see what he might have, and you should also look in the pile by the shop. Now let's measure for roof tin and get a list to your mother before she heads to town."

Dad and I measured and made a list and I gave the list to Mom. Since Dad had other things to do, Fuzz and I checked out the lumber we had by the shop. This was prime time for Fuzz because you could sometimes get a barn rat out from the pile. Barn rats are a major nuisance and actually cause many barn fires. We try to keep them in check with Fuzz and the cats. It's not every cat that will take on a full grown rat, but our tom cat was a seasoned veteran when it came to rodents. I started digging through the pile while Fuzz stood guard at the other end. She was something special. She watched every movement I made, just waiting for a rat to come out. I threw a corn cob by her and she grabbed it instantly.

"Fuzz, that wasn't fair, was it?" I said, laughing at her. Pretty soon I saw some movement between some boards.

"Fuzz, get ready!" I shouted. She could tell by my tone of voice I meant business. Somehow in the excitement I lost track of where it was. The next thing I knew it was headed for my pant leg!

"Holy buckets!" I hollered and jumped clear to the moon. "Fuzz, that was close!"

Mr. Rat snuck back into the board pile. I went back to moving boards, only this time I was a little more careful. Fuzz and I were on pins and needles. I finally saw the rat again, so I made sure it would head towards Fuzz when I poked at it. Sure enough, out came a big Norway rat.

The rat took off across the drive running for all it was worth. When a rat runs it just gives you the creeps, humpbacked, with that famous hairless tail. Fuzz was on it like greased lightning. She grabbed it with her teeth, shook it violently, and flung it in the air. She did it as fast as possible for two reasons: so she wouldn't get bit, and because sometimes two rats come out and she gets them both. It's a sight to see how quick she is. Very few rats get away from her. I took the dead rat to a cat and off she went with it.

"Fuzz, that was pretty good. It's about time you did some chores today." And of course I had to rub her ears for awhile. It was then I realized I hadn't called Mr. Olson about pitching manure. I ran to the house and called him but there was no answer.

Mom said, "Jude, I'm leaving for town. Is there anything else you need?"

"Maybe check with Dad, but I don't think so," I hollered back.

I thought about what to do about going to Mr. Olson's and decided to check with Dad. I found him in the machinery shed putting silage equipment away. I helped him with the last couple items.

"Dad, guess what Fuzz and I got out of the wood pile?"

"I suppose you found some boards. Isn't that what you usually get in a wood pile?"

"Old Fuzz and I caught a rat," I said. "It almost went up my pant leg. Say, Dad, when are we going to the sawmill? I'd like to stop at Mr. Olson's on the way."

"And may I ask why?" Dad replied sarcastically. "I suppose you want to see that Molly creature."

"Gee whiz, Dad, don't you want to see her? And we have to tell him what we decided about Molly's foal."

"All right, son. Let's go so we can be back for dinner."

We loaded up and headed out. We went to Grady's sawmill first. Grady had bought the old circle blade buzz sawmill at an auction and cut timber on the weekends. A sawmill is very intriguing so Dad was always looking for excuses to go over there. The blade is three feet in diameter and powered by a stationary cat diesel engine. The carriage is cast iron and works by pulleys and cables that run back and forth. As the blade goes through the log it hums, and the cat engine adjusts its speed by a governor. It sure is something to see, and I love the smell of fresh cut wood in the air. They had plenty of oak boards and slab wood we could use. We gave him a list and asked if we could pick up the boards later since Mom had the pickup.

I paid Grady for the lumber and he said he would put it on a hay rack we could pull home. It was funny, he was wondering why I had to pay for the lumber. I explained to him what we were building and why.

Dad said, "Son, let's head south. We've got other things to do before lunch."

"Thank you for the lumber, and we'll be back later to pick up the rack. See ya later."

As Dad and I headed for Mr. Olson's place, I was curious to

see how Dad would treat Molly, now that she was pregnant.

Dad said, "You know, son, you can learn a lot from this foal because it won't always be fun and games. You also have to remember that Molly could lose the foal this winter or at birth."

"Dad, I try not to think that way, but I suppose it could happen."

"Jude, I hope you make the best of this opportunity. Have you thought of getting your Grampa Warden to help you with the horse pen and training?"

"Holy buckets Dad, I completely forgot about Gramps! He'd be great help! I'll call him tonight."

"I know he would enjoy helping, but remember he's very fussy on doing the job right. So make sure you pay attention. Then someday you can be just as fussy on projects you do."

"Thanks, Dad. I hope he wants to help."

We were just about to Mr. Olson's when a car full of my classmates screamed passed us like we were sitting still!

"I take it they have somewhere to be in a big hurry?" Dad asked. "They'll be lucky if they don't kill themselves or someone else at that speed."

"They drive that way all the time. They're a bunch of jerks. If they crashed not too many people would miss them."

"You mean you know those kids?" Dad asked. "Do they drive like that when you're with them?"

"They go to my school, but they're 'popular kids', so I really don't spend much time with them."

"Who are they?"

"That was Nick Grudden's car, which means Greg Shants, Bill Masters, and Judy Clemons were probably with him."

"It's too bad they're in the 'in crowd' but those type of cliques were in school even when I was a kid."

"You know what I don't understand, Dad? Judy Clemons is really pretty but her personality doesn't match her looks. She is a total jerk."

"Remember what the Bible says about judging others. Just think Jude, you only have to be around her a couple hours a day, whereas she has to live with herself twenty-four hours a day, seven days a week. Just make sure you treat her good at all times and throw a few prayers her way. God has special plans for everyone."

We pulled into Mr. Olson's driveway and he was just starting

to harness Molly and Ladd. I could hardly wait for the car to stop.
I ran over as fast as I could while Dad just took his time. But I
guess that's okay; Dad lost his running legs a few years back.
Molly and Ladd were standing outside the tack room waiting
patiently for a harness. You see, Mr. Olson trains his horses to
stand without being tied to anything while he puts the harness
on them. That takes some discipline to do that. I blew in Molly's
nostrils and she whinnied like always. Mr. Olson heard Molly and
came out of the tack room to see what her problem was.

"Well, old girl what seems to be the matter?" Mr. Olson asked.
"You know, Molly, that neighbor kid was supposed to be over by
now, but I guess he really doesn't care for you." As Mr. Olson
pretended he didn't see us. "Yes Molly, if that Jude Bonner kid
ever shows up, you tell him to curry you and Ladd so we can get
to harnessing.

I could take a hint, so I ran to get the curry comb and brush. As
I brushed Molly and Ladd, they leaned into the curry comb trying
to absorb as much as possible.

Dad finally made his way over and said his howdy do's to Mr.
Olson.

"Bud Bonner it's been a coon's age since I saw you last."

"Well, Quin, you know how it is when a guy has no help at
home," as Dad winked at Mr. Olson.

"What's this I hear about a free foal for helping with chores
this winter? I'm pretty interested in filling out a job application.
I've always wanted a Percheron foal," Dad responded.

"Why certainly, Bud, I'd be glad to interview you. But you've
got some pretty stiff competition. There's talk of that Bonner kid
applying for the job too and he's quite a horseman."

I couldn't take it any more so I blurted out, "Dad and Mom
said I can take you up on your offer, Mr. Olson."

Mr. Olson said, "Why certainly, Jude, but what if your Dad
wants the job?'

"Oh, Mr. Olson, Dad probably couldn't work for such a slave
driver."

"So, come spring, God willing, you'll be in the horse business.
Now remember what my Dad always said, 'wild and woolly and
full of fleas, never curry below the knees." With that Mr. Olson
let out his hearty laugh and repeated the phrase again. I harnessed
Molly while Dad harnessed Ladd. We helped Mr. Olson hook up
to the spreader before heading home to get the lumber and start

on the horse stall.

When we got home, Mom and Rebecca were back from town. We also had company, Grandma and Grampa Warden. They said they were just passing by so they thought they would stop. I think Mom called them from town and suggested they come out for Saturday supper and to hear the news about me being in the horse business.

"Hi, Granny and Gramps!" I hollered. "What brought you out this way?"

"We heard a rumor that some kid might need some help with a pony shed." Gramps knew I wasn't getting any pony. "Now, is this pony going to get a home built or are you just going to stand here all day?" Gramps teased.

I beamed, "I suppose we might as well get started. I sure don't want to pay you for idle time." Gramps helped us many times and never took a dime for it.

"Gramps, Rebecca come on. Let me show you where the horse lean-to will be."

"Jude, Rebecca and I stopped by the library and picked up a book on draft horses you might find interesting. It has measurements on a stall and manger." Mom said.

"Great idea, Mom, Thank you! Please leave it in the truck and we'll look at it in a little while," I replied.

Granny went in the house with Mom while Dad went to start chores. Rebecca, Gramps, and I went to the south side of the barn to look things over.

Gramps said, "This looks like a pretty good area, wouldn't you say, Rebecca?"

"Gramps, I don't know all that much about horse stalls, but it looks good to me," Rebecca responded.

Dad and I were thinking the lean-to with the stall over against the barn, and we would fence all the way to the chicken coop and back. I think that will give the colt plenty of room.

"Looks good to me." Gramps replied. "Okay you two, let's go to the shop and get some tools so we can get started on this pony shed." As we headed for the shop, Gramps quizzed us on what we would need for tools. We loaded all the tools we thought we needed on a hay rack and pulled it over to where we would start.

"How big should it be, Gramps?" I asked.

"Well, how many stalls are you building?"

"Gee Gramps, I'm only getting one foal."

"Well, what if you get a mate for her some day? Now's the time to build for a team."

"Geepers, I never thought of that."

"That's why you are paying me the big bucks, so we can build a two-stall pony shed." With that we all laughed.

"Back in the day when I had horses, we allowed about a six-by-ten foot area for each tie stall. We also need to decide if you're going to have a hay manger in front of each stall. What does the book give for stall dimensions?"

Rebecca said, "I think it would be great to have hay mangers in front. It would also give you something to tie them to."

"Good thinking Rebecca!" Gramps said.

I said, "The book talks about the mangers being high enough so the horse doesn't get its feet up and over. The width of each stall should be five feet and the length seven feet. They also talk about a minimum of eight feet in height."

We started measuring and putting a few stones on the ground where the walls would be. We would step back to look and readjust the stones over and over again! We finally agreed on the total size and started stretching mason lines out. Gramps showed us how to make sure it was square by measuring the diagonals. I grabbed the post hole auger and proudly started digging the first corner post in.

"I'm going to run and get the camera for some pictures!" Rebecca shouted.

When she got back, she brought Mom with her so that Rebecca could be in the picture with Gramps and me. We were just ready to put the corner post in, so we asked Mom to wait until we had it in for the picture. Gramps, Rebecca, and I grabbed the post and put it in while Mom took a few action pictures. Then we all stood by our corner post, including Fuzz, and Mom took a still shot. That's when Granny brought out some warm chocolate chip cookies that she and Mom had just baked.

I said to Mom, "How do you expect us to get anything done with warm cookies to eat?"

We got the corner post plumbed and tied back to the main barn and the spreader lean-to. By then it was almost supper time, so Gramps helped make a list of what we were missing for parts. I did my calf chores while Gramps and Rebecca put the tools away. By then Mom was ringing the dinner bell.

As we stepped in the back door you could smell the fragrance of Mom and Granny's labor. Mom and Granny had fixed pork roast, mashed potatoes, green bean casserole, and lemon poppy seed muffins. Put all that on the table with milk right from the bulk tank and it's pretty hard to beat.

"Well Jude, when shall we work on the pony stalls again?" Gramps asked.

Dad chuckled, "What's with the pony stuff? And how many stalls does one colt need?"

"Dad, Gramps suggested we build two stalls while we're at it, just in case I get a mate for Joe some day."

Rebecca said, "How can you have a name for the foal that isn't born yet?"

"I've asked God to give me a little stud colt out of Molly."

Dad responded, "Jude, don't go counting your chickens before they hatch. Are you guys building pony stalls or Percheron stalls?"

"Bud Bonner, you know Gramps is only pulling Jude's leg about those pony stalls! Now who left room for pecan pie with homemade whipped cream?" replied Mom.

Well, I don't know of too many people that can turn down Mom's pie and homemade whipped cream. We all had a piece of pie and a few more laughs. After that Granny and Gramps went home while we cleaned up the dishes.

Chapter 6
"The Record Breaking Hunt"

The phone rang. It was Harold Posey.

"Dude, are you going rat hunting or not? Perry and I are ready to go. Should we come pick you up?"

"Harold, let me check with my parents first. Hey, Mom, can I go rat hunting with Harold and Perry?"

"That's fine but remember you have church tomorrow so don't be out too late."

"Harold, it's a go. See ya in a little bit."

I asked Mom if I could skip the last part of dishes so I could get my gun ready and my flashlight. Of course, she said that was fine. It's great to have a mom who understands the importance of rat hunting. I hurried upstairs and got my old twenty-two rifle out and some bird shot shells. I found a good flashlight and made sure the batteries were okay. Next I called Mr. Gabe Anderson to see if we could go through his barn. Gabe was a person who wasn't the neatest farmer around and didn't use any poison or baits. He also didn't have any cats, so the rats had the run of the place.

"Jude, you be careful tonight. Always know where that gun barrel is pointed," Dad said.

"Okay, Dad, maybe we'll break the record tonight."

"And just how many is that?"

"Last year around this time we shot fourteen in one night," I answered proudly.

"Well, good luck and remember we have church tomorrow."

I went outside to wait for Harold and Perry and grabbed some twine for our pant legs. You see, we always tie binder twine around the bottom of our pants so rats or mice can't climb up under our pants. Dad always tells the story of his uncle who had a rat go up his pants while shoveling corn. Dad said he never saw such a dance or heard such hollering before!

Harold and Perry finally arrived and we all packed into the cab of Harold's truck. I told them we could go to Gabe's place.

Perry said, "What if we go to Gabe's first, then over to my uncle's place, and then maybe hit Gabe's a second time."

Harold shouted, "It sounds like a plan. We're going to break the record tonight. Mr. and Mrs. Rat, you'd better look out! Yeehaw!"

"Did you bring the bucket with a lid on it to put them in?" I asked. One night we had shot nine rats and threw them in the pickup box for pictures when we got home. Before we knew it, the cats at Perry's uncle's place had jumped in and helped themselves.

Harold said, "Dude, I forgot to grab the bucket so we'll have to throw them on the cab floor for now."

I was kind of glad Harold was driving his truck since I knew Dad wouldn't appreciate a bunch of dead rats in his pickup. We got to Gabe's place and we headed towards the grainary as quietly as we could. We were loaded for bear; two rifles and one good flashlight. We had a certain pattern that we would follow, each taking turns on the flashlight. The person running the light always felt a little helpless with no rifle in his hands. With the rifles ready, we would turn the flashlight on and shine it along the top sills and hallways. Some rats will freeze in the light and others try to run. We all got to be pretty good shots over the last couple years. The tension and excitement is very thick during these episodes.

We chose the perfect night. We had a full moon, with a sharp fall bite in the air, and the rats were out in full force. Dad said rats could sense winter coming on so they were always more active in the late fall. We shot eight rats on the first trip to the grainary. We headed towards the drive-through corn crib, another hot spot. It was raised up off the ground about ten inches for air movement and this was usually a highway for rats. The worst part was that you had to lay on your belly to see the rats. It always gave me the shivers to lay down on their level.

We all snuck up as quiet as church mice, laid down, and got ready as I turned the flashlight on. All you could see was eyes and gray fur running for cover. Harold and Perry let the lead fly. They each hit two rats, which brought the total to twelve, and we hadn't even been to Perry's uncle's place yet. We loaded up the dead rats in the back of the truck for the trip and off we went. We were pretty pleased with our catch so far.

As we drove Harold sang, "You're a mean one Mr. Rat, you're evil when you run, you're as slimy as a scum, you're at the bottom of the rung, Mr. Rat, I want to fill you with a lot of lead. Yee Haw!"

"That's a great song, Harold!" Perry yelled. "When did you think of that?"

"Perry, that's one of God's gifts to Harold. It's like you or me chewing gum."

As we pulled into Perry's uncle's driveway, we saw a rat running down the driveway right in front of us.

"Floor it Harold!" Perry yelled. "Run that bad boy over!"

Harold grabbed that steering wheel like he meant business, gritted his teeth, and put the pedal to the metal. That rat looked back and tried to run faster just as the tire was making him part of the driveway.

I screamed, "We got him! Awesome dude, he's a pancake, your average road kill!"

We all jumped out with the flashlight and loaded our latest victim, number thirteen, in the back of the truck. We remembered we needed to put the dead rats in the cab so we didn't donate any to the cats. After loading them into the cab, we started towards the hog barn, again as quiet as possible and ready for action. We opened the feed room door and got one rat trying to run up the grain. It was like he was on a tread mill. We were now tied with last year's record. Things were looking pretty good. We got one more big one in the grainary. We headed to the pickup, threw all the rats in the box, and headed back towards Gabe Anderson's.

Harold was driving and just starting to sing his new song when he yelled, "Dude quit playing with my leg! What's your problem dude?"

"I'm not playing with your dang leg!" Perry shouted back.

"Sure Perry, you're trying to play footsie with Harold."

Harold was just starting into the rat song again when he let out a war whoop! "Holy crap! Something is climbing up my leg!

Turn on the flashlight!"

I turned on the flashlight and there it was, Mr. Rat climbing up Harold's pant leg with a nasty look on his face. Harold was losing it!

"Not good, not good!" Harold screamed. He was going crazy, legs flying, eyes the size of saucers, and arms swinging. Needless to say, it's pretty hard to drive and fight a rat at the same time. In the excitement, Harold went off the road and into the ditch as we all were hitting our heads on the head liner of the truck. We caught an embankment, and launched into the air. I didn't think we'd ever come back to earth!

I yelled, "Hit the brakes!"

When we finally hit the ground again Harold locked them up. You never saw three guys get out of a truck so fast in your life. You'd think someone threw a stick of dynamite in the cab.

Harold hollered, "Dudes is this legit or what? Where did Mr. Rat come from and where is he now?"

We got to thinking and the only thing we could come up with was he was the one we hit with the truck and was only stunned.

Perry said, "Harold, it's your truck so you have to be the first to get back in, you big baby."

"Get lost, Perry," Harold yelled back. "You have a rat run up your leg as you drive and see how you handle it!"

"Okay, guys, I've got an idea. "One guy opens the door, and the other two just start shooting in the cab!" I said trying not to laugh!

"Hey, that's a great idea!" Perry added.

"Not in my truck you dirt bags! You ain't throwing lead inside my cab, no way!"

"Okay guys here we go. We'll open one door and try to get him with the shovel handle." I said.

We all agreed that was the way to get him. We opened the door and looked in with the light. There he was, sitting on the middle of the seat like he owned the truck. At the time he basically did. Harold swung at him with the shovel handle and he ran under the seat.

Perry said, "Let's shoot him in the truck or we'll be here all night."

"No way! Jude, you've got Fuzz at home. Let's borrow a truck from Perry's uncle and go get Fuzz."

"Gnarly dude, gnarly," I said. "Let's do it."

So we hiked back to the farm place and borrowed a pickup to get reinforcements. When we got to my place Fuzz was pretty excited. She could sense something was up. We made our plan as we drove.

I said, "When we get there, we'll let Fuzz in the cab with Mr. Rat. That should put a crimp in his evening."

Harold questioned, "What if she can't get under or behind the seat? You know that's where it will be."

Perry explained, "If Old Fuzz can't get him out, we'll shove the shovel handle at him."

"Keep in mind Harold, we can always flood him out with a garden hose!" I was only kidding but I wanted to get Harold's dander up!

Harold yelled, "Are you crazy? I'll go in there bare handed if I have to!" Harold was foaming at the mouth. "We'll see if Fuzz is as good as you say she is."

We arrived at the scene of the crime and looked in with our flashlight. There he was on the seat again, proud as a peacock. He had also left a few deposits on the seat, right where Harold sat! Perry and I could hardly stop laughing. Harold was pretty mad.

"Mr. Rat, nobody craps on my seat. Let's get Fuzz in there before he poops all over my truck!"

Harold opened the door and I threw Fuzz in as fast as I could. We watched with the flashlight. At first Fuzz didn't know why she was in there. She just stood there for a while until she got wind of Mr. Rat, that put some wag in her tail. Her tail was going crazy as she tried to get under the seat. She couldn't fit so we ended up opening the door and poking around with the shovel handle. Mr. Rat finally came out where Fuzz could grab him. With a quick shake and a fling the rat flew through the air right into Harold's face as he was watching the action! Perry and I were laughing so hard we ended up rolling on the ground. We'd never seen Harold move so fast as that night! He was spitting and sputtering, and even had a few curse words!

After Harold gained his composure Perry said, "Harold what does the Bible say about being slow to anger? God is watching you, and besides it was one of God's creatures that hit you in the mouth!" Perry and I exploded with laughter again.

Harold grabbed some grass to wipe the seat off, and we headed back to Gabe Anderson's place. That's when Perry calmly stated how nice it was to sit on a clean seat, I of course chimed right in

of was hatred towards Herbie. Fear and anger took over as I kept re-hashing the whole fight with Herbie. I just wanted to hit something as I seemed filled with rage. Every muscle in my body was tense. I tried to pray but I wouldn't allow myself to give up the Herbie ordeal. As you can imagine sleep was scarce that night!

The next morning was kind of eerie as I looked at Herbie laying there with a few cats sitting on top of him. I had thoughts of going over and beating on him with the shovel handle thinking I could even the score for Fuzz and me. Yes, after calf chores, with shovel handle in my grip, I paid a visit to Herbie. It was scary, as I knew it was wrong, but I couldn't stop from wailing on him. I swung that handle as fast and hard as I could while I cried like never before. I stood over him until I was soaking wet with sweat. As I put the handle away Pa was waiting for me, he didn't say a thing.

We finished chores and headed to church. Pastor Hanson's sermon was on grace and how most of us don't show enough to others. I had to assume God was talking to me regarding me and Herbie! After church, we went out to eat to give Mom a break from cooking. When we got home, we had time for some Frisbee tossing before chores.

Fuzz limped along as I did chores. Fuzz and I helped Dad with the milking while Becky helped Mom with supper. I was dreaming of the future with Molly's foal when all of a sudden I got zapped by the cow trainers that hang over the cow's back. The hot fencer is connected to them so when the cow arches her back it causes her to back up and do her duty in the gutter.

Dad laughed. "Day dreaming again, I suppose, Mr. Bonner?"

"I guess so, Dad. It's pretty hard to stay focused at times."

"I reckon every boy has to go through what you're wrestling with, a yearning that just seems to burn a hole in your gut. I had it bad over two things when I was a kid."

"Really, Dad? I thought this stuff only happened to me. What did you yearn for?"

"Golly, son, it seems a long time ago. The first thing was a lever action twenty two rifle out of the Sears and Roebuck catalog. The second was your mother. If you think you got it tough now, just wait till you fall in love with the girl of your dreams. That's something I'll never forget. God gives you some nudges and places this woman in front of you, and all of a sudden it hits you—this is the woman he has meant for you. Then if a man treats her like God intended, she will have a gleam in her eye all her life."

"Dad, I think I'll stick to Percherons for now."

After chores we cleaned up in the house and sat down to a great meal Mom and Rebecca had prepared. After supper we all had milk shakes while we played a game of Monopoly. It seems I never do well in that game. Rebecca thrives on it and Dad always tries to take advantage of Mom.

"Okay kids, it's off to bed," Mom said. "You've got school in the morning."

Dad laughed, "Did you kids know that I don't have school in the morning?"

This was his way of bugging me since he knew I wasn't totally fond of school. We went to our bedrooms, said our prayers and tried to get some shut eye. This is when Dad would sing a song or two. Sometimes "The Lord's Prayer" or some song from a musical. He did this on Sunday mornings and just before we went to bed sometimes. Dad's voice is something I will have in my mind the rest of my life.

Chapter 7
"The Big Game"

The old alarm clock seemed to ring too early the next morning. I hit the snooze button and quickly hid under the covers, just hoping that the alarm was only in my dreams. This is the best time to get in that last bit of sleep. When it rang the second time I got up and checked Fuzz, she had pulled all her bandages off and shredded them. "Fuzz does that tell me you're doing okay? You scroungy mutt." As Fuzz followed me downstairs you could tell she was on the mend. I did my chores, cleaned up, ate breakfast, and Rebecca and I were off to school.

School was in the town of Belgrade, and it was your average high school. There were the different cliques of kids: the athletic people, the brainy people, the type to test the waters with bad attitudes, alcohol and parties, and the people who really didn't fit in with any of the groups. I guess Harold, Perry and I had our own group which consisted of a Christian background. We tried to hold each other accountable to a Biblical standard which seemed to be getting harder to do. We kind of did our own thing and tried to get along with most of them. The few that had the bad attitudes and partied were constantly trying to get more people to be a part of their little group. I guess misery loves company. If you didn't agree with their agendas, they attempted to make your life miserable.

We had coed gym class with Mr. Wright as our teacher. It was the time of year for field hockey in his class. We got along with Mr. Wright, so he allowed Perry, Harold, and me to be on the same team. It just so happened that Greg Shants, Nick Grudden, Judy Clemons, and Bill Masters were on the opposing team. I still wonder if this team selection was encouraged by Mr. Wright.

There was a new kid in school named Will Stevens who was also on our team. Will wasn't a real big person but he looked fairly athletic. Mr. Wright got us started and then refereed the match. Will was running up the court looking for a pass and Judy Clemons came in from his blind side and raised her stick right into Will's throat, knocking him to the floor. Will was totally caught off guard so he hit the old gym floor pretty hard.

Mr. Wright blew his whistle immediately. "Judy Clemons, what was that about?" As he helped Will off the floor. "Judy, you're disqualified! You can take a seat over there and I don't want to hear a word from you!"

As Judy proudly walked off the floor, Will gathered his senses. We huddled around him and made sure he was okay. Harold was twisting his stick back and forth in his hands as his eyes were bulging out. He was all red in the face and I wasn't in the best of moods either.

I spoke to our team quickly. "Will, sorry about that, we should have warned you about this crew. Now guys, God wants us to honor him but he doesn't ask us to be pushovers. Harold, Perry, Will, are you ready to rock and roll?" With that we met hands in the middle and yelled, "Team!"

Harold had a crazy faraway look in his eyes. I figured he was going to set the score straight. Mr. Wright started the game again and it didn't take long before Harold had Bill Masters on the deck. Greg Shants tried to come to his rescue but I cut him off. There we were, whistle blowing constantly and Judy Clemons screaming bloody murder from the sidelines. Greg Shants and I were toe to toe, Harold and Bill nose to nose. Greg Shants was standing there with his long greasy hair and a smirk on his face. How can anyone be that evil?

Mr. Wright decided to make us all run wind sprints for the next few minutes to take the edge off. After that, we finished the game without any other altercations. Mr. Wright dismissed everyone in the class except for Harold, Perry, and me, along with Greg Shants, Bill Masters, and Judy Clemons. We stood there at half court, them on one side and we on the other with Mr. Wright between us.

He spoke in a calm voice. "When I was a kid, our gym teacher would give boxing gloves out to kids that couldn't get along. He would ref the boxing match to keep it in line. Nowadays, we aren't allowed to do this. Now, you didn't hear this from me, but if you two groups want to get rough with each other, then may I suggest some type of competition that is fair to both parties and off school grounds? Both sides must agree to the event and the winner walks quietly away and the loser walks quietly away. Is that understood?" He looked Greg Shants right in the eye. "Greg, how about it? Maybe a little game of ice hockey will cool these tempers down! If you agree to this, I will come out and ref the match to help keep it civil. Greg, Jude, what's your answer?"

We all agreed to a hockey game with four or five of us on each team. We also agreed to play it on our slough when the ice was safe. With that said, it was lunch time.

Perry, Harold, and I were sitting at our usual spot when the new kid, Will, came along with his food tray. We were still pumped up from the gym class and our future hockey game. We were thinking who we could get to join us for the big match.

Will sat there not saying much at first. "Hey, guys, you can count me in on this hockey game," he said.

There was a hesitation as we all shot looks around the table, sharing our mutual concern that Will was just too small for this type of action.

Harold said kindly. "Will, you're new to this school and this feud has been festering for years between them and us so it would probably be better to stay out of it."

"Do you think I'm not part of this after that girl clothes lined me with her stick and knocked me on my can?" he said gritting his teeth. "Besides, hockey is my sport. I've played varsity since I was a freshman and was all conference last year at St. Cloud Apollo."

"As I was saying, Will, we'd love to have you as part of our team." Harold said casually. We all laughed and gave out high fives.

Just then Mr. Wright came by the table. "Guys, I've helped set up this big game of hockey. This is something that is important to me, so I'm just checking in to make sure I won't be disappointed in the outcome, if you know what I mean!" We all looked at each other and busted out laughing. Harold assured him that we would take care of business. The rest of the day was uneventful.

On the bus ride home, I caught myself dreaming of Molly's foal again. I decided right then and there I would have to be there when she foaled. I got off the bus and hurried to the house for some quick snacks. I changed my clothes, did my chores at home, and headed to Mr. Olson's to start my job. Old Fuzz was right beside me but not as spry as usual. When we got to Mr. Olson's, Molly and Ladd were in the barn.

"Mr. Olson, what do you want me to do first?" I was a hoping he had the horses in the barn for a reason.

"Jude, you harness them nags while I grease the spreader."

"You mean we're going to hitch?" I asked.

"Does the bear crap in the woods? And make sure you give them a quick run over with the curry comb. We've got to look our best when we drive Percherons."

I curried and harnessed Molly and Ladd while Mr. Olson greased the manure spreader. The whole time Old Fuzz checked the corn cribs out for rats and mice. Mr. Olson let me drive the team over the pole of the spreader and hook the neck yoke and tug chains. He dipped a couple four tine forks in oil so they would slide easily into the manure.

"Jude, drive them over to the calf barn and pull down the main center aisle, if you think you can handle such high spirited horse flesh."

I got up in that cold steel seat and grabbed the lines, double checked all hook ups, and felt pretty darn proud.

"Molly, Ladd, get up," I spoke to them in a strong firm voice.

Their ears spun back towards me wondering what happened to Mr. Olson, but off they went. I had a little too much slack in the lines so they got a pretty good jump on me, but I reined them in pretty fast. As I headed to the barn, Mr. Olson opened the door so I could pull right in. I can't describe the feeling when you've got almost two and a quarter tons of horse power in front of you and they are listening to your every word. The power you feel in your hands and arms is pretty sweet. They were right up in the bits and wanting to trot because they hadn't been hitched for awhile. Molly was almost prancing.

"Easy Molly, easy girl." I spoke to her in a soft soothing voice.

I pulled closer to the barn and they hesitated as they entered the door. "Come on Ladd, Molly step up, we've got work to do." As

I pulled in the barn aisle Mr. Olson was standing where he wanted them to stop.

"Whoa Molly, whoa Ladd. Stand," I commanded.

I jumped down and got right to pitching manure out of the calf pens. I looked at Mr. Olson. He was fussing with Ladd and Molly.

"Yes Jude, I've run an Armstrong loader for, I bet, fifty years now. I'm sure if I don't get in there and show you how it's done you're never going to learn. Why, when I was your age, I used to have a pitch fork in each hand. Now make sure you keep the load square. We can't be going to the field with no crooked load behind such fine horses."

Mr. Olson and I pitched four loads together and I pitched one by myself as he milked. Old Ladd and Molly would get down and scratch pretty hard when I'd first kick in the beaters, but they weren't so peppy by the fifth load. Kind of like kids, give them something to do and they are less likely to get in trouble. I backed the spreader into the barn and line drove Ladd and Molly back to their stalls. Mr. Olson had tie stalls for each horse. They knew which stall was theirs. I took their harnesses off in the aisle and soft brushed them as they stood there untied.

"Molly and Ladd, Quinn sure has you guys trained well," I said, speaking softly.

I blew in their noses and released them to their stalls. Ladd went right in his but Molly thought she would do a little exploring on the way.

"Molly, you old nag, you get your big butt where it belongs."

As I said this, I leaned on her back side as much as possible, pushing as she took her time getting to her stall.

"Molly girl, you think 'cause you're with foal you get special treatment?" I chided. "I think you're just out of shape, you old piece of mink food."

I tied them both up, blew in their noses again and went to the milking barn to see what was next. Mr. Olson had me do calf chores and then I was able to head home. Fuzz and I ran in to say good bye to Molly and Ladd before leaving.

On our way home, I decided to check the slough to see if it was frozen enough to skate on. When I got there, old Fuzz ran right out on the ice like she owned it. I weighed a few more pounds than Fuzz so I started out cautiously on the edges. With most sloughs, the water isn't very deep so if you break through you're only going to get a wet foot and knee. The ice seemed pretty safe so I was some thirty feet from shore when it started cracking! I turned around slowly and thought I could make it back to the edge without getting wet, but with the next step it was over and down I went. Old Fuzz was right there checking me out. Wow, I could feel the cold water instantly soaking my socks. I've had this experience almost every year.

"Fuzz, you're lucky I don't drag you in with me." I picked her up and held her, then lowered her towards the water. Old Fuzz was very tough but the one thing she didn't like was water, especially cold water. I let one paw get a little wet, and then threw her back to safe ice.

"Fuzz, I guess I've got to drag myself out of this mess. Mom's not going to see the humor in these dirty smelly jeans!" I dragged myself on top of the ice only to break through again. Seems like once you break through it weakens the rest of the ice, so I plowed my way back to dry land and started the long walk home in waterlogged boots, water sloshing back and forth with every step.

When Fuzz and I got home I slipped my boots off in the garage and tried to sneak in past Mother. I do believe God gave mothers radar screens.

"Mr. Bonner, what, pray tell, have you been up to, and what are you going to do with those pants and socks?"

"Mom, how did you know I fell in the slough?"

"Maybe it's that time of year for you to start checking the ice. Plus I could smell that slough water the second you stepped in the back door. Now put those stinky clothes in the utility sink and get in that shower." Dad always said God gave mothers better sniffers than fathers.

The winter was going along as I had planned: going to school, chores at home and Mr. Olson's, temperatures getting colder and dreaming of Molly's foal of course. Each day I would check Molly's belly to see if I could notice the foal getting bigger. I even started putting a tape measure around her once a week.

A week later the ice was now thick enough to play hockey so Perry, Harold, and Will would come over and we would skate around. Many times it would be in the dark with Coleman lanterns lighting the way. We even got Dad out there a couple times. I think he was better than what he showed us. And of course we used someone's boots for the goal markers. An unwritten rule is that the boot laces have to be tucked in; otherwise a skate will cut them off. I remember skating across Dad's shoelace years before and having to buy him new boot laces. That's how you learn responsibility.

The boys and I decided we were ready for the big hockey game with Greg Shants and his crew, so I said I would talk to them at school and try to line it up for that coming Saturday.

The next morning on the bus, I was wondering if Greg Shants would even come through with a team. I was also curious who would fill out the rest of his team.

"Hi, Greg," I said when I saw him in the hall. "The ice is ready and we thought we might play our little hockey game this Saturday, if that works for your guys?"

His eyes lit up and he gave me this strange look like I wasn't even there. His eyes were glazed over like he was still hung over from the weekend. He stood for a few moments and finally answered me.

"Sure, Judd, I can get the boys lined up for Saturday. I suppose you'll have your Bible out on the ice with you." He called me Judd instead of Jude thinking it would get under my skin. I have to admit it did bother me when he called me that.

I responded angrily, "Bring your guys Saturday right after lunch, 1:00 p.m. sharp at my place?" Greg agreed on the time and had a few adjectives to finish his thoughts. Greg was the kind of person who thought the world owed him happiness because of what he thought was a difficult childhood. I felt sorry for him to a certain degree, but I also thought he had to make up his own mind if he really wanted to be mean and hateful all his life.

I got a hold of Perry, Harold, Will, and Mr. Wright to tell them we were on for the match. I reminded them to get their skates sharpened Friday night.

The week seemed to drag on forever. Having the big game on my mind seemed to bring things to a crawl. I had been doing some squats, push-ups, and sit ups in preparation for our hockey game and felt good, both physically and mentally.

"Dad, can you help me flood the pond Thursday or Friday night after chores?"

"What's happening at the pond that makes it worth flooding?"

"Can I go with and skate a little?" Becky asked.

"Perry, Harold, Will, and I challenged a few boys from school to a hockey match on Saturday. It's time to get even with these guys!"

"Sounds pretty serious if you want to go through the hassle of flooding the old pond. Not sure if I understand what 'getting even' has to do with anything Jude."

"Dad, it is serious to us, these kids are total losers! If you only knew what they are like."

"Sounds like you should be praying for them instead of playing hockey against them. Jude, make sure you let God do the judging and don't underestimate these guys. Remember David and Goliath. In the past, I've counted my chickens before they hatched only to have my lunch handed to me."

"It sure has been gnawing at me all week, waiting for the big day. I think we'll do pretty well. We have Will on our team and he used to play at St. Cloud Apollo," I explained.

"He's that new kid that's kind of cute!" Becky said with a smile.

Thursday night after chores, Dad, Becky and I loaded the gas powered transfer pump, chain saw, and Old Fuzz into the truck. Of course Fuzz had to ride in the cab right on my lap, looking out the window. We both had our hip boots on because this process can get pretty wet. Dad had water flying everywhere as he cut two holes in the ice with the chainsaw. I carried the gas pump and hoses down to the first hole. We primed the pump, attached the hoses, and pulled the starter rope. The motor sputtered for a little while, then took off throwing quite a stream of water out the discharge hose. This is where Old Fuzz thinks she needs to help, by backing up and running through the stream of water coming out of the hose, then spinning around and running back through again and again. All the while she's forgetting that her hair between her toes is collecting ice every step of the way. Then she goes off to the side and lays for awhile biting at her own toes, trying to free them of the ice packs.

We moved the pump to the second hole and repeated the process, and old Fuzz did the same. Becky was skating around through the water chasing Fuzz. I like to watch the water go across the smooth ice. When it freezes it is as smooth as glass, as long as we keep Fuzz off of it. We loaded everything in the truck and headed back home.

"Fuzz, you old mutt, I suppose you want me to help thaw your toes on the way don't you?" So I held her frozen little paws in my bare hands to give her as much warmth as possible. You can't believe how cold that is, but she's my dog and that's part of the deal when you own a mutt. She looked up at me with her beady brown eyes and thanked me. "Fuzz, if I'm not careful I might spoil you and I suppose you taught that water a lesson it will never soon forget."

"Jude, as cold as it is, the old pond will be in pretty nice shape for your little hockey game! What time is this game supposed to start?" Dad asked.

"I told the guys to be here right after lunch, around 1:00."

I got up early the next morning to check the ice. It had a few bad spots where old Fuzz walked when it was starting to freeze. I planned to fix them after school with a few pails of water and the ice chipper. I hustled back home and caught the bus for school. As we went past Mr. Olson's, there were Molly and Ladd, black as the eight ball, laying down in the pure white snow. Pretty awesome!

When I got to school I caught up with Perry, Harold, and Will. They seemed ready for the big match, each with their skate's newly sharpened and new tape on their hockey sticks. I also checked with Greg Shants to be sure he was still planning on coming out with his boys. Greg made it sound like Judy Clemons might come to watch.

As you can imagine, I had a terrible time concentrating on school that day. I almost got in trouble with Mrs. Norman for daydreaming. After class I figured I owed her an explanation.

"Mrs. Norman, I'm sorry for the lapse in my attention today." I apologized. "For a minute I thought I might be singing 'I'm a Little Teapot' again."

"Well, I guess you're allowed a few time outs per year during class. Just don't make it a steady habit. Let me guess, is it related to a big black horse named Molly?"

"No, ma'am. Not this time, Perry, Harold and I have a big hockey game tomorrow against Greg Shants and his crew."

"Now, that sounds interesting. That crew could use a little ice time to cool down. By the way, how is that Molly horse doing this winter?"

"She's fine so far. I measure her belly to see the progress once each week and she seems to be getting awfully big so early. Even Mr. Olson thought she was bigger than other years. I was hoping for a filly, but now I think I'd rather have a big stud colt."

"I suppose you are counting the days till she pops the foal out."

"You bet ya, ninety days from tomorrow is her due date, and

I'm planning on sleeping in the barn when the time comes."

"I do wish you well with that foal. I know you've worked hard for Mr. Olson. And I will be rooting for your team tomorrow from home, but you didn't hear me say that. I try to reach out to Greg, but haven't gotten anywhere with him. He seems bitter about something."

"Yeah, I can't wait to take some of that bitterness out of him tomorrow! You just...."

"Jude?" Mrs. Norman cut me off. "Be careful with that attitude young man! Sounds like you've let the devil start a foothold."

Wow, that stopped me in my tracks. I didn't know what to say? I stood there silent and actually got a little mad at her. What gives her the right?

Mrs. Norman broke the silence, "Please let me know on Monday how the game went. You've got my curiosity piqued a little. Now get going before you miss the bus."

That night Mom fixed one of my favorite meals: big juicy cheeseburgers, baked beans, and lettuce salad. I went to bed early so I could get extra rest, but all I could do was lay there thinking of the next day. I finally dozed off and slept well till chore time. I did chores at home, and then had waffles and sausages for breakfast. Then I headed to Mr. Olson's for Saturday chores.

"Hey Jude, did you watch the news last night?" Mr. Olson asked. "The sports guy talked up some big hockey game scheduled for today at 1:00 sharp."

For a second I thought he was talking about some big college game, but then I realized he was talking about our hockey game. "They say there will be standing room only, so you'd better get there early if you want a good seat," I responded. "I'm sure there'll be several pro scouts attending also."

"Why certainly! Why certainly! Now let's head to the barn. We've got some horses that need their toe nails trimmed."

We started with Ladd and took turns. Mr. Olson would do one foot and I did the next with old Fuzz hanging around to clean up any frogs that we trimmed off the soles of their feet. Mr. Olson was on Ladd's last foot when Ladd decided to let Mr. Olson's back share some of his weight. Mr. Olson was usually pretty mild mannered but that was enough of that.

"Ladd, you old sack of bones, stand on your own feet and not on my back!" he shouted. He rapped Ladd on the belly with the rasp and got his attention. After that old Ladd did a whole lot better.

"Did you learn anything, Jude? You see, you don't have to beat a horse, but every once in a while they need to be reminded who the boss is. When they are this big, a person can't be their leaning post."

"Do you think Ladd got your message?"

"Why certainly, why certainly."

Now it was Molly's turn. I brought her out and cross tied her and blew in her nose a little.

"Easy girl, easy girl," Mr. Olson said soothingly as he picked up her front foot and started trimming. One of the many things I learned from Mr. Olson was the tone of voice to use around horses. It was rare that he raised his voice to the horses, only when necessary. Many people talk too loudly to their horses and then the horse is always on edge. They can even understand the tone of your voice when they are pulling a load that makes a lot of noise, like a manure spreader.

We took turns on Molly's feet and she gave us no grief. Mr. Olson was fussy on when they got their feet trimmed. He did not want any cracks appearing. When we were done, I heard Mr. Olson's famous quote again.

"Wild and woolly and full of fleas, never curry below the knees," he said and laughed.

"Jude, I suppose you need to get home and have a big lunch before the important match. If I was thirty years younger I'd be out there helping you today."

"Thanks Mr. Olson, but I think we have it under control."

"Play smart and fair and make sure you have fun, but remember you don't have to be a leaning post or door mat for those guys either," I nodded my head in agreement.

"Let's go Fuzz, I think you've enjoyed enough hoof trimmings for awhile. See ya later for chores Mr. Olson."

Fuzz and I hustled home and Mom had a big pot of chili going for lunch. Mom usually makes the chili one day ahead so it seasons out better. Add some shredded cheese and sour cream and it's hard to beat. I started inhaling my chili when Mom reminded me to slow down.

"Jude, don't you think you should learn to be a little more patient. You can't let this hockey game consume your every thought."

"But Mom, this is real important and I need to get down to the ice soon."

"Okay, okay, but if you wait just a couple more minutes I'll have some warm chocolate chip cookies to take to the ice with you for the guys."

"Mother! This is a hockey game not a bake sale."

"Jude Bonner watch your mouth!" Mom scolded. "Now go get the rest of your stuff and I'll get the cookies wrapped up."

When I got back Mom had sixteen cookies wrapped in some paper towels.

"Mom, there are only four of us. Why so many cookies?

"Now Jude, didn't you say the other team also had four players? You be sure to share them."

Mothers just don't seem to get it at times. This was a very serious hockey game against some real jerks and I show up with cookies.

I headed down to the pond with skates, stick, puck, Fuzz, and sixteen cookies. It wasn't too long before the rest of the guys started showing up. I noticed old Fuzz hanging pretty close to the cookies.

"Fuzz, you leave those cookies alone, or Mom will have a conniption." Fuzz pretended she didn't hear me but she knew dang well I meant business. It was funny how she acted when Harold, Perry, and Will showed up. She greeted them with tail wagging and tongue a licking. But when Greg Shants and his crew came by she growled ever so slightly and watched every step they took. As Greg and his crew were skating around to warm up, I saw Fuzz slip down to their end of the ice and squat over Greg's Mountain Dew pop can. I could barely contain myself as Fuzz quietly returned. "Fuzz I'm not sure if I should scold you or praise you, you little mutt!" I had to really bite my lip to stop from laughing. At least it was organic!

What took me by surprise was that Greg had a total of five guys for his team, plus Judy Clemons and her mouth on the sidelines. We only had four.

"Hi, Greg," I said. "How are you guys doing? Ready to play a little hockey? Dad and I flooded the ice the other night so it's in pretty good shape. My Ma made some fresh cookies if you'd like." They took them with not much to say, not even a "thanks." I introduced myself to them because Greg had two guys I'd never seen before. The one guy looked pretty serious with very nice Bauer skates. He seemed to be in an older class than Greg. I was thinking Greg had brought in a couple ringers.

"Are you playing with four guys, Greg?" I asked. Before he could answer, Judy piped in.

"You guys think you're so dang good that you should be able to play against five, or do you want to call it quits and run home?"

Well all I needed to fuel my fire was Judy hollering like an idiot. Greg sat there lacing his skates with a little smirk on his face.

"When you guys lined this game up, you said four or five guys! So we choose to play with five. Are you going to have it or not?"

"Yes, sir, we're going to have some." I said. "The games are up to ten and it's the best two out of three."

As I skated back to my guys I had a hard time controlling my emotions. I never thought they would show up with five guys. I had to tell myself it was just a game and God has surprises for us every once in awhile. Mr. Wright was just walking down to the ice. I was trying to figure what to say to my guys to get them fired up as I headed back. We were pretty good skaters but with Greg bringing in a ringer or two, plus their one man advantage, we might be in trouble.

"Boys, are you ready for some hockey?" I asked. "Four against five, I figure we'll have to play with the goalie at center ice when we're on offense."

Will piped in, "Well, I hope they packed a lunch because they'll need it."

Perry and Harold didn't say a word but you could see the determination on their faces. When they get mad they usually go silent. We skated around a little to warm up as Fuzz sat by my shoes and the leftover cookies. Harold placed a pair of boots at each end for the goals, spacing them with a hockey stick.

Greg shouted over, "Let's get this show on the road, or are you little boys just going to warm up all day?"

Mr. Wright shouted. "Any puck over the boot height is too high and doesn't count. Jude's team will bring the puck down first. Are you ready?"

We huddled quick and said a little prayer. "God, please be with us today and give us safety for this day." I prayed.

Will took the puck, flipped it in the air, caught it with his stick in mid air, and brought it to the ice. That was it, the game had begun. We spread out and skated towards the south end with the sun glistening off the skate blades. Will was pretty impressive. You could tell he had played before. I was playing back a little for the goal person. Will passed the puck to Perry, as the puck slid across the smooth ice, Greg put a huge body check on Will. Will was laying flat on the ice with Greg standing over him and laughing.

"Welcome to the big leagues, Sonny!" Greg shouted.

Mr. Wright flew onto the ice to check on Will. Will got up and went face to face right there. I skated between them as quick as I could. Will's eyes were like steel lasers. Greg laughed and spit a wad of tobacco on the ice.

"Now boys, this is not the NHL where a fight is an everyday practice!" Mr. Wright shouted.

As I was breaking up the fight, Harold and Perry were trying to score two against four. The guy with the fancy skates took the puck from Perry and skated down the ice and scored on an empty net. The score was one-nothing before we knew it. Will grabbed the puck and headed out, skating along and watching for the body check this time. Greg attempted the same hit but Will slid right past him. Will passed the puck over to Harold and we seemed to have it going our way. All of a sudden, Harold was checked hard, and was lying on the ice. Again Fancy Skates went down the ice with the puck and scored right past me. Two-nothing. We brought it up the ice again and this time it was my turn. I faked a pass and skated around Bill Masters and saw Greg headed my way full force. Well, I guess all those years of throwing bales and pitching manure paid off. He hit me square at my side, but I leaned into him and neither of us went down.

"Run into something?" I asked.

I passed the puck to Will and he put on quite a show. His feet were so quick as he juked and glided past two guys to score. The score was now one to two in their favor. We thought we had things figured out, but with one man short all the time we just couldn't cut the mustard. They ended up winning the first match ten to two.

We all took a little break between the games and talked strategy, drank water, and had a few more cookies. As we stood there I noticed Greg reach for his pop can. "Hey guys, watch this!" As I pointed to the other end. We all watched Greg take a big swig of Mountain Dew and it exploded right back out like a rocket as he spit and sputtered and threw his can off to the side. I stood there and laughed.

Harold asked. "How did you know he would spit out his pop?"

"At the beginning of the warm-ups I saw Fuzz go down there and squat over his Dew can." Harold, Perry and Will lost it after I said that! Perry ended up laying on the ice as he laughed and said. "Even if we end up losing to these losers, that was well worth it." I looked over at Mr. Wright and he had a smile on his face!

"If I'd known we needed a fifth man I could have asked my cousin to join the fun," Harold complained.

Just then we looked towards home and could see Dad and Becky coming across the ice. I wondered what they wanted.

"Maybe we could talk your Dad into strapping the old skates on for the fifth man." Perry suggested.

"Don't you think he's a little too old for this kind of game?" Will asked. "Well, don't look now but Dad has his skates and hockey stick with him!" I said. "This is awesome. We'll show them now."

I'll never forget what happened next. Dad walking down to the ice in his old bib overalls, skates that seemed ancient, and an old homemade hockey stick. I snuck a look at Greg's team and could see them laughing as Dad passed by them.

"Jude, do you mind if Becky and I skate a little today?" Dad asked "We'll just stay on the back edge over here and won't interfere with your little game."

"Sure thing Dad, no problem."

I knew what Dad was up to. He had every intention of playing that day. I figured I better ask if Dad could play, so I skated down to their end.

"Greg, is it all right if my Dad plays a little hockey for us?"

"Sure thing, Judd, nothing I'd like better than whopping two Bonners on the same day!" Greg laughed.

I bit my lip. "Now you boys take it easy on Dad. As you can see he's not a very good skater."

As I said this, there was Dad attempting to skate and looking pretty shaky. He was going really slow swinging his arms in the air for balance every so often. I knew what he was doing but no one else did.

Harold came over to me. "Are you kidding me? I thought your Dad skated better than that! He won't be much help to us. Sure hope he doesn't get hurt."

I played along with Dad's decoy game and just agreed with

Chapter 8
"The Waiting Game"

I was plenty stiff as I got out of bed the next morning. I hustled over to Mr. Olson's for chores and back home for breakfast before church. As we pulled into the church parking lot, there stood two coach buses. Minnesota Adult and Teen Challenge was there to put on a concert for us. This was one of my favorite worship services. The group is made up of teens and adults that have some type of chemical dependency. It is a faith based treatment program with very high success rates. The members sing and give testimonies, it takes a lot of courage to stand in front of total strangers and admit your sins. Dad always said everyone is addicted to something, these people happen to be addicted to something that is illegal. After church, Granny and Gramps came over for dinner and to help finish the horse stalls.

Mom served pork roast and a sweet potato dish along with blueberry pie. After lunch we started on the "pony pen," as Gramps called it. By the end of the afternoon the horse pen was looking pretty good. Grampa Warden was real fussy on every detail. We followed the recommendations from the library book on stall length, manger height, and tie chain length. All those dimensions are important so when the horse is tied it can't get hung up. We even took a router and cut the date on one of the boards.

The closer we came to Molly's due date the more excited I got. Sometimes God would slow down my daydreaming about the foal with thirty below zero temperatures. On several mornings I had second thoughts on whether it was all worth it. Spreading manure at thirty below is rather difficult to say the least. Mr. Olson had no cab on the spreader tractor. I drove with one hand while placing the other over my face to block the wind. To top it off, I had to make sure the apron did not freeze down for the next day, so I had to spend time with a pitch fork cleaning the bottom of the spreader out. The wind shows no mercy; it bites very hard when it blows at twenty miles per hour. Every time you just pray to get back to the barn without some chain jumping off a sprocket or the tractor stalling in the middle of the field. The only thing that kept me going on those bitterly cold days was thinking of that colt in my arms and praying to God.

Mr. Olson and I started leaving Molly in the barn more often, especially on the frigid days. Each day I would spend time running the curry comb and soft brush over her. She was looking very pregnant as she stood there with a bloated belly.

"Jude, have you noticed that Molly is starting to breathe a little harder?" Mr. Olson asked. "The bigger the foal gets the more pressure it puts on her lungs."

"What do you think she'll have Mr. Olson, a stud colt or filly colt?"

"Well, I don't rightly know, Jude, but the last two colts she threw were stud colts and she was pretty ornery on each of those pregnancies. I figure, as calm as she is, she'll throw you a filly colt. I suppose you can hardly wait for the big day? Think about it Jude, creation is written all over this! Molly has a foal in her belly surrounded by fluid in a sack that is hooked up to an umbilical cord. Through that cord the foal gets all its nourishment. Molly has the room in her belly for a 120 pound foal. Then at just the right time, Molly's body says it is time to go, she waxes and the birthing process starts. Molly has all the correct muscles to push a 120 pound foal out and then the foal just happens to know that it needs to nurse very soon or it will die. To think that some believe this whole process evolved after two rocks collided! Why certainly."

"I never thought about creation from that angle before.

Anyway, I can't wait much longer Mr. Olson, I just hope she has it when I'm home and not at school. I plan on sleeping in the barn when she gets closer."

"Why certainly, why certainly," Mr. Olson chuckled. "Maybe you should start sleeping in the barn right away so she gets used to it. Some people say a horse will hold their foaling off if bothered two much."

"Do you think so, Mr. Olson? She's still one month away! That's a long time in the barn."

"As much time as you spend with Molly, I don't think she'll hold the foal on your account. Well, I'm headed inside. Make sure you catch the barn lights when you leave. Good night."

Fuzz and I spent a little more time with Molly before heading home. It was funny how docile she had gotten.

When we got home we gathered some things together for when the foal came. The book from the library suggested iodine, string for the umbilical cord, and a few towels. I grabbed my camera and a journal to document the different times things would happen, like when her water breaks, when the first hoof shows, etc. Mom even suggested a few granola bars if I got hungry. I also threw in our best flashlight and an alarm clock. I reread the chapter on assisting at foaling time. I read that chapter so many times I could have said it word for word. I grabbed my sleeping bag and an old pillow.

"Jude, it looks like you're moving in at Mr. Olson's with all that stuff," Dad said.

Old Fuzz was already asleep in the utility room so I checked her water and food and rubbed her ears awhile before I went to bed. Fuzz usually waits for the coast to clear before sneaking up to my room to sleep alongside my bed. I brushed my teeth, read my Bible, and checked off one more day on my countdown calendar. It was February 16th, so I only had approximately twenty days to go. I jumped into bed as the wind howled outside. It was hard to sleep with my mind full of a black colt running around kicking in the air. I kept running the whole foaling process through my mind. It's funny how you can think of something you want so much that you work yourself into a tizzy. My mind was working all the different scenarios when I heard Fuzz sneaking up the stairs. She lay beside my bed so I could reach over and rub her ears.

That next Monday at school, Greg Shants was walking awfully

slow. He must have still been feeling the effects of Dad's hockey check. Judy Clemons was back to her normal loud mouth self and acting like she owned the place.

"Hi, Greg, thanks for the game Saturday," I said as we passed in the hall.

He ignored me and went on his way. You could see the anger in his expression. But I still had a hard time not laughing as I watched him limp away. Then in Mrs. Norman's English class, she noticed Greg limping.

"Greg! What on earth happened to you?"

"I kind of ran into something skating Saturday, Mrs. Norman."

"I hope you get better real soon, Greg. I'll make sure I pray for you tonight," Greg glanced at her with a scowl on his face.

Mrs. Norman was a Christian and I admired how she lived her faith out. After class we talked about Molly's progress. Mrs. Norman seemed almost as excited as I was.

"Oh by the way, did the right team win the big game on Saturday?"

"Yes, Ma'am." She gave me a high five.

"Jude, I would like to bring my family out to see your colt when it's born?"

"That's fine with me but I'll have to let you know when Molly is ready for visitors. Mr. Olson said there is a good chance Molly will be very protective of the foal and could even bite or kick us. If a mare has too much activity right away, she gets too nervous and doesn't nurse the colt well. It gets better once the colt is around five days old or so. I also better check with Mr. Olson."

"Jude, I suppose you feel like these days are going in slow motion, waiting for that little black foal?"

"You betcha, Mrs. Norman. The closer it gets, the harder it is to sleep and pay attention at school,"

Those last few days before Molly's due date were hard to handle. Winter was in its latter stages so you could feel the temperatures getting a little warmer each day. The excitement was unbearable. I think Mom and Becky were getting sick of me always talking about Molly. Molly was also getting more and more restless. Her udder was getting full and tight. I recounted the days to make sure we had the right due date, and I moved my sleeping bag and other items over to the barn. It was now getting very close to when I would start sleeping in the barn. As soon as she was showing wax on her teats, it was the time to do the nighttime vigils.

Mr. Olson and I bedded down the maternity pen with knee high straw. I chose the bales that were the cleanest and covered the entire area. I cleaned her water fountain so it sparkled and lined up some of Mr. Olson's best hay.

When I got home from school, I bolted over to the maternity pen. Mr. Olson was standing with Molly, stroking her neck. Molly looked like she was standing there sleeping.

"Hi, Jude," Mr. Olson said. "Well, you're not in the horse business yet. She is still seven days away from her due date. You head off and do your chores and we'll talk after milking."

I did my chores in record time and checked on Molly several times. I even had to chase a couple steers back in their fence. The snow had built up enough that they could jump the fence. Old Fuzz certainly helped those steers understand that it was easier to stay in the fence. I shoveled the snow away from the fence so the steers could not get out again.

Double checking to make sure I'd done all my chores, I joined Mr. Olson in the barn as he finished up milking.

We each carried a milker into the milk house and as Mr. Olson ducked under the pipeline he said. "Jude, what does a guy look for in a mare just before she foals?"

"You look for waxed teats and the tail head muscles getting loose."

"Why certainly, why certainly. I would think that a fine horseman like you would check things like that when you first come in the barn."

"What? Are you saying Molly is showing wax?"

"You tell me."

I ran to the maternity pen, grabbed my flashlight and checked Molly's udder. Sure enough, there was wax! I checked her tail head muscles and they seemed pretty limp. She paced in the stall like she was very uncomfortable. I gave her a big hug and blew in her nose just a little.

"Molly girl, how are you doing? Are you going to pop that foal soon? I guess that means you'll get a roommate tonight!"

She was acting as if I was not even there, pacing around the stall from one end to the other. I offered her hay and a little grain but she wasn't interested. This was looking pretty serious. Mr. Olson always said they lose all interest in food and water when they get really close.

"Jude, I think you might be in the horse business by morning. Now you get home and line your things up for sleeping here, and make sure you tell your parents. I'll stick here until you get back."

Chapter 9
"The Birth of _____?"

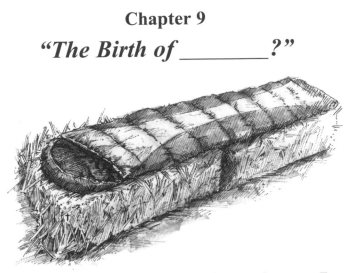

I ran home as fast as I could through the crunchy snow. Fuzz was with me every step of the way. I blew in the back door like a hurricane, ran upstairs, brushed my teeth, and grabbed my watch. Mom, Dad and Becky met me at the bottom of the stairs.

"Jude, is it that time?" Dad asked.

"Yes sir, Molly is waxed, tail head muscles are soft, and she is really restless. Mr. Olson thinks I'll be in the Percheron business by morning. I've got to get back as soon as possible."

"Make sure you grab the cell phone. If you have any trouble you can call us," Mom said. "Be sure you let us know if you're going to school in the morning."

"Fuzz needs to stay here tonight. Molly will accept you but not Fuzz," Dad said. "Good luck and be careful. We'll check on you right away in the morning before chores."

"I can't wait to see what she has!" Becky said with a huge smile on her face.

Mom gave me a hug and Dad gave me one of those looks that lets me know he's proud of me. The way Mom hugged me you'd think I was going off to college or something. I ran out the back door and headed towards Mr. Olson's. It was a cold, dark and damp night. The closer I got to the barn, the more nervous I got. I stopped and asked God for strength, warmth, and courage. The old adrenaline was pumping hard by the time I got to the barn. I had worked up a pretty good sweat by then. I changed my T-shirt quickly so I wouldn't get the chills. Mr. Olson was in the barn fussing over Molly.

"Jude, are you calling me or your parents if you need help tonight?"

"I'll try my best to get it done without interrupting any of you, but I'll knock on your window if I need your help. If Molly has her foal tonight, I'll be a proud owner of a Percheron colt in the morning."

"Good night, Molly. Night, Jude." Mr. Olson left the barn.

I was in the barn alone with Molly. Mr. Olson had gone to bed and Fuzz was at home. I stood beside Molly, consoling her, with her head on my shoulder, her eyes closed. Then a strange feeling of peace came over me. I looked around and the barn was silent. It took me awhile but I finally realized that God was with Molly and me. I fell to my knees and thanked him immediately, and God surrounded me with warmth that seemed to say, this was the night and everything would be okay.

I brushed Molly for awhile and then headed to bed myself. I set the alarm to wake me in an hour. I lay there staring at the hay loft floor boards with all the dusty cobwebs between them. Was I nuts or what? I couldn't sleep with all the events running through my mind! Molly was restless and pacing in the background. I got up ten minutes later and decided to scrape the barn alley for something to do. I would scrape for a minute and take a peek at Molly. I was so pumped up I don't think that alley was ever that clean before. I checked on Molly time and time again but no change. I decided to set up the milk house for milking in the morning to save Mr. Olson time. When that was finished I set the alarm for one hour of sleep and crawled in the sleeping bag again. I actually dozed off that time and was awakened by the alarm one hour later. It startled me so much I fell off the bales I was lying on.

I grabbed my flashlight and shone it towards Molly. She was standing there like she always did. I set my sleeping bag back on the bales, reset my alarm, and laid back down. It was now 2:00 a.m. and I was pretty tired. I dozed off and started dreaming of Percheron foals running everywhere. I had one all picked out in my dream. It was a little stud colt lying there fast asleep. I was walking up to it and for some reason I couldn't walk anymore, like I was stuck or something. Just then a big nasty looking old barn rat was heading towards my foal, and neither the mare nor the foal realized the rat was there. I still couldn't help since I was paralyzed as the rat got closer. I screamed as loud as I could but neither Molly or the rat cared. That dream was so powerful, I tossed and turned fighting my sleeping bag as I slid off the bales again. As I hit the ground I quickly opened my eyes and inches away from my face lay a dead rat on the floor with the Tom cat standing over it! I tried to roll away but ran into the bales so I scurried out of that sleeping bag as fast as I could, as the Tom cat picked up the rat and headed up the haymow ladder. Wow! That had me all shook up as I stood there in my stocking feet on the ice cold barn floor. I quickly crawled back into my sleeping bag to keep from freezing to death. I got myself all tucked in and was trying to get some heat going when I heard a big moan out of Molly.

I looked over and Molly was lying down. I tore out of that sleeping bag and pulled on my boots as fast as you can say "Jim Dandy".

"Molly, old girl, how are you doing?" She was lying there fairly restless and had a faraway look in her eye. She would lay her head to the ground, then bring it back up to her side and moan. I stroked her neck and tried to soothe her.

"Well, girl, at least you're lying in the correct spot to have a foal pop out, versus having your big butt against the wall or gate!"

I checked the straw behind her to see if her water had broken. I sat back and observed for awhile. This looked like the real thing. I set up a bale in the stall with all my towels, iodine, and other supplies. As I was doing this I heard her water break. It sounded like gallons came out. Molly was in full labor now, and groaning and pushing became her main objective. I placed dry straw behind and tied her tail off to one side.

"Hey, Molly girl, I see one foot. You keep pushing, girl, you are doing fine." Pretty soon the other foot followed. Things were coming along just fine. Molly would groan and push and push and groan. I could hardly believe it was finally happening. I could see the nostrils now, pressed up against the front legs. It is amazing how God lined up the birthing process. Molly was working pretty hard. The head and shoulders are always the worst areas for getting through the birth canal. As Molly pushed, the foal kept showing more and more of itself, eyes, and ears and now its slimy little head were completely out.

"Molly, old girl, you're doing fine. The head is out, keep at it girl." I cleared the birth sack from the foal's nostrils and eyes so the foal could breathe. It was so cute! It was moving a little bit. As Molly was pushing to get the chest out, I pulled on the foal's front legs. They were all slimy and hard to keep hold of. I wrapped an old towel around the front legs so I could keep my grip. We soon had the entire chest cavity out with only the hips left to come.

"Come on Molly, only a few more pushes and we'll have this little bugger out." Molly let out a huge groan and out it came. It was amazing, the little guy was soaking wet from the fluid in the sack. The foal lay there, moving ever so carefully. I just stood there in awe as I marveled how precious this time was. "Well Molly, we are in the Percheron business now. I suppose I'd better get this little bugger up to you so you can clean it up." I pulled the foal up to Molly's head. Molly gave a little whinny and smelled it real close and started licking the foal dry. I dipped its navel in iodine and then grabbed a towel and helped Molly dry her foal.

"Molly, old girl, this foal is mousy colored so it will be black when full grown. Molly, you did yourself good, old girl." I finally realized I hadn't checked the sex of the little bugger. "Molly, I'm sorry! We didn't even check to see if it's a boy or girl yet." I pulled the tail up to see what plumbing it had.

"Molly, it's a stud colt you rascal!" I shouted, giving Molly a big hug. Molly and I were busy drying when I noticed a wide white strip on the foal's forehead. I checked the colt closely for any flaws. I checked its feet, eyes, tail, ears, and even its tongue. Everything seemed to be in the right place.

"Molly, we've got ourselves a fine specimen of horse flesh here. I can't wait to see the look on Mom and Dad's faces when they get here." The foal was trying to gain control of his head. Right when he would get his head up in the air, Molly would lick him and he would have to start all over again.

I started to clear things out of the stall so when Molly stood up she had room to maneuver. I was just about done when Molly let out a big groan and seemed to push again.

"Molly, are you all right? I'll bet you're getting rid of the afterbirth. You get that stuff pushed out and then we'll get you up to nurse this little stud colt."

When I was done clearing the stall out. I went back to the foal and the little bugger was trying to get up already. First his back end would bob unsteadily up, then his front end, it was kind of funny. He would tumble left, then right, or get most of the way up and then fall on his face. As close as he was to standing, I figured I better get Molly up to start the nursing process. The quicker you get the milk in the foal the better the effect of the antibodies.

"Okay, Molly, time to get up, old girl. You've got a little shaver that's awfully hungry." I tugged on her halter a little and she let out another big groan and push. Something didn't seem normal here. I decided to check in the horse book on mares foaling. It stated that the mare usually gets up fairly soon after foaling. Molly foaled over an hour ago. Then I read what shook me to the bone: "A mare that has twins will often have the second foal in the breech position."

"Molly, are you having twins? Is that what you're doing? I better call Dad."

I grabbed the cell phone and called home as fast as I could dial. It rang for what seemed like hours. Finally I heard, "Hello."

"Dad, you have to get over here right away! I think Molly's having twins!" I yelled.

"Dad? I don't have any kids" A very groggy voice mumbled back. "Who is this?" Oops. In my haste I dialed the wrong number!

"I'm so sorry I woke you! I dialed the wrong number," I said sheepishly. This time I got to some better lighting and dialed home. Again it seemed to take forever for Mom to get to the phone.

"Mom, I need some help right away! I think Molly is having twins and one of them seems to be in the breech position." I yelled into the phone and hung up.

Mom and Dad hustled over as soon as they could. Mom came loaded for bear with water, towels, liquid soap, and a flashlight. Dad surveyed the situation and started to wash his right arm up to the shoulder.

I asked, "Are you reaching in to check for another foal?"

"Got to, son. Now get a towel and wrap it around her tail and hold it out of my way." Dad proceeded to reach up into Molly. "I feel a pair of hooves." After a little more time he said, "They seem to be upside down. Let me try to locate a head." This whole time Molly was pushing like crazy against Dad's arm. "Easy girl, easy," Dad reassured Molly. "Sure enough, she's upside down. I'll have to flip her over."

Dad adjusted his position and started pushing his arm in

farther. He grabbed Molly's left thigh with his left hand for additional leverage. Dad started groaning as he added more torque. "She's starting to go. Come on girl, stay with me. Oh no, she slipped just as I almost had her flipped."

"Honey we don't have much more time before we lose that foal." Mom said anxiously. Dad reset himself. "Jude, get a couple bales of hay that I can pry my feet up against." I hustled up the hay mow as fast as I could go and threw down three bales. I think I hit the floor the same time the bales did. I positioned the bales so Dad could push himself into Molly better. Dad started in again, the veins in his arms bulging, his brow full of sweat. Dad was a very powerful and determined man. He seemed to be using every muscle in his body.

"Come on, baby, keep coming, you're almost home." With one last burst of energy and a big groan from Dad the foal flipped. Dad was totally exhausted from the strain and lay there a few seconds. "Jude, get over there and wash up so you can help pull this little rascal." Mom held Molly's tail back and I grabbed hold of those little legs and pulled when Molly pushed. It didn't take long and out popped a little mouse-colored stud colt. I cleared its nostrils and dragged him over by his mother and brother. I think Ol' Molly was wondering what was going on. Mom, Dad, Molly, and I started drying the little buggers off. Mom was even smart enough to take some pictures of this special occasion.

We all sat on the bales just staring at the spectacle in front of us. Each of us, including Molly, was mentally and physically exhausted. It was so rewarding to see Ol' Molly nuzzle each foal with her massive head. For all the power she had in that neck, she was gentle as she went from one foal to the other.

"Mom, it looks like there's going to be little black stud colts running around Quin's pasture. And look, one has a wide strip and one has a narrow strip on the forehead."

"Jude, you can be awfully proud of these little guys. By golly, who would have ever guessed Molly would throw twins," Dad said as he wiped his brow.

"I've got chores to do Jude. I think you've got things under control here, so I'm going to grab Mom and head home." I gave each one of them a hug and thanked them for the help.

"Fuzz, we better clear some of these things out of this stall for when Molly gets up." Just then I heard Mr. Olson open the barn door. I couldn't wait to see the look on his face, he'd probably think he was seeing double. Sure enough he came right into Molly's area to check on her.

He stood there surveying what was before him with a blank look on his face. He gradually cracked a grin and shook his head. "Jude, what have you got here? Am I seeing correctly that you have a pair of twins on your hands?"

"That is up to you, Mr. Olson. If your offer is still good I reckon one of them is mine," I answered.

"If you recollect, I stated that anything that comes out of that mare is yours so it looks like you got yourself a team. But you got your work cut out for you, for twins have a very high mortality rate. Now the sooner we get some colostrum in these little shavers the better their chances. I'll get a couple bottles and lamb's nipples. You head to the house and get a good clean ice cream pail. We'll milk Molly as she rests and bottle feed them right away."

As I hurried to the house I thanked God for these little foals and also thanked him for people like Mom, Dad, and Mr. Olson. When I returned, Mr. Olson washed the bottles out well with the high temp water in the milk house and we started milking Molly. Colostrum is the early milk from a mare or cow, and it contains extremely important antibodies. We filled the two pop bottles and brought them to the mouths of the little foals.

"Now dip your finger in the colostrum and see if you can sneak it into one of their mouths," Mr. Olson instructed. "If it works, then replace your finger with the lamb nipple."

"Okay, little guy, let's get something in that little tummy of yours." The foals didn't understand what was going on. They kept pulling their heads back and we kept re-dipping our fingers. The colostrum is very thick and sticky so we were getting messy real fast. Mr. Olson and I kept trying, and we finally started getting them to accept the taste. Soon we each had them working over the lamb's nipple. They would gulp some down than lay there and look around for awhile and shake their head. We'd bring the nipple back to them and they would latch on for another round. They had colostrum all over their faces and necks by the time they each took a bottle and a half. It was a pretty special time, something I will never forget.

The barn door opened again and it was Becky with her camera. She was all smiles as she took many pictures. "Mr. Olson have you ever seen twins before?" she asked.

"When I was about six years old we had a mare throw twins, I'll never forget that! We lost the mare and both foals."

"How terrible!" Becky complained. "I've got to get to school, bye."

"Jude, we need to get Molly up before she gets too stiff." It took a little prodding and she staggered up slowly but seemed to be okay. She stood over the twins licking and nuzzling them.

"I've got milking to do and you have chores waiting. I'll watch for Molly to drop her afterbirth this morning and call Doc Strand if she doesn't. I have a feeling she won't clean proper after what she's been through," Mr. Olson said.

"I'm going to talk Mom into letting me stay home from school today. After chores I'll go home and get a little grub, and then I'll come back and check on the foals. Thank you, Mr. Olson! See you later!"

"Jude, you need to read that horse book of yours and maybe even check the internet for advice on raising twin foals. Do that before any grub time or nap time. Twins can be very troublesome and we'll be lucky not to lose one or both of them."

I hustled through chores and all I could think of were the haunting words Mr. Olson said, "We'll be lucky not to lose one or both of them." I prayed all the way home. Mom had a hot breakfast waiting for me.

"Jude, how are Molly and the foals doing?" Mom asked.

"Fine, but Mr. Olson says we need to research raising twins. I guess their mortality rate is very high. Mom, we can't lose those little guys after all that work. They're my first team!"

"Have you taken it to prayer?"

"Yes ma'am, that's all I've been doing! After breakfast I'll get on the internet and see what it has to say."

The information I found confirmed Mr. Olson's threat. Mortality rate is over eighty percent for both foals. They talked of the IGG count, which is a test to see how well they received the anti-bodies from the first colostrum. You need to feed them every two hours, and they will probably need a stomach tube to ensure each feeding. It also stressed the need to watch for navel infections.

"Mom, I need to get over there right away and check on the boys. Can you run to town and get a tube feeder in case we need it?"

"Yes Jude, is there anything else you can think of?"

"No. I'm calling Doc Strand either way so we might need to make another trip after we see what she says." Doc Strand was a one-person vet clinic but she specialized in equine. Mr. Olson said she was one of the best around.

Mr. Olson was just finishing milking when I got there. "I called Doc Strand and asked her to come right away. The information on the web wasn't real encouraging and said the foals probably need a shot to help clear their lungs. We need to feed them every two hours around the clock and watch super close for navel infections."

"Why certainly, why certainly." We checked on the foals and they were both sound asleep with Molly standing near them. Doc Strand arrived and stood there by the stall in silence for a minute.

"Quin and Jude, you've got your hands full with these little jewels," Doc stated as she whistled quietly. "Quin, will Molly be okay with me in the stall? Some mares are pretty fussy after they've foaled."

"I think she'll be fine, but let me get a lead rope on her and hold her just in case."

I grabbed a rope and handed it to Mr. Olson. Doc entered the stall slowly as Molly let out a light whinny. She listened to lungs on the foals and Molly. She checked the navels and Molly for the cleaning process. "We need to give these little boys an injection that will help clear their lungs and Molly a shot of oxytocin to see if she'll drop that afterbirth."

"Why certainly."

"Jude, Quin says you're the proud owner of these little guys. I wish you the best, but try not to get your hopes up too high." she put her hand on my shoulder and looked me in the eye. "The cards are stacked against these guys right now. You need to keep them warmer than what they are, so head over to Crow Creek Kennels and see if you can borrow some insulated dog wraps. You'll need to figure some type of schedule that feeds these boys every two hours. You'll also need to call me right away if there are any signs of weakness or scours in the foals. Lastly you need to say your prayers," Doc instructed.

As she was packing up to leave, Doc said, "It is very easy to think you're helping the foal by giving additional milk. That is only hurting. You need to carefully measure each feeding. I drew blood from each foal to check the IGG counts, so I'll let you know as soon as I get the results."

"Thank you and let us know what the tests come back as." I said fighting back tears.

"Sure will, I'll stop when I'm in the area just to check in."

Mom stopped by with the tube feeder and dog blankets. She offered to help with the next feeding. I was pleased that Mom offered to help because God equipped mothers with that special touch with little ones. Mr. Olson got a measuring cup from the house so we wouldn't overfeed. We milked Molly and tried the lamb's nipples with pop bottles again. Each foal seemed uninterested and weak.

"Jude, I think we need to use the tube feeder," Mom said. Mom filled the feeder and dipped the end into the milk to add lubrication and taste. Cradling each foal in her lap, she gently slid the feeder through their mouths and into their little stomachs. It seemed to go pretty well. "Jude, while I finish here you'd better run to the truck and get those dog blankets." Mom said.

I ran to the truck and got the two insulated dog blankets. We were lucky that Crow Creek Kennels raised Boerboel dogs. Boerboels are a large breed of dogs around 140 pounds so the blankets would fit well. I got back to the pen and put the blankets on the boys right away. Molly had just finished cleaning so I grabbed a pitchfork and threw it in a bag for the vet to check. The foals were fast asleep again. So peaceful...

"Molly, ol' girl, you did yourself proud. You and I got a lot of work ahead of us, but we'll make it," I whispered to Molly. I cleaned the dirty straw out and added new straw, took a few pictures and headed home for lunch.

Mom and Dad were ready for lunch when I got home.

Dad asked as he stirred his coffee, "How is the horse farmer and his horses doing?"

"I don't know, I just don't know." I said with a shaky voice. "Doc Strand doesn't give them much hope."

Mom said, "Bud when we just fed them they seemed very weak. Jude has a mountain to climb. I just pray for those little guys, they are so precious."

"Yes, ma'am, we do," I stated.

"What's this we stuff? Do you have a turd in your pocket?" Dad laughed.

"Bud Bonner, watch your manners," Mom hollered.

"Son, did Doc say how long we have to feed them every two hours?" Dad asked.

"Depends on how soon the colts start nursing on their own, if they even live. Doc said these first twelve days are very critical. She took a blood sample to see how well their systems accepted the antibodies."

Mom asked, "Jude, have you thought about school and the extra time these little guys will take?"

"Not yet." Deep down I really didn't want to think about that. "What do you think I should do?"

"Your Dad and I have been talking, and we think if you get your school work done at home you could take a week off."

"Are you kidding?" I asked.

"Now, let's work out a schedule so we can help with feeding them little rascals," Mom said.

Chapter 10
"The Grind"

We put together a schedule the best we could. I took most of the night feedings since I couldn't ask my mom to sleep in the barn. When we first started, it seemed to be going well, but after a couple of days it was getting pretty old. Working on very little sleep was harder than I had thought it would be. It was the same old routine everyday: clean pen, feed the twins, curry Molly, and do school work. It seemed like I was a slave to everything. I was starting to accept that the colts were going to die. It was one of God's tests for me, and I don't think I pleased him with my attitude. And, of course, a mother can tell real fast when you need an attitude adjustment. I was home, late for a feeding, and ready to give up!

"Jude Bonner! Aren't you late, young man?"

"It's no use Mom."

"No use! You've got to realize the world does not revolve around Jude Bonner. Yes, Sir, you're tired and overworked but it could be a whole lot worse. Now you need to start thinking of the positive things God has done for you and quit feeling sorry for yourself," Mom scolded.

"But Mom…"

"Don't you 'but Mom' me! Those little guys need you in the worst way, and you told them you'd be there for them. Are you going to go back and tell them to just go ahead and die?" She shouted as she pointed her finger right in my face. "God has given you a responsibility. Are you going to let the devil tell you that you're not man enough to do the job? Now get your butt out that door before I slap you! And you decide if you're going to listen to God or the devil!"

That was the worst tongue-lashing I'd ever had, and it came from my own mother. I headed towards Mr. Olson's with my tail between my legs. As I walked, I realized Mom was right. I was too busy listening to the devil and letting him tell me I wasn't good enough. Philippians 4:13 came to mind: "I can do all things through him who gives me strength."

"God, thank you for my wake up call, and I'm sorry for not trusting you. Please forgive me," I prayed as I walked.

It was the night shift again, but I felt this new hope. I prayed over the colts and started the process of feeding them. I continued to pray as I fed each one. It was going pretty well when I finally realized that I wasn't doing the work, but it was God working through me. God also spoke to me about naming these colts. I had so little hope before this that I hadn't even named them. Shame on me! I sat right there with a colt in each arm and thought up their names, Pete and ah... Joe.

"God, please forgive me for taking the credit for all the work here." I cleaned up the feeding bottles, washed Pete and Joe's faces with warm water, and headed to my hay bale bed exhausted but with a new hope.

It seemed like I had just fallen asleep when the alarm reminded me, two hours later, that the colts needed another feeding. I was surprised to see Pete standing up on his own shaky little legs.

"Hey, big guy, you're looking pretty strong. Now we just need your little brother to do the same." This was the fourth night of the feeding marathon but it seemed like we were getting over the hump.

Early the next morning, I was still sleeping soundly when I was startled awake with the opening of the barn door. It was a good thing because I was late for the next feeding. I assumed it was Mr. Olson, but in walked Doc Strand.

Yawning and stretching, "Good morning, Doc. Glad to see you."

"It's time we checked these twins to see how they're doing. I believe this is day number nine, am I correct?"

"Yes, Doc"

"Have you seen any progress, Jude?"

"Pete stood up a little on his own at about three this morning."

"That's good. The tests for the antibodies came back pretty positive. You folks did a fine job early on."

Doc took their temps and checked their eyes, hearts, navels, and lungs. I helped her weigh them with a platform scale and they had both gained a couple pounds.

"Jude, they're looking pretty good. I would try to get them on their feet a couple times a day. This will stimulate leg muscles and help with their digestion. Increase their milk by five or six ounces each feeding. I'm sure you will see them nursing on their own in a couple of days. Now let me check over their mother and be on my way." She took Molly's temperature, checked her lungs, her tongue color, eyes, and her heart rate.

"Molly looks in great shape for keeping up with these two guys. I would take her out daily for a little walk. Realize she will be pretty nervous without her little shadows, so make it brief. You need to work on a bigger area for them that is high and dry and out of the weather, which will allow Molly some more freedom. I will check back early next week, but I think we might be able to see the light at the end of the tunnel."

Praise God! I could have done back flips down the barn aisle after she said that. I finished my other chores and went home.

Rebecca and I headed to Mr. Olson's right after school to help with a bigger pen area. Rebecca was great help and she loved spending time with Pete and Joe. Mr. Olson thought it best to move them into the old hog barn. We had to move some items he had stored there, sweep the floor clean and bed it down good with clean straw. Mr. Olson hooked up some plumbing so Molly could have an automatic water bowl, and we were ready to move the horses in.

"Jude and Rebecca, before we move them in, is there anything else we need to check?"

I thought for awhile but didn't really think of anything. "I think we're fine, Mr. Olson. Let's go get Molly."

"I disagree. How's bout you, Rebecca?" Becky stood there thinking.

"You guys are forgetting the most important detail when bringing animals into a new area. We all need to stand back and look for areas where the colts or Molly could get into trouble. For instance, lying under a gate or nails sticking out, areas where they could get their little heads stuck, stuff like that."

"Good thinking, Mr. Olson." Becky said.

We all went over the pen with a fine tooth comb looking for any snag that could cause harm. When we had all given our final approval, we went to get Molly and the foals. Mr. Olson lead Molly while Becky and I guided the foals along. Those little rascals didn't let Mama get too far ahead, and Molly was watching every move we made. Molly would whinny softly as she got nervous and side stepped. She even started prancing with her head held high. Of course the foals had to mimic her every move. We closed the gate behind them and just stood silently watching them explore their new home. Molly would whinny every once in a while and nuzzle them oh so gently. The colts were sticking to her like glue.

"Becky and Jude, I could stand here all night and just marvel at those little fellars, but chores are a waiting. Thanks, kids, for helping."

Doc Strand was right. Pete and Joe got stronger each day and started nursing on their own. This was a sight to behold! Of course they couldn't figure out that Molly had two teats, so they would stand and jockey for the same one on the same side. If I was there I would play referee and push one to each side. Each day brought something new to discover for the colts. They would spend some time each day play fighting with each other, kicking each other and pawing with their front legs. Occasionally they would even send a stray hoof into Molly. Molly would just stand there and maybe put her ears back for a few seconds. Mr. Olson fed Molly heavily so she could support the foals. We were lucky she had the milk supply. Pete and Joe were growing like weeds.

Our Minnesota winter was letting go and you could feel the power of the sun getting stronger each day, so Becky and I led Molly and the foals out daily. I would lead Molly and Becky would chase the colts. I had to laugh a couple times as the colts would kick Becky. Each day they would get more confidence as they explored the barnyard. Becky and I couldn't believe it when Pete got stuck in a snow bank. He just stood there waiting for Becky to save him, like he was totally helpless. Molly whinnied as she thought her colt was in a world of hurt. Becky lay beside him and gave him a big hug and then helped him get out. Joe stood and watched this whole episode and jumped in the same snow bank as soon as Pete was out.

Pete and Joe soon learned they could chase Fuzz and the cats around. Fuzz understood and would just sidestep them. The cats were not as forgiving and they would head for the high country as we led the colts out. Ladd stood in the pasture and would whinnie at Molly each time he saw her.

Molly was doing well and allowing the colts more freedom, but she still wanted to protect them from any danger. One afternoon, with Mr. Olson we led them into the main pasture and let Molly roam with the colts. As we stood there watching them, Molly suddenly raised her head and looked to the north. She soon took off at a full gallop with ears pinned back, snorting the whole time. She was on a mission. We noticed a muskrat running ahead. Molly was there in seconds and reared up and stomped that muskrat into the ground with her huge front feet. She was relentless as she cocked her head to one side with her ears folded all the way back, stomping over and over. She would back up and snort and then go at it again. Nothing was going to hurt her foals. It was something to watch as she gradually eased away from the pancake she had created.

Mr. Olson chuckled. "He won't do that again!"

Just then Doc Strand pulled in. Becky told her what Molly just did as I led Molly back to the barn so Doc could check everyone over.

Doc shook her head. "Yes, mares can be very protective of their little ones! Several years back a mare pinned me against a wooden fence. I was lucky that I was able to slip between the boards when she let up a little. Now, I'm anxious to check these guys over and see what their weight is."

Molly was still wired from the muskrat episode so I held her back as Doc checked the foals. "Jude these little guys are doing very well! I guess I shouldn't say little, look at how they have grown. Would you believe this is the first set of twins I have seen live? You and your family have done a remarkable job!"

Chapter 11
"Training and Church Youth Group"

At supper that night Mom said, "Jude, I brought home some books from the library about early training and handling of foals. I put them up in your room. And by the way, you can thank me for cleaning that area you call a bedroom, but don't think it's going to become a habit."

"Thanks, Mom. I can't wait to read the books." After supper I helped with the dishes, grabbed a couple horse books and headed over to Mr. Olson's to read in the barn. I started working with Pete and Joe that night. It was really fun to see them respond to handling their feet and legs. I had to be real gentle and patient so they wouldn't pull away too fast. The books stressed it was a whole lot safer for me to work with their legs and feet early on in their lives. This would make trimming feet much easier when they weigh in at two thousand pounds. Pete and Joe seemed to be fast learners. The main problem was when I worked with one, the other would be biting me or his brother. I would push one away while working with the other, only to have the one I pushed turn and kick me. Those little feet packed a pretty good wallop. Sometimes if you walked up behind them and pushed down on their rumps, they would start crow hopping with their back feet prepping for a hoof to fly.

The time spent with them seemed to go so fast. Mrs. Norman visited with her grandkids and husband. This was the first time

Pete and Joe saw little kids. They were looking at them eye to eye. It seemed like Pete and Joe had to put on a show for those kids. They would prance past them like the kids were judges. Mrs. Norman stood and laughed at both her grandkids and Pete and Joe. Molly allowed me to put the little kids on her back for a few pictures.

The local paper 'The Observer' came out and did a story on them. They took tons of pictures and asked Mr. Olson and me a lot of questions. That next week Pete and Joe made the front page! The writer did a great job on the story with history of the breed and statistics on twins foals. Pete and Joe were getting famous.

Now that spring was in full bloom, we moved them out into the main horse pen with Ladd, where they could get inside if the weather was bad or lay in the sun. I felt sorry for Ladd. Those colts would just torment him to no end with their play antics. They spent most of their time soaking up the sun, bugging Ladd, or filling their bellies.

When school was out for the summer, I spent many hours with Pete and Joe. When they were three months old it was time to start training. Training to lead was pretty interesting. Pete caught on right away. Joe was a different story. Joe would lock his little legs as stiff as a board. I had to keep reminding myself to take it slow and keep the sessions short. After a week or so they were both leading and backing pretty well.

That summer flew by. Between training colts, making hay, finishing our horse pen, trapping gophers, and Wednesday night church youth group activities, my life was a whirlwind.

Youth group at church with our youth pastor, Carl Toney, was always a good break midweek. In the summer Carl would mostly plan games like tennis or softball. One night we played softball against our parents. The score was closer than what Perry, Harold and I thought it would be. Despite Dad putting a couple over the fence, the kids prevailed.

God works all things out for His good, so I thought it interesting that during the big game, Greg Shants and his crew including Judy Clemons, drove by and stopped. They actually got out of their car and watched for several minutes. During inning changes Carl asked them to join us, I caught myself hoping they wouldn't play.

Carl was definitely using the gifts God gave him to reach many different kids. He knew when to laugh and when to be serious. Jesus used Carl to bring several kids to the Lord, including Harold and Perry. Carl wasn't afraid to wrestle with the guys. Dad always said he thought it was great that Carl would get physical with the boys, because guys need that kind of roughhousing.

Carl was very aware of my activities with Pete and Joe, so he asked me, "Jude, would Mr. Olson allow the youth group to meet at his place next week?"

"I can ask him, I'm pretty sure he wouldn't mind."

"Maybe we could do a hayride and bonfire, if that works for him."

"Fair enough. I'll check with him and let you know."

I checked with Mr. Olson that next morning during chores, and he was fine with Carl bringing the kids out for a night on the farm. Mr. Olson seemed to be pretty excited about the whole thought.

I knew Mr. Olson liked kids but rarely had a chance to mingle with them. Most kids just thought of him as an old Minnesota bachelor.

I called Carl when I got home and told him it was a go.

The next morning Mr. Olson was quite different. He seemed more energetic and happy. I truly believe it was because the kids were coming out. He was humming a few tunes and had an extra spring in his step.

"Jude, we have to get the place looking good for Wednesday night!," he said as he rattled off a long list.

I just smiled at how he was a changed man. You could tell he was brimming with joy.

"Do you think we have enough time to get this all done before Wednesday?" he asked.

"Well, it's a pretty long list but we want to look our best, so how about I call Perry and Harold to see if they have time to help."

"That would be nice if they could help."

Perry could help but Harold was too busy so I called Carl to see if he had time. Carl could help also, so the next two days we worked on Mr. Olson's list and then some. Carl made the work even more fun because he was kind of a city slicker.

Perry whispered to me, "Hey man, let's jump Carl in the hay mow and work him over a little!"

"Awesome, but we'll probably get our butts kicked." Carl had played college football and was very quick and strong.

Carl, Perry, and I headed up to the mow to throw bales down. Sure enough, Carl sensed trouble brewing.

"Now boys I wouldn't want to have to hurt…"

That was the only warning he gave before he jumped us. We were supposed to jump him. He grabbed Perry by his arm and slung him into the bale pile. I jumped on his back piggy back style, hanging on for dear life. Carl wasn't exactly your average pushover, you could see the sparkle in his eyes as he was fighting us. Well, I didn't stay on his back very long, because he backed hard into some bales and I let go. Perry and I both got on our feet and charged him at the same time from two different directions. Before we could think, Carl grabbed me and placed me in front of him so Perry ended up hitting me. We both went down again laughing.

Carl laughed, "Now, children, I warned you." That was it, Perry and I had to redeem our dignity. Perry got up first and started doing Ninja moves. I grabbed a bale and charged at the same time. We all met in the middle. I felt a sharp object hit my eye, as I was going down. When I looked up Carl was holding his elbow. Perry tripped over my bale and lay there laughing as I held my eye. It hurt pretty bad.

As Carl stood there rubbing his elbow, "Sorry about that elbow? Are you okay?" Carl asked, while he tried to stop from laughing.

"Carl, if I get a shiner from this what will all the girls say?" I asked him jokingly. We threw the bales down, then Perry and I came down from the loft licking our wounds.

Mr. Olson was there to greet us, "So, I sent some boys to do a man's job, huh? Why certainly, why certainly." We all laughed. I could feel my eye swelling tighter by the minute.

"Looks like you better head up to the house for a little ice on that eye," Mr. Olson said.

"Yes Jude! Get some ice on that while we finish up here." Carl said.

We finally got all the items checked off Mr. Olson's list. Perry and I headed home as Carl talked to Mr. Olson.

"Perry, Carl showed us who's boss. It sure will be fun to get the best of him, someday." I said.

"Your mother is gonna skin you for that eye of yours. It's looking pretty gnarly."

"If it looks as bad as it feels, then it could be the worst shiner I ever had."

Perry and I walked home. "Jude, wash your face and get ice on your eye right away." Mom stated as we stepped in the back door. "What did your eyeball run into this time?"

"Carl's elbow," I answered sheepishly.

"Now don't tell me that Carl gave you boys another thrashing?" Neither Perry nor I would even answer that question. It was a dignity thing again.

I was surprised when Perry actually tried to schmooze Mom. "Mrs. Bonner, did I ever tell you that you make some pretty mean sugar cookies?"

"Now, Perry Carper, don't you go buttering me up with that kind of comment, and yes, you may have one. And Jude how about getting that ice?"

It was time for the big hayride at Mr. Olson's. The weather seemed perfect for the hayride and bonfire. You could feel that hint of autumn in the air and there was not a cloud in sight. To top it off, the moon was on schedule to be full that evening. I went over to help with chores so everything would be ready.

"Jude, as soon as we get milking chores done we need to get them horses ready. Wild and woolly and full of fleas, never curry below the knees," Mr. Olson mumbled to himself.

"What are we doing with Pete and Joe during the hay ride, Mr. Olson?"

"I think they'll be fine just tagging along. We'll see how it goes."

Mr. Olson and I had Ladd and Molly looking pretty sharp. We even curried Pete and Joe. Those little fellars would just stand there as you brushed them and act like you owed it to them. When you would quit brushing one and start on the other, the first one would come back seeking more attention. It was hard to get anything done. Mr. Olson was pretty jolly as he worked with Molly and Ladd.

"Now Ladd and Molly," he said, "you have to be on your best behavior tonight. Why certainly. Who knows, you might even be hauling Jude Bonner's future wife," he laughed. "You know Jude, many a romance has started on a hayride," He said as he peeked around Molly.

Carl brought a bunch with him and other kids showed up on their own. Mr. Olson was all smiles. Even I was all smiles despite my shiner that Carl had to mention to everyone. Carl had the kids watch as Mr. Olson harnessed Molly and Ladd. A few kids asked questions and Mr. Olson answered as he worked. I helped hitch to the wagon and we were off. Mr. Olson was pretty proud up there driving his team. Pete and Joe stole the show, prancing around Molly as she did all the work. Mr. Olson had a beautiful trail he used for hayrides and sleigh rides. It meandered through the woods and along a spring-fed stream. Along the stream were a couple of huge Cottonwood trees with some Hackberry trees on the ridges. A few hills to go up and down added to the experience as Molly and Ladd leaned into the load as they fought to get us to the top. Molly and Ladd could probably drive this trail on their own as many times as they've done it. Molly and Ladd were trained to work together very well. Mr. Olson even let Carl drive for a stretch. Carl got us singing a few songs as we rode along.

We got back to the barnyard and Carl started the bonfire. Just before Carl started his message, he asked Mr. Olson to bring Molly and the foals back out from the barn. Molly and the foals followed Mr. Olson along, kicking and high tailing the best they knew how. They would run ahead and suddenly stop, look at the kids, and run back to Mom. Many times they would stop in front of her so she would have to alter her direction. Molly of course took this all in stride.

"Mr. Olson," Carl asked, "how much does Molly weigh?"

"I suppose she is around two thousand pounds." Most of the kids couldn't believe Molly was that heavy.

Carl asked, "How old is Molly and how long have you owned her?"

"She was ten years old this spring and she was born on this farm."

"Mr. Olson, I notice Molly stands quiet while Pete and Joe are nervous and anxious. Why is that?"

Mr. Olson laughed a little. I think he thought it was a silly question. Before he could answer, Carl asked the youth group to give their opinions of why Molly was more controllable than Pete and Joe. Several kids stated that it was simply the age difference between them.

Carl looked back to Mr. Olson. "Mr. Olson, is that the only reason?"

Mr. Olson said with a smile on his face, "You see, the difference is ownership. I own Molly and Mr. Jude Bonner owns

Pete and Joe." Mr. Olson laughed, "Carl, the real answer is the age difference and training. With all animals, it is important to train them so they understand who's in charge."

Carl asked, "Could you explain to the kids at what age this training should start, how long it takes, and what gives you the right to be in charge of Molly?

"Yes, I can explain that."

We listened to every word Mr. Olson said. I think Carl was pleased at how well Mr. Olson captured everyone's attention.

Mr. Olson answered, "In the book of Genesis, God gave us the responsibility of ruling over all of his creatures. As far as when this training starts, Jude and I started with Pete and Joe when they were just a couple of days old. How long does it take? Normally about two years."

"What if a horse receives no directions or very bad training?" Carl asked.

"Then you would have an animal that would be of little value, dangerous, and not a joy to be around. And I would add that you would not be honoring God's plan for man to rule over all creatures."

"So Mr. Olson, does the word training, have anything to do with discipline?" Carl asked.

"I think they go hand in hand, one in the same. You can't have training without discipline."

"Mr. Olson can you explain discipline please?" Carl asked.

Mr. Olson hesitated, then responded, "It is very important that you discipline an animal at the right time and place and for the correct length of time. And that discipline needs to come from your heart, for the good of the animal. And what's most important, correct discipline is not beating an animal; it is getting the animal in a situation that makes the wrong thing hard and the right behavior easy. The horses end up disciplining themselves if you are consistent with your approach. I have never beat Molly and I never will because beating would only teach her to work with me out of fear. Trust would not be part of the relationship." With that answer, all the kids focused back to Carl like this was a tennis match.

Carl pressed on, "Mr. Olson, did Molly always like this discipline?"

"No she didn't. You know it's funny, many people have defined discipline as something negative. I can look back at the discipline I received from my parents and laugh, even though at the time it meant my butt was sore." He chuckled.

"Mr. Olson can you relate this relationship between you and Molly and a relationship between kids, parents and God?"

"Oh I guess I would say it's simple. Molly and I have mutual respect for each other. That was created by God's plan for man to rule over all of his creatures. Kids and parents need that same mutual respect. One of the ten commandments talks of honoring your parents. I feel respect is taught through proper discipline. Molly would be dangerous if I hadn't worked with her. Kids can end up dangerous also if they have no discipline. Look how God disciplined Adam and Eve. With that said, Mr. Olson turned and walked Molly towards the barn. The colts weren't paying attention and stood there for awhile. Molly looked back and whinnied, and soon the colts were high tailing it to the barn.

We sat there laughing at the little guys. Carl finally broke the silence with a prayer. We all had some s'mores and hot chocolate and old time stories from Mr. Olson and a few of the adult leaders.

Chapter 12
"Weaning and Early Training"

As we all know, time disappears. Before I knew it Pete and Joe were six months old, old enough to wean from Molly and bring home to our place. That was a very special day. Dad, Fuzz and I decided to lead them home through the field right after morning chores. This would allow us more daylight time if we had any trouble. As we walked to Mr. Olson's the Bluebirds were flying ahead of us in groups of six or so getting ready to fly south. Dad led Pete and I led Joe as Mr. Olson watched us from his line fence. When we got to our property line Mom and Rebecca were there to get our picture. I was so proud that day standing by my first team of Percherons on our property. Pete and Joe did pretty well on their trip home. They whinnied back to Molly every once in awhile. They pranced and pawed at the ground. Since they had each other they didn't seem to miss Molly all that much.

First thing I did when we got them to the barn was measure them to see how tall they were. I vowed to do this every four weeks and mark on the barn wall to keep track. Dad and I stood them in the barn alley as Rebecca and Mom helped measure with a level and tape. Pete was one inch taller than Joe.

Dad and I led them to their new home. Rebecca and I had done all the finishing touches on it so it was all ready for the new guests. The water was full, hay in the manger, hot fence plugged in, and knee deep straw in the shelter area.

"Remember, Jude, to be ready to move out of the way once you let the lead rope go, in case they turn and kick," Dad warned. Rebecca closed the gate as Dad and I went into the paddock with the colts. Dad and I led the colts around the perimeter of the paddock to let them see their new boundaries. When we got back by the gate we let them go at the same time. To our surprise they just stood there awhile, gazing at their new home. Dad and I slipped out and stood with Mom and Rebecca. I could have stood there the rest of the day just staring at those colts.

"Jude," Mom said, "you've got some pretty nice colts. I wonder if I'm going to have to bring supper out here to feed ya? A team of wild horses couldn't pull you away from them little fellars right now."

"Be sure to come back and check them often. Later on you should pull their halters," Dad said. We left the halters on at first, so that just in case they got out we could catch them more easily.

Dad and Mom went on their way and Rebecca and I stood there watching and waiting. Joe was the first to make a move, with Pete right behind him. They explored the water trough and rippled the water with their upper lips, then the hay manger where they took a few nibbles of hay. Before we knew it, Joe took off full blast towards the other end of the paddock. Pete followed suit. I prayed they would stop at the end. As they got closer you could tell they were considering their options: turn around or go over the fence.

The option they chose caught Becky and me off guard. They both locked up the brakes and stood like statues right next to the hot fence. Sure enough, like clockwork, they both placed their muzzles closer to the hot wire. Snap! Snap! They each took a zap in the nose before spinning around, looking to check if anyone was watching! Pete took off and headed around the paddock, his head held high and awfully proud, with Joe a mirror image right behind. Becky and I just laughed.

Joe and Pete settled right into their new home. This would be home until next spring when we would give them their own pasture. Their first winter was pretty cold and long, and Pete and Joe looked like woolly mammoths with their winter coats.

The winter seemed to last forever. Sometimes I came out to find frozen water in the horse trough. You could tell right away when you had frozen water, because Pete and Joe would be standing at the water trough pawing it with their hooves. They expected it to be fixed the second I stepped foot into the paddock. They would crowd me as if I had water for them in my back pocket. I would bring two five-gallon pails full of water out from the barn and let them drink from them. It was amazing how much they could drink! Dad always said livestock need more water in the cold than on hot summer days. The colts did well their first winter and soon we were celebrating their first birthday.

"Jude, I've invited Quin and Granny and Gramps over for supper tonight to help us celebrate the colts' first birthday," Mom said.

"Thanks Mom, good idea!"

Becky asked, "What are you getting the colts for their birthday, Jude?

"Gee, Becky, I hadn't thought much about it."

"How about some apple treats from mixed in with their oats?"

"Great idea, Becky!"

Off to the Farm & Fleet we went to buy some apple treats. As we headed up the aisle of the store we ran right into Greg Shants and his crew, Judy Clemons, Nick Grudden, and Bill Masters. It was a little strange, but Becky and I said hi and weaved through them. I don't believe we heard any "hi's" back.

As I got further down the aisle, I glanced back and caught Judy looking back at me. Much to my amazement, she actually gave me a little smile.

Pete and Joe's party went well. Becky mixed in the apple treats with their oats and they gobbled them up. Gramps was busy trading horse stories with Mr. Olson. Mom made a birthday cake for us and we had homemade ice cream to boot.

"Jude, have you thought that next year at this time you could be training these boys for harness and hitching?" Gramps asked. "Quin and I think it best to eventually hitch with Ladd or Molly, after you've done the proper ground work."

"Why certainly, but I'll have to figure what type of fee to charge for using such fine horse flesh." Mr. Olson laughed.

Gramps and Mr. Olson quizzed me on how often I was trimming feet, worming, and when I would be cutting them. Cutting is another term used for castration. I had actually kind of forgotten about it.

"Some believe the sooner you cut them the taller they get," Mr. Olson stated.

"You really should avoid the fly season also." Gramps added.

The next day before school, Becky and I stopped by Doc Strand's office to get her opinion on when would be best to cut Pete and Joe.

As I walked in the back door I heard, "Well, if it isn't that kid who owns that fancy pair of hitch geldings south of town. How are you doing, Jude?" Doc Strand asked.

"Oh, we are doing just fine, and I trust the same for you?"

"Couldn't be better! Now what can we do for you and Becky on this fine morning?"

"We need to check with you on when is the best time to cut Pete and Joe?"

"I see." Doc paused for a moment. "Have you checked to see if they have all dropped down?"

I wasn't sure what she meant. "What do you mean by 'dropping down'?"

Doc stopped what she was doing and smiled. "Jude, you have to check if the hardware has dropped down on each colt. Sometimes one stays way up there and makes the retrieval much more difficult. You go home and check after school if all four are down. Then call and schedule an appointment for next week so we can beat the oncoming flies."

Sure enough, all four were down so that next week Pete and Joe became geldings. "Fuzz, that bill won't be cheap from Doc. You and I will have to hit the gophers extra hard to pay her." Fuzz just wagged her tail.

The colts were getting bigger every day. Each month the marks on the barn wall went higher. I was doing some simple foundation work with them; leading, backing, and sacking them out. Sacking them out means getting them used to having ropes and bags against all parts of their bodies. Pete was more docile than Joe and accepted sacking out better. I had to spend twice the time with Joe to keep him at the same level.

One day I took the chain saw in the paddock and fired it up to get them used to the noise. That got their attention right away. They ran the perimeter of the pen several times before they realized it was easier to just stand there and look at the noise.

The one area I didn't spend enough time working on was their feet. One morning I was in the barn alley getting ready to trim Joe's feet, but he had other plans. I had trained them to stand still untied. I started reaching for his front foot when all of a sudden, down the barn alley he went. I went down and brought him back, so far keeping my cool. I reached for his front foot again, but Joe decided it was going to stay on the floor. Superman could not have picked it up. This was starting to get on my nerves! When Dad walked into the barn, he could tell something was not going well.

"Jude, what seems to be the problem?"

"Well, Joe is being real stubborn. He won't give me his foot and I'm losing my patience!" I shouted.

"Sounds to me like you need to go back to the basics a little and review with Joe picking up his feet with the rope. Do it with confidence, without losing your temper. The Bible says to be slow to anger. Remember also that the horse is your best teacher. Joe tensing up is telling you that he doesn't understand this right now. You need to cool down and look at it from his side of the fence."

Dad was right! Joe was not as far as I thought he was with his feet. I worked him through some basic stuff on picking his feet up, and then we got the job done. I was learning important lessons as I worked with these colts. I couldn't be a pushover but I couldn't be too firm either.

Most of the time I really enjoyed the foundation work with the colts. Mr. Olson suggested separating them from each other for short periods. This would teach them to accept being alone. Every once in awhile I would take one out for a lesson in the side yard or lead him down the road so he would get used to traffic. At first they each went crazy when they couldn't see each other, but with time they started to realize it wasn't that big of a deal.

It was amazing to see them learn new things. We walked through puddles, stepped over bales, walked on plastic tarps, walked through real tight areas between buildings, walked beside a tractor, and I even taught them to walk down a plank one foot off the ground. The most fun I had was teaching them to go into water down by Mr. Olson's stream. They would walk real slow up to the edge and then they'd back up like crazy. I kept at them and made sure I praised them when they did move toward the water. Pete was the funniest. When he finally got ankle deep in water, he stood still for a long time. Then, all of a sudden, he lunged and went the wrong way and was belly deep before he knew it. He looked at me like it was my fault and came running out.

Mr. Olson would come over and check on my progress every once in awhile. Becky and I were out lunging Pete one day when Mr. Olson pulled into the yard.

"How are you kids doing?"

"Oh we're fine Mr. Olson, how are you?"

"Becky, how many times have you handled these colts?"

Becky was surprised by his question. "Well, Jude lets me lead them in and out of the pasture sometimes, otherwise not much."

"Jude, I think it would benefit Becky and the colts if you allowed her to work them at times. The colts need to learn to take commands from other people besides you, and it would teach them to take commands from a girl. Also, it is a great learning opportunity for Becky."

"Gee, Mr. Olson, I never thought of that. I guess it sounds like a good idea," I added doubtfully.

"Becky, it will only work if you have a pretty keen interest in horses. If you think about it, many of the best trainers are ladies, usually because they have more patience than men. Imagine if you were home alone and the colts got out, wouldn't it be nice if you had more experience leading and handling them?"

"I guess that does make sense, Mr. Olson. I would love to work with them more if it's okay with my brother!"

"Well, Jude, you have the final say!"

I had to admit that deep down I was a little jealous. Becky was my kid sister, these were my colts, and this was my gift from Mr. Olson. Plus, she was just a girl and what if she was better than me? This was my real concern. All of a sudden I heard a stern voice say "Jude." I looked at Mr. Olson but it wasn't him who said it! I looked at Becky and it wasn't her. It must have been God! God was checking my attitude! I looked at Becky. Seeing the excitement in her eyes, I made a decision. "Sure, let's do it. It makes sense to me,"

"Now, kids, the most important thing is to be consistent together. Jude, you have to tell Becky what you expect, and Becky, you have to agree with what angle Jude is working. That doesn't mean Jude is always right, but these are his colts and he has the final say. If you both agree on the approach and give it to the colts in pretty much the same method, then you won't confuse Pete and Joe," Mr. Olson explained. "Now if you are willing, let's have Becky work with Pete and Joe while I'm here to oversee."

Mr. Olson first had Becky run Pete through some basics that he was very used to. This way Becky could gain confidence. Pete seemed a little confused that the commands were coming from a different voice and he didn't seem to pay much attention to Becky. In fact, Pete was getting a little unruly.

"Okay, Becky, you have to get a little more firm with him. Show him you are in charge and mean business. That means when you want him to turn to the left, you decide where and when and then make it happen," Mr. Olson coached.

Becky got right in his path and stared him down, pointed the next turn to him with authority and sent him on his way. Becky looked over to me, I think to see my reaction, so I gave a thumbs up and she grinned from ear to ear. I could tell Becky was really enjoying this and she seemed to be a natural.

"Becky, bring him in to the center now, please. Jude, could you get a thirty-gallon drum or two?"

Fuzz and I went to get some drums while Becky and Mr. Olson waited in the round pen. As I was grabbing the drums I had visions of Pete weaving between them, but Mr. Olson had different plans. Becky and I were about to find out what he needed the drums for.

"Jude, place the drums lying on their sides along the inside of the pen."

"Mr. Olson, are you thinking of jumping those drums?" I asked in total amazement.

Mr. Olson stopped, looked at me for a second, and then quietly said, "Well no, I think it would be better if Pete were to jump them." Then he laughed! Of course Becky joined right in. I have to admit it was a pretty silly thought, Mr. Olson running and jumping those drums.

"Now Becky, this is something Pete has never done before, so it will be important for you to be patient but firm. You need to be in charge of Pete. This earns you respect when done correctly, Also, make sure you pay attention to his every move. You're going to circle him in one direction and gradually force him into a bigger circle till he is forced to go over the barrel. Now you force him out with your body language and when he comes to the first barrel he will try his best to sidestep it. That's when you place extra pressure on him to get up and over the barrel. Understand?"

"I'm not sure I can do this, Mr. Olson."

"Have you ever helped Jude and your pa chase the pigs or

cows into a pen?"

"Yes, many times."

"And when you're doing that, have you ever had to step in front of an animal to change its direction?"

"Well, ah, I guess."

"Why certainly you have, Becky. When Pete comes to that first barrel and wants to side-step it, you need to get into that area so you change his path. You need to be ready on the first couple jumps to get out of his way in case he does something really stupid, but chances are he will sail right over the barrel." Mr. Olson smiled. "When you're ready, lead Pete in at a walk and let him smell the barrels and get used to them."

Becky and Pete headed around the pen and Pete got more and more nervous the closer they got to the drums.

"Becky, lead him up to one until he stops, then stand there and praise him. Okay, now back away and approach the barrel again and try to get closer each time. Be sure to take your time and praise him when he stands close to them."

It was hard watching from the sidelines as Mr. Olson and Becky were doing what I usually did. I had to swallow my pride and support Becky. Pretty soon Pete had accepted the drums as common items.

As Becky continued to lead Pete around, Mr. Olson said, "Remember, a horse is a prey animal so they first look at a new object with fear. Pete was probably thinking that barrel was a bear or something," he laughed.

"Becky, I will step out of the pen now. That gives you complete control over Pete, so start whenever you are ready. As you increase his circle and he gets closer to the barrels, you will probably have to increase your pressure gradually so he starts to think more about going over instead of around. Good luck."

It was pretty sweet. Becky started Pete to the right at a walk. She gradually gave more lead rope to increase the circle. Pete was walking pretty close to the barrels but he still allowed them to change his direction somewhat.

"Good job, Becky, good job! When you're ready, work him up to a trot. It will make it easier for him to jump," Mr. Olson encouraged.

Becky looked at me with a grin of excitement. What would Pete do with this new challenge? Becky sent Pete to the right again, only this time in a trot. Pete was high stepping pretty well as he circled. I think he sensed something was different. She gave him more rope and his circle got bigger. Becky was changing body position each time Pete came close to a drum. Pete increased his speed as he got closer and closer. It was kind of like a chess match, Pete against Becky. Pete's circle was now right next to the barrels and his pace was not getting any slower. Becky was hustling to keep him tight against the barrels on each revolution.

"Next time, Becky," hollered Mr. Olson. You could see Becky grab the rope tighter. She jockeyed for position and Pete came around the bend headed right for the barrel. You could see the intensity in his eyes and every muscle in his body rippled. All of a sudden, all four of his brakes came on. Pete stopped with his shins touching the barrel and just stood there. Becky didn't know what to do, nor did I.

"Just lead him to the middle of the pen again," Mr. Olson suggested. "Okay, Becky, what do you think went wrong?"

Becky had no answer.

"Becky, you cut off his path going forward too much. You need to position yourself so he can't go around it, and you need to be directly behind him, almost chasing him over the drum at the same time."

"Gee, Mr. Olson. I don't think I can do this," Becky complained.

"Becky, just think of this as a test from God. There are going to be many more tests from God in your life and you can't walk away from all of them. Now, collect yourself and stand in there and get'er done, as they say. Understand?"

"Yes, sir."

I wasn't sure what Becky's attitude was, but she started Pete to the right again, first at a walk and soon into a trot. Becky seemed to be giving more rope faster this time. Pete was soon approaching the same barrel he balked at before. As he rounded the corner Mr. Olson yelled, "Stay with him Becky!" Nostrils flaring, Pete charged towards that barrel, skidded just a little, then sprang into the air like you wouldn't believe. He cleared the barrel and then some. It was a spectacular sight to see that big of a horse, that high in the air. He approached the next drum and flew over it like an old pro. You could see the relief in Becky's expression.

"Keep him going a few more rounds to the right, then swing him to the left and send him over that way!" Mr. Olson hollered.

Pete did great both directions and Becky was grinning like a fox eating thistles. I wanted to go in and have Pete jump with me on the lead rope, but I knew this was Becky's turn. Becky brought Pete to the middle of the pen and gave him a huge hug.

"Good job! Becky you're going to be a fine horseman. You did well," Mr. Olson praised as he rubbed Pete on the neck. "I've got work to do at home, guys. I suggest you bring Joe out and do the same with him. You seem to understand the program now. Why certainly!" Mr. Olson headed out the driveway.

Becky ran Joe through the same routine as I watched. As usual, Joe took more time than Pete to accept the drums. Becky led him around three times before he finally cleared the first barrel. Mom came out and got some pictures of Joe and Becky. That night I lay in bed just picturing Pete and Joe catching air.

Chapter 13
"The Auction and Work"

One afternoon Becky and I got off the school bus and started walking up the driveway. Of course old Fuzz met us in her usual spot, happy we were home. She would lie on her back so we could rub her belly, and then she would get up and run to the house and back to us, darting around Becky and me like a barn swallow. We would chase her as she made big circles around us. This was pretty much an everyday occurrence when we got off the bus. Today, when Fuzz was done with her escapade, Dad jumped out from behind the chicken coop! Becky screamed and we took off running for all we were worth. Dad was too slow to keep up with me anymore, so he grabbed Becky and roughed her up a little and then tried to get me. I was safely in the house before he got there.

"Jude Bonner, what are you doing so out of breath?" asked Mom. "Did that Father of yours chase you up the drive again'?"

I stood there, hands on my knees, sucking air and laughing at the same time. Dad and Becky came in and we were all laughing.

"Mom, you wouldn't happen to have any hot brownies for a working man and his two kids, would ya?" Dad asked.

"Bud Bonner, yes I do, but I have to wonder who is the working man and who are the kids," Mom teased. All three of us bellied up to the breakfast bar and had some hot brownies with ice cream on top.

"Jude, you've got a pair of year-old colts out there, and next year you'll have a pair of two-year-olds," Dad said.

"Yes, sir."

"Your Mom is a real good seamstress but it would take a month of Sundays to convince her to sew you a set of harness," Dad said, laughing.

"Dad, what are you saying?"

"Jude, have you thought where you're going to get the money for a harness and where that harness is going to come from?"

I sat there dumbfounded. A harness hadn't really crossed my mind.

"Dad, do you have any ideas?"

"Think about it this way, you worked hard for Mr. Olson for the right to get them colts, but the work doesn't end there. You still need money to support Pete and Joe. My suggestion is to pray about it and see where God leads you. Now let's start chores before the cows get restless."

Dad headed out the door and I gathered my thoughts and followed. I was thinking about what Dad said and wishing he'd just tell me what to do, but that wasn't his style. He and Mom would only give Becky and me little thoughts that required us to think for ourselves. This was their way of teaching us how to make decisions and learn from our failures or successes.

As Fuzz and I did our chores I racked my brain for money ideas. I sat down on some bales and asked God for guidance.

"Dear Father God, thank you for all that you have given me. I need your help in getting more money for a set of harness. I ask you to check my heart for pure motives and lead me in your will. I pray, amen."

As I finished chores, I came up with a game plan for more money. Fuzz and I could trap more gophers, I could bale hay for the neighbors, pick rocks which I detested, and check with Mr. Olson if he had any extra chores.

I pedaled my bike as fast as I could to all the neighbors I could think of that might need hay baled, rocks picked, or gophers trapped. It was late April and we still had some snow left, but most of it was in puddles. The first place to stop, of course, was Mr. Olson's.

"Hey there, Jude, haven't seen you for awhile! How you been?"

"Oh, fine Mr. Olson, just fine. I came over to see if you needed any help this summer with rocks, hay, and stuff like that. I need to earn extra money so I can buy a harness for Pete and Joe."

"Why certainly, why certainly." Then he hesitated. "No

promises on how much work I can give you. I have a nephew who also wants to come out and help. I will keep you in mind if he can't make it. Fair enough?"

"Fair enough," I responded, even though that really wasn't the answer I was after.

"Where are you planning on buying this harness?"

"I have to get the money before I can think of that. I have to get going. I'm heading over to the Millers to see if they need any help."

"I just got my latest edition of the draft horse sales and auctions coming up this summer. They list an auction in Paynesville late summer where you might find a harness or two. If you want, you can take the catalog home with you."

"Gee, that would be great, Mr. Olson. I'll stop on my way back and get it. Thank you!"

Fuzz and I were off as fast as I could pedal. We headed down the gravel road to the Millers. The road was full of mud puddles from the snow melting, so we were dodging them as I rode. There was a huge low spot that was totally under water where the culvert went under the road. The culvert must have still been frozen. The water was only around five inches deep so Fuzz and I started through it. Old Fuzz wasn't a big fan of water, especially cold snow melt water, so she was hopping through and looking at me like I owed her for making her do this.

We were halfway through when we heard a truck with loud pipes, and big mud tires coming. It seemed the driver picked up speed when he saw us instead of slowing down. Sure enough, it was Greg and Judy. Fuzz and I picked up our speed the best we could. The roar of the engine was bearing down on us. As it got closer I looked back and saw Judy and Greg laughing as the big mud tires threw water sideways. Fuzz and I didn't stand a chance. I waited for the splash.

I hunkered down knowing I was going to get a mighty cold bath. The ice cold wall of water hit me like a tidal wave. I lost my balance and landed on my right side. How can water get that cold without being frozen? I jumped up as quick as I could and picked up my bike. I had water in my ears, down my pants, in my shoes, and everywhere else. The shock was almost unbearable. I had worked up a little sweat from riding, so it seemed that much colder.

As I looked up, Judy hung out the window, waving her arms

and laughing hysterically. Fuzz chased the pickup to the edge of the dry land and stood there waiting for me. I sat on my bike and started pedaling towards Fuzz. The more I pedaled, the colder I got and the angrier I became. I was boiling with rage when all of a sudden my front tire hit a big washout in the road and into the frigid water I went again. I guess this was God's way of cooling me off.

Of course, as I picked myself up, I checked to see if anyone was watching me. "Fuzz, we came this far, we might as well keep going. Just think Fuzz, it was just last night that I read in James, 'Consider it pure Joy when you face trials and tribulations of many kinds. Perseverance brings on character,' etc." I mumbled.

We weren't far from the Miller's driveway and the more I pedaled the warmer I got. As Fuzz and I were pulling into their driveway, Greg and Judy were pulling out. As they passed us, Greg honked his horn and you could hear them laughing again. When I got up to the Miller's yard, I caught Mr. Miller walking towards the house after chores. Fuzz and I startled him as we approached.

"Jude, my Lord is that you under all those wet clothes? Isn't it a little early for swimming?"

I could tell he was having a hard time keeping from laughing at me. "Fuzz and I had a little trouble at the culvert."

"You need to come in and let me get you some dry clothes to wear. My goodness you'll end up catching your death of cold."

"Thanks for the offer, but this is something I need to finish myself. I just need to ask you something and I'll be on my way."

"Sure, Jude, what is it you need?"

"Well, I'm wondering if you will need help with gophers, picking rocks, or baling hay this spring and summer. I'm trying to earn money to buy Pete and Joe a set of harness."

"Funny that you would ask, Jude. Greg Shants just pulled in and asked the same thing right before you got here. I told Greg that I would call him when needed. Sorry, but I really only need one person. If something else comes up, I'll let you know. Are you sure you don't want some dry clothes to go home with?"

"I'll pass, Mr. Miller, and thank you for your time. Tell Mrs. Miller I said hello."

"Sure thing, Jude, and be careful going through that water this time," he said, laughing a little.

Fuzz and I left with our tails between our legs. I had come with grandiose plans for this job seeking mission and ended up with nothing but a cold, wet fanny. That was the longest bike ride I ever took in my life; I didn't think I would ever see our place on the horizon. Even Fuzz ran ahead and left me behind! She knew a warm barn with dry straw was waiting for her. As I pedaled, I kept thinking of Greg and was having a hard time keeping a positive frame of mind.

"Lord Jesus, I ask for strength to get home and please help me with my bitter attitude towards Greg. Amen."

The sky was crystal clear, which leads to colder temps, and I could feel the temperature dropping. My clothes were freezing as stiff as a board and my leg muscles were cramping up. As I pulled into the driveway, my toes went into muscle spasms. Yes, I had an old fashioned Charley horse in my toes. I had toes going in every direction and it was mighty painful! I dove off the bike to stand on them to try to get them to straighten out. Ooh man, God did not design toes to do that! I ended up walking the rest of the way up the drive because it was the only way I could stop my toes from going in opposite directions. When I got to the house, Fuzz didn't even greet me as I stiffly walked inside, frozen from head to toe. My frozen pants made noise as I walked and, you guessed it, Mom heard them. This was a time I wished God hadn't given Mothers bionic hearing and bionic sense of smell.

"Jude Bonner, what is that funny noise and what smells like a slough?" Mom hollered down from upstairs.

"I was doing a little testing to see if gravity still worked, if water was still wet and cold, and if water from a slough still smells like a slough."

"Don't you drag them clothes any farther into this house! Jump in the shower and I'll bring you down some clean ones."

That shower felt great. My body thawed out one layer at a time as I stood under that shower head, The slough smell still lingering in my nostrils. Mom and Dad were in the living room with Becky when I got done.

"Son, did you have any luck finding work?" Dad asked.

"Not really, it was pretty much a waste of my time."

"Remember, God has all things planned out. He probably knew you needed a little cold weather biking mixed in with some slough jumping," Dad laughed.

I wasn't really in the mood for jokes, but I had a hard time not laughing along with Dad, Becky, and Mom. When all the laughing was over I did feel a little better.

"Have you thought of detasseling corn this summer?" Mom asked. "If that is something that would work for you, you should get your name in soon."

"I guess that is something I should consider," I said. "I'll get a hold of Garth Tanner on Monday to see if they have any openings."

It was movie night, so Mom fixed buttered popcorn and we all watched a movie. The next morning I got a hold of Mr. Tanner and was able to sign up for detasseling corn. It wasn't what I had in mind for summer employment, but it would at least put a set of harnesses on the geldings.

That summer was pretty hectic with trapping gophers, detasseling corn, baling hay, and youth group at church. I did earn $2,000.00, which I figured should buy a pretty nice set of harness and then some.

I was just getting ready for bed after a long day when the phone rang. "Jude, it's for you!" Mom yelled.

"Hello?"

"Jude, have you saved up enough to get that harness? That auction is in two weeks," Mr. Olson said.

"Yes, sir, I have, Mr. Olson! Will you go with Dad and me to look it over?"

"Why certainly, why certainly."

The night before the auction I could hardly sleep.

On the big day of the auction, it was lightly raining with a pretty good wind. Dad and I picked up Mr. Olson. As we drove to Paynesville, Mr. Olson talked so much I wondered if he was more excited than I was.

The auction was one busy place. Dad told me I had to do my own bidding so I was pretty nervous. Mr. Olson, Dad, and I looked the harness over carefully. Mr. Olson was pulling and flexing the leather in certain spots.

"Jude," Mr. Olson said after his final inspection, "it is in fair shape. It has some areas that have dry rot and need repair. It's been too far away from the harness oil."

Dad asked, "What do you think it's worth, or should we even bid on it?"

When Dad hinted that we might not even bid, I was shocked. In my opinion we came here to get a harness, and that is what we were going to go home with. I was just about to give them my opinion when Mr. Olson spoke.

"Bud, as you know the harness can be fixed, it just depends on what Jude is willing to spend."

"I brought two thousand dollars with me!" I blurted out. Right then it seemed like everyone at the whole place went silent and was looking at me. I felt pretty foolish.

"Jude, lower your voice a little. Now you need to decide what you are willing to bid and tell yourself that you will not go any higher," Dad said.

"Jude, this harness is not a two thousand dollar harness, not even close. Now remember, you asked your pa and me to come with for our opinions, so that is my answer." Mr. Olson said.

Wow, reality hit hard. I had my mind set on getting a harness that day and now the people I had asked to help were throwing wrenches at my plan. I have to admit, I wanted to just ignore their advice and get this harness.

"Son, Mr. Olson and I are going to look at a few other things. I think it best if you study that harness alone for awhile and decide what you're willing to spend. I know you had your heart set on getting a harness this day. It is your money and decision." Dad paused, "Please remember one thing that my Dad taught me; it is always easier to buy something than it is to sell something."

I was standing there almost in a trance, my head just spinning.

"Dad, what do you think it is worth?" I asked as I turned towards Dad.

Well, guess what? Dad wasn't there anymore. A total stranger was standing where Dad was. I was pretty embarrassed asking a total stranger what he thought it was worth. The funny thing is, the stranger answered me.

"Four hundred dollars at best," he chewed on a cigar. I looked back at the harness and figured I'd ask this stranger another question.

"How long have you been around harness stuff?" No answer came. Well, maybe he hadn't heard me, so I stood up and looked his way. Much to my surprise, the stranger was gone just as fast as he had appeared.

I had another thirty minutes before the auction started, so I caught up with Dad and Mr. Olson. Dad gave me some advice on when to bid and even my stance when bidding. He said body language was important and to remember the limit I had chosen. My stomach was turning all directions and I didn't think the bidding would ever start.

The auction finally started and it took them about one hour before they got to the harness. I picked a spot to stand that would give a good view of the other bidders. I thought for sure I would see the stranger bidding against me, but he was nowhere in sight. Dad and Mr. Olson stood back a ways, making me feel like an island.

"Okay, folks, we have a set of good draft harness here. Who will give nine hundred dollars?" the auctioneer asked.

I have to admit it was hard not to open the bidding but Dad warned me to never give what they first suggest as the opening bid.

"Someone start me out here folks. What is it worth?" prodded the auctioneer.

From way in the back someone hollered, "Two hundred dollars."

Well, that got it started.

"Who will give me three hundred?"

"Two fifty," I bid.

I had to stop and collect my thoughts. I had actually bid. Well, it was pretty neat, and I had one of the spotters checking my eyes on a regular basis after that. Best I could tell there were three, maybe four guys bidding. I set my top dollar at four hundred twenty-five dollars. I was there right up to that point, but the other gentleman either had more money or didn't look it over that close. I finally shook my head "No" to the spotter and I was out of the bidding. Much to my amazement, two guys took that harness to twelve hundred dollars. Needless to say, I was pretty discouraged. I made my way back to Dad and Mr. Olson. Not much was said on the way back to the pickup truck.

Dad was driving us home, but the funny thing was he drove away from home. To tell you the truth, I was too busy feeling sorry for myself to even ask why. We drove to Sauk Centre and had some lunch. I was still not in the mood for much talking.

"Bud, I can't wait to see what this fella has for a harness!" Mr. Olson said. "If it looks good, I think I'll buy it on the spot."

I was still in a daze so I barely caught what Mr. Olson had said.

"What do you mean, harness?" I asked.

"Mr. Olson wanted us to drive up here to see a harness that he is thinking of buying," Dad replied.

"Why certainly, why certainly."

"Now Jude, you can wait here while your dad and I go to the harness shop. We'll pick you up on the way back through." Mr. Olson laughed.

Come to find out there was a new harness shop north of Sauk Centre and Dad said they had some good used harness for sale. It's funny how my attitude changed from despair to thoughts of grandeur in a matter of seconds. I couldn't wait to get going.

We pulled up to a mail box that had a sign near it stating "Peterson Harness Shop" I was just about frothing at the mouth. Much to my surprise, the stranger who told me what to bid at the auction was the owner of the shop.

"Well, what can we do for you fellars today?" he asked.

"I'm looking for a set of used harness for draft horses," I answered.

"You're just in luck. I have three sets right now, over on the south wall."

I hustled over there while Dad and Mr. Olson chatted with the owner. This was pretty special. Each harness was cleaned real nice. There were two sets with two britchen and one with three britchen. Most people prefer a three britchen harness because it looks better on the horses' rumps.

"Sir," I asked the owner, "what are the prices on the used harness?"

"You can call me Brad," he said as he chewed on his cigar. "Now let's mosey over there and take a look. How big are these colts of yours?"

"They are seventeen-two right now as two-year-olds so we think they will get eighteen hands when mature."

."Wow, that sounds like some pretty serious horse power. It takes a big pony to reach eighteen hands." Pulling the cigar from his mouth, he looked at Mr. Olson to double check that I understood how big eighteen hands really was.

"Yes, they should get that big when all is said and done."

"Jude, that last harness is too small for those boys, it's more for the smaller drafts. The other two will fit just fine. The two strap britchen is six hundred and the three is seven fifty.

"Does that include collars?" Dad asked.

"Nope, harness, bridles and lines only."

Dad, Mr. Olson, and I started going over the harness real close. The shop owner left and went into his back room.

"Jude, both these harnesses are in better shape than the one at the auction, and they are less money," Mr. Olson stated.

Dad agreed with Mr. Olson. Just then the owner wheeled a harness cart out to us from the back room. On the cart was a brand new three strap britchin harness with chrome hames and all!

I just stood there staring. It was beautiful.

"Son, I know you asked for used harness, but I just finished this and thought you might like to see it."

"What kind of money do you need for that set?" I asked as I was reaching out to touch it.

"Sixteen hundred."

I looked at Dad. He said, "Jude, this is your money, and remember, neither harness comes with collars."

"What size collars do those colts wear?" the shop owner asked. "You might consider adjustable collars while the colts are still growing. When they're done growing, I will give you a good trade in price for regular collars. Used adjustable collars are around one hundred apiece."

Decision time. All I could think about was how nice that new harness would look on Pete and Joe. After seeing the new harness I really didn't want to even look at the used ones anymore. My palms were sweaty as I kept staring at that shiny new harness.

"Jude, we got chore time coming, so do we need to come back another day?" Dad asked.

Dad always told me not to do creative financing with my money. That's when you create money you don't have and justify buying something you really want but don't really need. Dad would ask, "Is it a want or a need?"

I really wanted to take a harness home that day, so I bit my lip and told the shop owner I'd take the used two strap britchen harness. I told myself one day I'd own a fancy harness, but for what I needed right now the used set would work just fine. Even so, it was the biggest check I ever wrote. We loaded up the collars, bridles, and harness and off we went. I was feeling much better than when we had left the auction.

We dropped off Mr. Olson and headed home ourselves.

Dad said, "Jude, that took real courage. I want you to know I'm proud of you and I think you made the right decision twice today."

"What do you mean, twice?"

"First, when you walked away from the harness at the auction and second, when you decided against the brand new harness. That took courage."

"Thanks, Dad, and thanks for going with today."

Chapter 14
"Training To Harness"

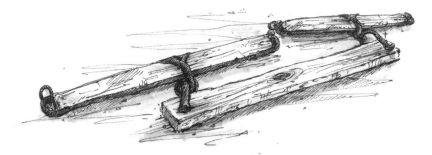

In the springtime when Pete and Joe were two years old, it was time to start them into the harness and pulling light loads. I didn't think we would ever get to this part of their lives. They were around seventeen two hands tall and looking pretty good.

"Mom and Dad, today is the day I start getting the colts used to the harness," I said at breakfast that morning. "I've been waiting for this part of the training a long time."

"Those colts will look pretty sharp pulling a wagon," Dad said. "Just remember not to rush this part of the training. They're only two-year-olds."

Dad was right. Both Mr. Olson and the training books I read talked of going slow with two-year-olds. One book even suggested training steadily for a good thirty days and then letting them go until they were three years old. Many people say a horse doesn't mentally mature until roughly age six.

Becky and I headed out to catch the colts. Becky caught Pete right away but Joe had different plans. As I went to put on his rope halter, he sidestepped me and walked away. Since I had plans of harnessing, I had a hard time not getting mad at him.

"Becky, please take Pete to the tack room. I need to stay with Joe till he lets me halter him."

So there we were and it would be my will or Joe's will. If I let Joe get away with this he would never let anyone catch him. I just walked right at him in a fairly aggressive posture and he knew exactly what I wanted. I had to keep constant pressure on him so he could not rest until I wanted him to. I walked very fast and he would trot off, then I would cut corners on him and keep him moving. Horses like to run from their predators and then stop and rest. The key for me was no rest for Joe. We shuffled around that paddock for I bet ten minutes before Joe began to realize this was not a lot of fun. Just when Joe thought his game was over, I increased my speed and aggression to make him move all the more. When I finally thought he learned his lesson, I backed away, then stopped and looked away from him, still watching him out of the corner of my eye. Joe stopped and looked my way but made no effort to come to me, so off we went around the paddock a few more times. I stopped and walked away again and this time Joe turned and followed me. I slowly turned and rubbed his neck. I rubbed him with the rope halter. Just to make sure he got the point, I sent him around again and he easily let me halter him. I was all sweaty from that episode but it needed to be done.

Becky was already working Pete in the round pen when I led Joe to the tack room. I tied Joe to his stall and took Pete's harness to the round pen.

"Becky, what have you worked on with Pete?"

"Oh, turning on a walk and trot and a few leading workouts."

"Is he doing okay with them?"

"Yes, yes, he is."

"Here is the fourteen-foot lead rope. Snap it onto his rope halter and take him to the middle of the pen. Then fling it over his back, neck, and rump from both sides of him with very consistent timing. I will watch from here and when I think it is okay I'll bring in the harness and keep getting closer to him." Becky did as I asked and soon I was in the round pen with harness on my shoulder, walking the perimeter. Pete didn't pay much attention until I got closer.

"Okay, Becky, stop flinging the rope and just hold him," I instructed. I brought the harness up to Pete to smell and he stretched out his nose and smelled it. I immediately retreated to take any pressure off of him. I came back and let him smell it again. After he smelled it, I circled him with the harness still on my shoulder. Pete was watching every move I made. It's amazing how horses can see straight behind them without turning their heads. He started sidestepping as I got closer. I went back to his front side and just stood there so he could see and smell the harness. After awhile the harness became quite heavy, so I walked away and switched shoulders.

"Becky, I need to take the lead rope now and you'll have to stand back and watch."

I headed back to Pete's front and let him smell it again. I started walking right along his neck. Pete sidestepped so I immediately followed him, harness and all. Pete needed to learn that he couldn't walk away from the harness, so I had to stay right with him. He would snort and sidestep, sidestep and snort, all the time watching me with a hard left eye. I just kept the same pace, waiting for him to tire. Walking in a tight circle for a big horse is somewhat cumbersome and tiring. Soon Pete's eye softened and he started to slow down. I had to make sure that when Pete stopped I also stopped immediately, rewarding him by taking the pressure off. I worked Pete from both sides and advanced to rubbing the harness on all sides of him. With the lead rope over his neck and me standing near his left front shoulder, I lifted the harness up and down in the air again and again. I walked around him, lifting it up and down. I was feeling pretty good with his progress. He was even licking his lips with his head relaxed. This is a sign that a horse feels no fear.

"Jude, I'm running up to get the camera, so wait until I get back before you put the harness on!"

"Okay!"

While Becky was getting the camera, I shook the harness by Pete and even dropped it on the ground on all sides. Becky got back and took a picture of me placing the harness on Pete's back for the first time. Pete sidestepped a little, but I stayed with him. We did it! The harness was on his back! Becky whooped and started clapping, but I could tell that what I did next surprised her; I took it right back off.

"What did you do that for?" Becky shouted.

I ignored her for the moment so I could stay focused on what I was doing. I gave Pete a few seconds before I approached with the harness again and successfully placed it on his back. This time he was much better at standing still. I took it off again and back on again, off and on, off and on. Soon Pete didn't even think about it.

"Sorry, Jude," Becky said after I led Pete over to her. "Now I see why you took the harness off and on so many times."

"Becky, I'll go get his collar if you want to lead him around the pen a little."

I brought out a couple collars, not sure which would fit. It's best to slip them over their heads, but for today I chose slipping it around his neck to save a little time. We still needed to work with Joe. Becky and I found the collar that fit the best, hooked the hames into the hame groove, and slid the britchen straps over his rump. Becky hooked the martingale and then we started adjusting all the buckles.

"Jude, I must admit, Pete is looking sharp! Let me take more pictures!"

Mom even came out to take a look. Mom took some pictures of Pete, Becky, and me. We took some of Pete alone as well. It was another moment I wouldn't forget. Pete seemed to understand that this was a special time also as he stood tall.

"Jude, should I get Joe while you finish with Pete?" Becky asked.

"Sure, good idea!" I needed to work Pete with the harness on so he got used to it as he trotted and walked. As Pete was circling me I sent a quick prayer and thanked God for his help.

Becky brought Joe out and I headed in with Pete. Becky started basics with Joe while I led Pete back to the tack room. I brought Joe's harness back with me and was ready to start the whole process again. Becky knew what to do this time which helped save time. Joe was his usual self, eyes of steel, feet a-dancing. He just didn't like that harness. I think it took twice the time as it did with Pete.

After we finally got Joe to the level Pete was, we took pictures of Pete and Joe together. With their harnesses on, we let them go in the pasture where they could really run. They needed to accept the harness in all gaits. Joe was the leader, thinking he could run out from under this leather contraption, and Pete wasn't far behind. They made a couple of complete circles and came back to Becky and stood there. I think this was their way of saying, "Hey, we give up! Can you please take these things off?" Becky and I led them around a little, pulled off the harnesses, curried them and led them back to the pasture. Sure enough, as soon as they got in the pasture they lay down and rolled in the dirt, eight legs swinging in the air back and forth. I'd heard that most horses do this because it scratches their backs.

The next day we started with Joe first. It was time to introduce them to ground driving in the round pen. Ground driving is using lines on a halter or bit to steer the horse while you are behind them. It's best to have two people for this, so it was great to have Becky's help. Becky ran Joe through some basic stuff before we started.

"Becky, you start leading him but let me give all the vocal commands to Joe from back here. As soon as you hear me give the command for Joe to walk, give him a tug on the lead rope if needed. Remember, you need to be ready to jump out of the way if he decides to do something stupid."

I grabbed the lines and got all squared up and gave Joe a kiss sound to move forward. Joe seemed to ignore my voice command. Becky gave him a little tug and we were now in motion. Since we were moving, things were going fine, but I don't think Joe really understood what I was doing. This was only the third time he had a bit in his mouth so I was trying to be very soft with the lines.

"Becky, without stopping, try to fade back slowly while draping the lead rope over his back while I keep him going ahead," I coached. Becky gradually eased herself back and pretty soon Joe stopped because she was no longer leading him.

"When we get him going again I want to practice turning him a little. When I say left and right, be ready to go in that direction. Remember to always try to fade out of the lead role as much as possible."

I kissed to Joe again as a cue to move forward. Becky again had to lead him to get him started. After two rounds in the pen I said, "Right!" and turned him towards the center of the pen. Becky was right there and helped Joe through that first turn. At the other side of the pen I said, "Left!" and we all turned to the left. Joe was getting a little fired up and snorted to let us know. "Easy, Joe. Easy, Joe." I tried to soothe him. Becky kept fading farther and farther away. Next thing I knew, it was just Joe and me going around the pen. Praise God! I went around the pen four times and tried a left turn. It wasn't pretty but we got it done. Five rounds that direction and a right turn, again we did it. "Good boy, Joe. Good boy, Joe," I reassured him.

Joe and I made many revolutions around and across the pen before we tried our first stop. When you ask a horse to walk for a longer time he is more likely to want to stop. "Whoa," I spoke in a firm voice. Joe didn't understand this very well but he did eventually stop. Both Becky and I stood with him and gave him praise for doing such a good job. The two most important things to do when training a horse are to praise and release pressure at the correct time. I suspect, Becky and I went overboard with the praise, but we didn't want to shortchange him either.

"Okay, Joe, let's see how you do starting up again without

Becky helping you." I eased back with the lines in hand and kissed to Joe. He snorted once and spun right around and faced me. This was not what he was supposed to do. I looked at Becky and she was trying hard to hold back a smile. I grabbed Joe's halter and turned him back forward, but as soon as I started to go back to his butt Joe turned and followed me. Becky burst into a laugh and I stopped and glared at her. I was getting mad and Becky's laughing didn't help my mood. I stood there for a moment looking at Joe.

"Joe, you and I got to get this right. Now you go forward and don't follow me," I commanded. I was annoyed at Becky, so I wasn't about to ask for her help. I decided to start Joe by leading him with the left rein and gradually easing back to the driving position. Joe and I went halfway around the pen with me leading before I was able to gradually slip back and drive with the reins. I was grinning from ear to ear. It was my first time driving a colt with no outside help. I was so proud. Joe and I made several stops and starts and he was definitely understanding what he was doing. I was so excited I could have driven till dark. I had to remind myself of what Mr. Olson said about working the colts too long in one session.

"Becky, please open the gate and I'll drive Joe to the barn. We'll get Pete and work him the same way."

Once the gate was open I drove Joe past it several times. He wanted to go out right away, but I made him go past the open gate three or four times to remind him that I'm the one who decides when we go through the gate. Each time we went past the gate Joe got more excited so I put more pressure on him to do what I wanted. I drove Joe out the gate and towards the barn, all of a sudden he wanted to trot. "Easy Joe, easy Joe," I said. Joe had different things on his mind! The next thing I knew, Joe arched his neck as he turned his head, fighting my lines. He spun around and faced me and then took off, harness and all as I dug in my heals. I did a basic face plant and was being dragged down the gravel driveway. I hung on for awhile but soon lost my grip. Joe really took off after I had no pressure on his bit, he was in the middle of the west hay field before he stopped and looked back. I stood up and dusted myself off and went running his way as my anger was building.

I hustled his way as he stood watching every step I took. He let me get about six feet from the lines on the ground and took off again. "Whoa, Joe, whoa, you stupid jerk!" It wasn't long and Joe was galloping east down our road. I took off at an angle through the field trying to cut him off. Believe me God did design horses to run faster than man! When I got up on the road I thought I could see him turning into Mr. Olson's driveway.

I don't think I ever made it to Mr. Olson's that fast before, but I was mad! As I came up over the knoll in his driveway there stood Mr. Olson holding Joe by his halter at the edge of the barn. I slowed down and started to think how I would explain this to Mr. Olson. Dad always says 'when in doubt tell the truth'.

As I got closer I could see Joe's harness had been dragging on the ground. I was mad yet feeling stupid at the same time.

"Jude, you hold him while I get this harness off him."

"I'm sorry Mr. Olson! But Joe was being a jerk as I drove him out of the round pen."

Mr. Olson scratched the back of his neck. "Joe, what is the problem here?" As he looked Joe in the eye, "Is that so? Why you think Jude is a jerk. Why certainly, I guess I can't blame you!" I couldn't believe it, Mr. Olson seemed to be siding with Joe!

Mr. Olson finished taking the harness off and then looked my way. "Jude what do you think you did wrong?"

"Why are you asking me what I did wrong, Mr. Olson? Joe was not..."

Mr. Olson cut me off. "Proverbs 14:17 A quick tempered man does foolish things. Jude, I have seen very few runaways that you could blame on the horse. I would guess you had Joe in a situation that he wasn't quite ready for and neither were you. It is very important to always be sure of the level of training they can handle, and remember to be in a position that you can always win. Now as you walk him home you think how you should have done this differently and maybe check your attitude and add more praise when training. Now, I have to run to town."

Mr. Olson headed towards the house as I stood there a little confused. I stood there still fuming as Joe nudged me in the back. Gradually Joe and I started down the driveway. I was having a hard time not blaming Joe for this mess. I was thinking the whole way home, busted harness, busted pride, starting over with Joe. We got home and I led Joe to his pasture, I stood there and held him as I looked him in the eyes.

"Joe, what do you think? I guess if I'm honest with you, I did you wrong. Mr. Olson is right, it's me that is the jerk here." I rubbed his neck hard. "Please forgive me." Joe trotted off slowly, I think that was his way of saying he wasn't sure about forgiving at this time.

The next day Becky and I hitched Pete to his harness and worked him the same way we worked Joe. Soon I was driving Pete around the pen like he'd done this many times before. The next couple of weeks were spent on driving Pete and Joe individually. I had to earn Joe's respect back after our little runaway. I would start them in the pen each day and then drive them out of the pen. We drove down the driveway, through the grove, down the road ditch, and around the barn. Becky started taking her turns at line driving too. We even took them out at the same time, Becky driving Pete and me driving Joe. We drove them side by side as if they were a team.

It was now time to introduce them to obstacles. I placed a hay bale, a full garbage bag, the old pickup, the lawn mower, and the horse pole in different spots in the barnyard. The idea is to drive each colt around the objects until they accept them and don't shy away from them. I started with Joe first while I had the most patience, knowing he would take longer. I drove Joe around the grove first and then headed to the barnyard. As soon as Joe spotted all those things in the barnyard, he stopped and stared. I gave him a little time to observe and then kissed to him to go forward. We headed towards the hay bale first. He was pretty wired as we got close. I stopped him before we got there so he wouldn't stop on his own. You want all ideas to be yours, not theirs. Soon I kissed again and we went closer to the bale. With his nostrils flaring, Joe snorted and sidestepped. I didn't press him hard since this was all new. We went on to the horse pole and the other objects. It took longer than I thought, but finally Joe was driving around all the obstacles with no fear. To make sure, I had Becky take him for a few rounds also.

Becky and I did the same with Pete. Pete caught me off guard as we approached the garbage bag. The next thing I knew, his front legs were in the air and when they came down he was ready to bolt to the barn and I mean right now.

"Easy, Pete, easy, boy." I leaned back on the lines as Pete had my feet skidding on the gravel. For a second I thought I was going to lose him. Pete and I went thirty to forty feet in what I'd call "road gear" before he settled down. Pete was actually worse than Joe when it came to accepting the obstacles, so Becky and I quit before too long because Pete was just getting more and more wired. He was prancing and sidestepping big time, and it was all I could do to hold him back.

The next day we worked Pete on some basics and then brought him back to the obstacles. He was much calmer and we got him to accept each one in time. As we were unharnessing Pete, Becky said, "Jude, do you remember that Granny and Gramps will be here tomorrow?" In my busyness I had totally forgotten.

"Golly, Becky, I forgot about them coming. Gramps will want to work with the colts some. What do you think we should do while he's here?"

"Well, I think it would be neat if we each line drove them out of the barn as they pull up the driveway."

"Great idea, Becky."

That evening Becky and I told Mom and Dad of our plans with the colts. We were both pretty excited about our idea until Dad intervened.

"Jude, are those colts traffic safe? What are they going do when they see that car heading down the driveway right at them?" There I was caught off guard again.

"Gee, I guess I hadn't thought of that, Dad."

"Why don't you get started early in the morning and have Becky drive up and down the driveway while you lead the colts," Dad suggested. "Becky can use the practice driving and it will start the colts on traffic sounds. Make sure you blow the horn at them too."

So that's what Becky and I did early the next morning. Becky started driving back and forth while I led each colt and slowly worked closer and closer to the pickup truck. She would swerve, honk the horn, stop close to them, and close doors hard. We had a few snorts out of them and sidestepping, but we got to where I was leading the two together as Becky bussed us. We went from leading to line driving them with bridles. The blinders on the bridles make it hard for the horse to see what is happening behind and beside them. I finally figured out that it would be best if Becky drove in front of us first, allowing Pete and Joe to see what was going on. After a couple of hours, Pete and Joe were doing fine with the traffic noise.

It was now time to get the colts ready for Granny and Gramps coming over. We decided to give them a complete makeover, bath and all. Becky curried them while I used my pocket knife on the manes and tails. I even trimmed their feet quick. It was now time for their first bath.

Becky got some Ivory soap mixed up in a five-gallon pail of warm water while I got the garden hose hooked up to the barn hydrant. I led Joe out near the hydrant and held him while Becky turned the hose on. As air and water shot out, Joe seemed to want to shoot to the moon. His eyes went to steel hardness and he was a-snorting like a machine gun. Becky emptied the hose a couple times to allow air back in the hose so we could do it again. Joe was getting better, so I took the hose in one hand and his lead rope in the other and started hosing him down. Joe was sidestepping as fast as he could go. As soon as he stopped, I took the water away. Several rounds of this and soon Joe was standing there enjoying the cool water. It is funny how some horses respond to the water when you spray them in the face. Joe stood there play biting at the water. Now that he was saturated with water, Becky and I scrubbed him with the Ivory soap. Joe was all foamed up from the soap and looked pretty silly. He seemed to enjoy the stiff bristles of the scrub brushes against his hide. I rinsed him off with the hose and led him back to the barn. Boy, you should have seen him prancing his way to the barn. Joe was one proud colt. His wet coat glimmered in the sun. Of course Ol' Fuzz had to run beside him to show him the way back to the barn.

Pete was next. He was a little better than Joe at accepting the water and air noise from the hose. Pete was even more animated when I led him back to the barn, high stepping his way back like he owned the world. I must say I was pretty proud of Pete and Joe.

I walked up by the manger. "Pete and Joe," I said as I looked them in the eye, "you guys are really special and this is your first big show, so I ask you to be on your best behavior and show Granny and Gramps what you're made of." I gave them each a big hug and rubbed their necks. I think they could tell by my tone of voice that I needed help.

That next hour seemed to take forever. Becky drove Pete out and I followed with Joe. We stood out by the driveway waiting for Granny and Gramps. When they finally headed up the driveway, Pete and Joe watched as they came closer. Gramps slowly pulled right in front of them and they hardly moved. I was awfully proud. Granny got out and took some pictures and then headed up to help Mom with supper. Gramps took time to drive each colt a little and helped unharness them.

"Jude, I have to say these colts seem to be doing very well. Your training sessions are paying off well for you," Gramps praised.

"Thanks, Gramps. Becky has been a lot of help."

"I guess you better get a step ladder out here for harnessing these colts! My goodness, how tall are they?" Gramps asked.

"We just measured them and they are a strong seventeen two."

"For two-year-olds, that's pretty tall. And they are well matched in weight also. It will be nice to see them hitched together heading down the road."

"Mr. Olson said we could hitch them with Ladd to get them used to pulling stuff behind them."

"I see, I see. Just take things slow and easy. They are only two years old." Gramps paused. "If it's okay with Mr. Olson, I would love to come over and give a hand when you hitch to Ladd."

"Becky or I will let you know when that happens. We'd love to have you there."

Chapter 15

"Pulling as a Team"

I couldn't believe it. I was entering my senior year of high school. Harold and Perry were also seniors, and yes, we still hung out together. They weren't real interested in horses so that did somewhat affect the time we spent together. Mrs. Norman was still a cornerstone of the teachers and Judy Clemons, Nick Grudden, and Greg Shants were still the rebels of the school. In fact, several times this past summer they drove past our place with their arms hanging out the window as we were working with Pete and Joe. I don't think they were waving hello.

I ran into Mrs. Norman in the hallway on the second day of school. "Jude Bonner, how was your summer?"

"Oh, it was pretty good, ma'am. I worked a couple different jobs and was able to buy a set of harness for Pete and Joe. I even started them driving."

"Now, Jude, don't go spending every minute with those colts and remember that I signed you up for singing the National Anthem at our first home football game."

I thought she was just kidding. I choked and snorted a little, but I looked her in the eye and realized she was serious. "But Mrs. Norman…"

"You need to use that set of pipes the good Lord gave you, so what better place than at the first home football game your senior year of high school! Now you are on the schedule as we speak, so are you up for it or are you going to let the devil talk you out of it? Which voice are you going to listen to? The 'I can' or the 'I can't!' Let me know by tomorrow." Mrs. Norman walked away.

I stood there in a daze for awhile until Perry came by. "Bonner, what is wrong with you? You look like you just saw a ghost, pal."

I snapped to and said slowly, "Oh, nothing, nothing at all. I'll call you tonight."

It was hard staying focused the rest of the day, but the Lord got me home in one piece. As Becky and I arrived home, Mom was in the kitchen fixing supper. I figured I would just slip past Mom and head out to chores. As usual Mom somehow read right through me.

"Jude, what is ailing you honey?" she asked abruptly. I pretended that I didn't hear her and kept walking.

"Jude, maybe you'd like to skip supper tonight!" Now that got my attention. Mom never plays fair. She barters with hunger to get her answers.

"Mrs. Norman signed me up to sing the National Anthem for the first home football game," As I moaned out my answer shaking my head.

Mom hesitated, then said, "Are you pleased with how Pete and Joe are doing so far?"

"Yes, I am, but what does that have to do with the National Anthem?"

"Did I see you leading them colts over a sheet of plastic a couple days ago?"

"Yes, ma'am."

"Did I see you getting them used to the tractor a couple days ago?"

"Yes, ma'am."

"Talk to me. Why did you work on these things?"

"It's for their own good, so they learn not to be afraid."

Mom continued, "Did the colts always want to do these things, or did you have to make them?"

"No, they weren't real keen on most new things I introduced to them, especially Joe."

"If they didn't want to do these things, why did you make them do them?"

"It makes for an overall well rounded horse. Besides, I know they are capable."

Mom got a small grin on her face. "Think about what you just said. Mrs. Norman is a fine Christian woman. Now she's asking you to do something she knows you are capable of, but you don't really want to do it. But it's okay to make Pete and Joe do things against their will."

"Gee, Mom, some kids will make fun of me for singing."

"Jude, if you're going to seek the approval of all your peers before doing something in life, then good luck. Remember what your Gramps says, If you want to be criticized, do something. People's natural sin brings about criticism no matter what you or I do, the sooner you learn that the better. Now get upstairs and change into your chore clothes, and while you're up there have a talk with the man upstairs!"

"Yes, ma'am."

I dragged my hind end upstairs with my mind spinning. That was a pretty good sermon Mom just handed out. I went to my Bible and looked up a verse I learned in 4th grade Sunday school. Philippians 4:13 "I can do all things through Christ who strengthens me." Mom was right and so was Mrs. Norman.

I knelt down to pray and as I was praying I felt this warm presence come over me. It had to be the Holy Spirit. "Heavenly Father, thank you for godly women like Mom and Mrs. Norman. Lord, I have sinned with selfishness, pride, and self-pity. Please forgive me. If it is your will, I would love to sing for your glory. Please give me your heavenly strength that evening. I pray this through Jesus Christ our Lord, amen." I stood up right there and sang the National Anthem with God on my side. The peace I had afterward told me God was in charge, not Jude Bonner or his peers. Praise God.

Mom was at the kitchen sink when I got downstairs, so I hugged her from behind.

"Thanks, Mom. Thank you for helping me stay strong."

After chores, Fuzz and I went over to Mr. Olson's to check with him on hitching Pete and Joe with Ladd for the first time. As I walked over there, I sang the whole way.

"How is the proud owner of hitch geldings doing?" Mr. Olson asked.

"I'm just fine. Hope you are too."

"Why certainly, why certainly."

"Mr. Olson, I think Pete and Joe are ready to be hitched with Ladd, if that is okay with you."

"Are they line driving single pretty good and do they understand 'whoa'?"

"I've driven them around tractors and along the road with traffic, and I've dragged tin cans behind them and they seem pretty good."

"Jude, you make the call, but from what I've seen and heard I would agree they are ready. Bring them over Saturday morning and we'll see what they've got."

After chores Saturday morning, Dad, Becky, Gramps, and I harnessed Pete and Joe and led them over to Mr. Olson's.

Mr. Olson met us outside his barn and talked to Pete and Joe. "My, my, look how you colts have grown. Pete and Joe, we are going to hitch with Ladd this morning and work the heck out of you, but without bridles that could be a pretty tall order."

"Golly jeepers!" I shouted. In my haste I left home without the bridles. I handed Joe's lead rope to Becky, and Fuzz and headed home to get bridles. While I was gone they must have pulled the manure spreader out by the manure pile because they were pitching a load when I got back with the bridles.

"Jude, throw a harness on Ladd while we finish this load of manure," Mr. Olson said.

Ladd was out in the pasture. I ran out to retrieve him and, of course, Molly had to tag along. Mr. Olson had four tie stalls for horses so I let Molly follow us in. That was a pretty awesome sight, four big black rumps in a row. I curried Ladd quick and threw a harness on him. I was just finishing when the manure-pitching crew walked in.

Dad chided, "Jude, you timed that just right. Of course you wouldn't want to get any blisters on them dishpan hands of yours."

Mr. Olson responded with a Bible verse, "Lazy hands make a man poor, but diligent hands bring wealth. Proverbs 10:4."

"Jude, bring one of your colts out to the bobsled and we'll see what he can do. He will be the right hand horse for now. I'll follow you out with Ladd, the finest hitch gelding this side of the Mississippi!"

I was pretty excited as I grabbed Joe and headed that way. Becky was taking pictures as the rest of us hitched Joe and Ladd to the bobsled. Pete was putting up quite a fuss in the barn now that he was alone in a strange place. I guess he didn't think of Molly, his own mother, as good company. It didn't help much that Joe whinnied back to him. We were hitching to the bobsled for a little less noise at first and a stable, steady pull. It also made room for all of us to ride. Joe had gotten pretty worked up by the time we got everything hooked. Ladd had done this so many times before that he stood there like a statue. We were about ready to head out with me standing in front of Joe, Mr. Olson standing with the lines, and Gramps, Dad, and Becky on the rack.

Mr. Olson said, "Let's ask for a little help from the man above before we get too far into this."

We all bowed our heads. "Dear Lord, you created all creatures and in Genesis you gave man the right to rule over all created things. Lord, please protect us and these horses as we take this ruling power to the next level. And Lord, we thank you for all the creatures that you surround us with, and help us keep this training in line according to your holy plan. We pray this through Jesus Christ our Lord, amen."

It is pretty awesome to have God on your side when dealing with one of his creations.

"Jude, slowly work your way back to the rack. If Joe gets fidgety, try calming him with voice commands. Remember, we want Joe to hear your voice today, not mine. Now when I hand you the lines, that means you are in charge so be ready. The other thing you will need to remember is to keep him moving. A lot of colts think if they stop, everything will get better. Only stop Ladd if I say so, otherwise keep them moving. Joe has to learn to keep moving and not let what's going on behind him affect his work. So you need to be on Joe right away if he shows signs of stopping."

I quickly made my way to the rack and was trying to calm Joe as I left him. "Easy boy, easy."

"Jude, the other thing to remember is even if they trot or almost gallop, that is better than stopping. Ladd will not run, so don't be afraid if Joe lunges or bucks or steps over the pole. Don't even calm him with your voice. He'll soon learn it is easier to walk with this load than to trot. And I feel that lesson is best for them to figure out on their own. Now here are the lines. Make sure you start them when you are ready, don't let them decide when to start."

I did one last visual check to make sure all straps and lines were hooked up properly.

"Joe, Ladd, get up there." There was some hesitation from Joe, but he did start to move. It wasn't a perfect start but we were actually moving forward. After about ten feet though, Joe tried stopping. I hollered at him pretty sternly and he lunged ahead at a trot. While Ladd was just plodding along at a walk,

Joe was everywhere, too far ahead and too far behind. Next thing I knew, Joe had both front feet off the ground. I guess that was the last straw for Ladd. As soon as Joe got all four feet back on the ground, Ladd reached over and bit him right on the neck. It wasn't any love bite either. Ladd meant business. That was the first and last time Joe reared up the rest of the day. We were coming to the end of the field so I asked Mr. Olson, "What do you want me to do?" Just the sound of my voice set Joe off on a good trot and even Ladd joined in. Before I had time to react we were right up by the fence. Ladd stopped on his own, and Joe followed his lead.

Mr. Olson quickly hollered, "Whoa!" Joe was dancing and prancing while Ladd just stood there.

"Jude, what do you think so far?" Mr. Olson asked.

"It is harder than I thought it would be. I thought Joe would do better."

"Jude, you're doing fine and Joe is doing what most colts do at this stage of the game. We will give them a brief rest here, but remember to keep them moving if at all possible. If for whatever reason they do stop, say 'whoa' right away so they think it was your idea. Now tell me what set them off into that trot?"

"I think it was when I started to ask you that question."

"If you notice, right now Joe is listening to every word we speak. Those ears were working overtime trying to catch every sound out there. Now we will start out again and we'll all talk more as we go. Hopefully they'll go into a trot again and make sure you keep them going. Turn right here so Ladd can push Joe if needed. Make sure to start them the same way as you did the first time."

"Joe, Ladd, get up" I hollered. Ladd started but Joe seemed to have no intention of moving, that is, until he felt Ladd's ivories sinking into his neck for the second time. Joe got with the program immediately after that. In fact we were going at a nice trot.

"Jude, give them some gradual turns both left and right," Mr. Olson said. Right when Mr. Olson started speaking, Joe lunged. Joe thought that every word we spoke was a command to him. He needed to learn the difference between normal talking and his commands. We all talked as we went and Joe was starting to get it. We were still trotting along at a good clip and it was pretty cool. Joe was fairly clumsy in the turns hitting the pole as he kept his eye on Ladd's teeth. We let Ladd and Joe determine whether to walk or trot.

"What's the deal with Ladd biting Joe? I've never seen or heard of that before." Dad said.

"Ladd is one of the best breaking horses I've ever seen. As you have noticed, he bites only when Joe is messing around. Notice Joe doesn't go back and try whatever he was doing again. Not all breaking horses bite like that, but I think it really helps a colt learn faster."

We had been out there about forty minutes and Joe and Ladd were starting to lather up with sweat. Joe was understanding turns a little better now. Both Ladd and Joe were huffing and puffing.

"Jude, stop them by that oak tree in the shade for a rest," Mr. Olson said.

"Whoa, whoa, boys!" Ladd stopped right away and Joe did right after Ladd.

"Jude, we are going to hook to the manure spreader soon and spread a load. I wanted to stop out here so Joe learns that you don't always stop by the barn. We will pull them up by the barn to unhook and then we'll head over to the spreader. I want you to drive them over the pole a couple times from both directions. Then we'll see how Joe likes the beater noise from the spreader." Mr. Olson chuckled.

I started them out again towards the barn. I smiled seeing Joe step right out when I gave the command. He knew if he didn't, Ladd would have his chompers heading Joe's way. We unhooked from the bobsled and I line drove them towards the manure spreader.

"Jude, let me tie Joe's halter back to Ladd's hame ring," Mr. Olson said. "With you being by yourself and the new noise, we don't want to take any chances. If Joe jumps ahead, his halter will hold him back to Ladd."

Wow! Until Mr. Olson said "by yourself" it hadn't registered with me that there was only one seat on a manure spreader. I would be heading out with no help, that is except from the good Lord, of course. We got Joe tied back to Ladd and now it was time to go over the pole a couple times. I put Ladd over first because he was used to it, and then we tried Joe. He sidestepped it more than I thought he would. I drove them around for several new approaches to the pole and Joe wasn't getting any better. Dad came up and helped lead him over as I drove with the lines.

That worked very well, so we did that a couple more times and I praised Joe each time he did it. We hooked up the neck yoke and tug chains and were now ready to spread the first load.

"Jude, remember that Ladd will not let you down. If necessary, holler 'whoa' and stop them. And if things really get bad, put them in a circle. Remember, you can ride just as fast as they can run. Ideally, even though Joe will be wired, try to keep them going just like before. Make several rounds with the spreader full and practice more turns, especially short turns. Then engage the beaters only and make several rounds before engaging the apron. After it is empty, make more rounds and tight turns with the spreader engaged. Give them a good reason to want to stop. Bring them up to the manure pile when you're done. You'll do just fine," Mr. Olson said.

I looked at Dad and Becky and they gave me the thumbs up. This was a steel wheeled manure spreader that made a lot of noise.

"Joe, Ladd, get up." Joe lunged as soon as he heard the steel wheels on the gravel driveway, but his halter being tied to Ladd brought him back in line quickly. Joe was dancing pretty good with his neck curved back towards us as we entered the field. We trotted, we turned, and we walked. Joe was doing okay until I engaged the beaters and that about sent him to the moon. He jerked on that lead rope tied to Ladd and started hopping with his back feet. Hopping with the back feet can mean he's thinking of kicking. When you are on a spreader and they kick, you are right where the action is! Luckily for me, Joe didn't kick. But the beater noise had Joe totally wired, especially on turns. He would pivot his ears, then lay them back, and then pivot them some more. He would look back to see what kind of monster was back there. It seemed to take forever, but Joe eventually started to understand that things were okay and the sun would come up tomorrow. I engaged the apron and spread the load. As the spreader got closer to empty the more noise it made, so we spent time on tight turns with it empty. I think Joe was hoping that he would never see a spreader again. When we got back to the barn, Joe was looking very rough. Mr. Olson had me try backing. Joe did okay with that, but he was pretty tired so I think he was glad to head into the barn.

"Mr. Olson and Jude, I have a few things to get done before chores. I'll help you get Pete hooked to the bobsled and then I think I'll head west," Dad said.

It was now Pete's turn to try the same things we did with Joe. Before we hooked him with Ladd, we pitched the spreader full again. Pete did better than Joe, as usual, being not as high strung. Even so we still tied him back to Ladd's halter when I went with the spreader. Becky took lots of pictures of us working both colts. Ladd was pretty tired by the end of Pete's training. I unharnessed Ladd and gave him a good currying and sent him out to pasture. As usual, it didn't take long and he was rolling on his back at his favorite dirt area.

"Jude, I think you have done well with these colts. I could tell you've done a lot of foundation work with them. I've seen many colts that were just plain crazy after running them through the hoops like we did. Pete and Joe did just fine for their first time out. Keep in mind, you need to hitch tomorrow and do pretty much the same thing, so we will see you after church."

As Becky and I led Joe and Pete back home, we could tell they were very tired.

"Becky, I want to thank you for helping as much as you have with Pete and Joe. They wouldn't be as far as they are without your help."

"I have enjoyed this just as much as you. Besides, I have another motive that I haven't told you about," she said hesitantly.

"And what might that be?" I asked.

"Remember when I was a little girl and wanted to get a pony to ride? If it is alright with you, I would love to train these guys to ride."

"Are you kidding, Becky? I never thought of that! I must admit it sounds pretty neat to me. Let's ask Mr. Olson about it tomorrow."

I unharnessed them while Becky curried. I gave them a big hug and thanked them before we turned them out to pasture. All in all, it was a good day for the colts.

Becky and I did our chores and headed in for supper. Mom had burritos ready. A guy gets pretty hungry after hitching horses all day.

"Mom that son of yours is close to having an awful nice team of Percherons on his hands," Dad had a gleam in his eye.

"Is that so? I was going to get over there to watch, but I got busy with some church stuff for Sunday morning."

"Mom and Dad, Becky is thinking of training Pete and Joe to

ride."

Becky asked, "What do you think of that? Can you imagine being up there that high going for a nice ride? That would be so awesome!"

Dad replied, "You'll need a step ladder to get up on them. It does sound pretty neat if you think about it."

"You just be careful young lady. Pete and Joe have a lot to learn yet," Mom warned. "Jude, have you thought about Friday night lately?"

"What do you mean, Friday night?" Right then it hit me, Friday night was the first home football game and I was scheduled to sing the National Anthem. "Mom, thanks for reminding me! I had plumb forgot."

"After supper might I suggest you practice while I do up the dishes so I can help you if you need it," Mom suggested.

Yes sir, Mom and I practiced until the cows came home. I was thankful I had a Mom who cared that much. She gave me some suggestions that really helped my tone and breathing. By the end of that session I was feeling pretty confident.

That night in bed I kept going over every detail of the day. I was looking forward to hitching the next day because Mr. Olson had said they make big gains each time you hitch them. I was dreaming of hitching them without old Ladd, just Pete and Joe. The more I thought about them the more excited I got and I couldn't sleep. It was one-thirty in the morning the last I checked the clock. Chores came pretty early that morning.

Pastor Hanson's sermon was on prayer so it was easy to stay focused. Sunday school was on different cults that are out there. A cult is a religion that doesn't recognize that man sins and Jesus died on the cross for man's sin.

After church Becky and I hustled over to Mr. Olson's with Pete, Joe, and Fuzz. I remembered the bridles this time. Mr. Olson had Ladd all harnessed up and even had Molly in harness.

"Jude and Becky, let's hitch Pete first with Ladd to the bobsled. If that goes okay, we might try Molly on the spreader with Pete while Ladd is with Joe on the bobsled," Mr. Olson said.

Mr. Olson had put a few cement blocks on the bobsled for more drag. He said it was good to teach colts to pull steady. We got Pete and Ladd hooked up in the barn and I line drove them out towards the bobsled. It was quite special line driving them. Mr. Olson had me drive around the barnyard several times before we got to the sled. I put Ladd over the pole first and then it was Pete's turn, but he had different ideas. He stood there like a statue until Ladd bared his teeth. His ears went back, his teeth came out, and he put the squeeze on Pete's neck immediately. Pete didn't know what hit him at first. He had missed out on Ladd's special training yesterday. Needless to say, Pete soon learned to step over the pole or lose a chunk of flesh. We hooked up the tugs and off we went. Pete was much better than yesterday. He stayed clear of the pole on turns and stopped right away on command. When he would lag behind a little, Mr. Olson would tap him with the whip until he got back to where he was supposed to be. We gave them a good workout with the sled, then hitched to the empty spreader. We wanted them to stand while we pitched a load on. A big part of training is standing quietly without being tied. Pete didn't set any records on standing; he would paw at the ground, walk ahead, and back up. Becky ended up with a set of single lines on him holding him back most of the time. After pulling that load of manure around for awhile, I spread it and came back for one more load. This time while we pitched it, Pete stood pretty quiet. He was tired!

"Becky, you go get Molly and bring her out here. We'll hook Pete with her for Jude to drive while you and I hitch Joe with Ladd," Mr. Olson said.

Sure enough, there I was driving Pete with his mother Molly on the manure spreader while Becky and Mr. Olson line drove Joe and Ladd. I drove close to them and while Joe didn't see the humor in that, Mr. Olson took it all in stride. It was amazing to watch Mr. Olson handle those driving lines and keep Joe in check. It wasn't long and we had two teams of Percherons in the field, Becky and Mr. Olson on the bobsled and me on the spreader. We drove side by side, crossed in front of each other, and drove straight on like a head on collision. Both colts were doing fairly well. I even had the beaters going as I came up behind Joe with the spreader.

"Jude, head Molly and Pete up a little grade and stop them. Then ask them to back a few steps. The pull from the hill will encourage Pete to back. Do that several times, but don't get in a hurry or ask for too many steps," Mr. Olson cautioned.

He was right. The hill seemed to help Pete understand backing. After that I headed back to the barn and pitched another load of manure. Pete was way better at standing than Joe. I only had to grab the lines a couple of times to settle him down. I even banged the pitchfork on the side of the spreader pretty hard. After pitching the load, I unhooked from the spreader and line drove Molly and Pete around the barnyard. It was going so well I wanted to just keep driving, but I had to help them get Joe and Ladd onto the full spreader. Joe and Ladd finished that day hauling two loads of manure themselves. Joe had his turn at standing still while we pitched a load. Joe was pretty wired so we hobbled his front legs. That changed his attitude about standing. Joe actually did better backing on the hill than Pete did.

"Jude and Becky, I think we've done well today. Praise God! We'll see ya after school tomorrow with these colts in harness. A couple more times and they will be ready to hitch as a team without Molly or Ladd," Mr. Olson said.

The next day, it felt like school would never end. All I could think of was driving Pete and Joe. Becky had lots of homework so I went to Mr. Olsons without her. As I led Pete and Joe east I could tell they were getting used to this routine. Mr. Olson claimed a horse never really forgets what he is taught. Molly and Ladd were in harness by the time we got there. Mr. Olson also had the hay wagon out with the three horse evener attached to the pole.

"Good afternoon, Jude. Tie one colt in the barn and bring the other one out," Mr. Olson requested. "We'll see how they like three abreast today."

I tied up Pete and put Joe between Molly and Ladd. We hooked everything up and off we went. Mr. Olson drove for a little while then handed me the lines. I assume you could see me smiling a mile away. To feel that much power in those lines was really special to me. We stopped and loaded up a chain saw, some pots and pans, a paper sack, tin cans on a string, and a plastic tarp. It seemed the only thing we didn't have was the kitchen sink. We tied Joe's halter back to the hame rings on Molly and Ladd. If Joe was going to try to run, he would have to drag Molly and Ladd with him. I drove out in the field and Mr. Olson started in with the noisy objects we loaded. Joe lunged ahead and came to the end of the ropes. The chainsaw set Joe off in a tizzy the most. Mr. Olson even had some firecrackers that he set off. We stopped by the barn to get Mr. Olson's pickup out and I drove three abreast as Mr. Olson buzzed us with the truck, honking the horn. Joe was somewhat used to this from Becky and me doing this at home, so he did pretty good. I drove out onto the road and Mr. Olson passed us and drove toward us at regular road speeds to get Joe used to that. It really helped Joe that Molly and Ladd ignored all this commotion. We got back in the field and Mr. Olson drove while I shook the plastic tarp at them. We even had them drive over the tarp. Molly and Ladd stayed cool and collected while Joe was all lathered up from the stress but soon learned life was better if he just ignored all the noise behind him.

We ran Pete through the same gauntlet with pretty much the same results as Joe.

Mr. Olson, Becky, and I hitched the colts to Molly or Ladd or both every night that week after school. Joe and Pete were showing good muscle tone and were really understanding what this was all about. Each night Mr. Olson had us hitch to a different farm implement like the hay rake, hay mower, hay loader, disk, drag, hay tedder, and even the stone boat.

"Jude and Becky, tomorrow is Friday. I think it's time to hitch Pete and Joe to the hay wagon as a team without Ladd or Molly. What do you think?"

"That sounds good to me!"

Becky, being more organized than I am, stated, "Jude, the first home football game is tomorrow night and you're singing the National Anthem."

"Golly, Mr. Olson, I forgot about that. I have to be there. Can we hitch Pete and Joe Saturday morning after chores?"

"Why certainly."

Becky asked, "Mr. Olson, what do you think of training Pete and Joe to be ridden?"

"That is an interesting thought, Becky. I think it is a great idea. However, they say a draft horse should not be ridden until four years of age. This allows their spines more time to fuse. So in a couple years you can start that process. You will have better behaved horses if you train them to ride."

Mr. Olson could tell Becky didn't like the part where she would have to wait two years, so he suggested, "Becky, if you wouldn't mind training Molly to ride while you are waiting for Pete and Joe to mature, I would sure appreciate it."

Becky perked right up and answered back with a big smile on her face, "Yes sir, I would love to work with Molly."

"You talk it over with your parents, but I would be willing to buy a saddle for you in payment for training Molly to ride."

I thought Becky was going to split at the seams! She had this huge grin on her face and she was speechless. She stuttered and stammered and finally said, "Yes sir, I will check with Mom and Dad."

Becky and I led the colts back towards home. As we walked, we talked of how the colts were bonding with us more and more each day. As I unharnessed them and curried them, I practiced singing for tomorrow night. The old barn has pretty good acoustics.

At supper Mom noticed Becky was sitting on pins and needles.

"Becky, what is it that has you all starry-eyed?"

"Mom, Dad, you'll never believe this! I asked Mr. Olson about riding Pete and Joe. He said it was a good idea when they get older and that he was going to buy me a saddle!"

"Why would Mr. Olson buy you a saddle?" Dad asked suspiciously.

"Oh, I guess I forgot one part. Mr. Olson wants me to train Molly to ride and to cover the cost of training her, he will buy me a saddle. He did say I should check with you and Mom. So what do you think, can you imagine? My very own saddle!"

"Now don't be counting them chicks before they hatch, young lady. Mom and I will talk it over and let you know in the morning."

"Thanks, Dad."

"Mr. Olson wants to hook Pete and Joe together for the first time on the hay wagon Saturday morning with no help from Molly or Ladd," I announced.

Dad smiled. "Jude, that's what you've been training for, so good for you. Becky should take some pictures and I'll try to be there too. I'd like to see them colts working together for the first time."

Mom asked, "Are you ready for tomorrow night, Jude? If need be, I can go over it with ya after supper."

So we did just that. Mom listened and I sang it through one time. She said it was sounding very good. I did a little homework, took a shower, and headed to bed. There I lay, my mind racing back and forth between driving Pete and Joe and thinking about singing in front of all those people. I finally got up and had a glass of milk, said some more prayers at the foot of my bed, and went to sleep.

It was hard to concentrate at school the next day. We had a pep session to get fired up for the big game. The weather was cool and rainy. That didn't help my attitude. Who wants to sing when they're cold and wet? I guess my attitude was showing somewhat when Mrs. Norman saw me.

"Jude, if it is raining tonight, I will hold an umbrella for you. Dress plenty warm and meet me down by the microphone at seven o'clock sharp. How are you feeling?"

"Pretty good. I'm a little nervous and anxious, but God will get me through this. Mom and I have worked on it several times so I'm feeling good about it."

"Remember Romans 8:31 Jude. 'With God on your side who can be against you'?"

"Thanks, Mrs. Norman, and thanks for prodding me along to do this."

"You're welcome Jude. It is kind of a selfish prodding because I love to hear a good strong anthem and I know you are capable of that. See ya tonight."

When Becky and I got home from school, I did chores quick and spent some time with Pete and Joe.

"Do you guys know that tomorrow you'll be pulling a wagon together for the first time?" I looked them in the eyes. "I know you can do it." They each put their heads over my shoulders and rubbed against my face. They could tell from my voice I was asking for help again. I rubbed their ears and scratched their bellies.

"Boys, I've got to sing tonight for the Lord. I guess since I ask you guys to be strong I have to be strong too. We should try to sneak you in so you can be there. You get your rest. We have a big day tomorrow." As I walked away they each softly snorted at me.

Before I knew it, Mrs. Norman was holding an umbrella over my head as I prepared to sing the National Anthem. I had said many prayers for this and I know others were praying right then and there. I was hardly nervous at all anymore. God took over for me and the song came out very well. I was just a vessel for God that night. It seemed like I was just standing there and God did everything else.

Mrs. Norman gave me a big hug and I believe I even saw a tear in her eye. "Jude, thank you for allowing God to use the gifts he gave you. You sounded great, and I mean great!"

I responded like Dad had taught me on compliments, "Praise

God, praise God." Dad always warned, "Be careful when someone compliments you. If you take the credit yourself then you'll soon be worshiping yourself instead of God."

The football team won the game that night. I was glad to get home and take a warm shower and head to bed. I was just getting in bed when Dad came up. "Son, you did Mom and me proud tonight. The good Lord has given you a gift in singing. Don't keep it under a basket, but instead use it for his glory like you did tonight. Who knows, someday I might have to hire you to sing at my funeral, that is if you don't charge me too much."

Dad gave me a hug and headed downstairs.

I got down on my knees. "Dear Lord, thank you for taking over tonight. I thank you for teachers like Mrs. Norman. I thank you for Mom, Dad, Becky, Pete, and Joe. Please be with us tomorrow and I ask for good rest tonight, Lord. I pray this through Jesus Christ your son, amen."

I think I was out as soon as my head hit the old pillow.

The good Lord woke me early Saturday morning. I did my chores and headed out to get Pete and Joe. When I got to their paddock, they were nowhere to be seen and the gate was open. My mind started racing. Had I not locked the gate the night before? Had someone stolen my colts? I ran to the barn to check with Dad, and much to my surprise Pete and Joe were in their stalls with Becky brushing them.

Becky smiled as she said, "Bout time you got up. Burning daylight, pal."

I had to admit it was pretty funny the way she said it and I was awful glad to see the colts safe and sound.

Becky continued, "Go in and get breakfast while I finish up here."

I started to ask why and was cut short. "Jude, you go in and get breakfast while I finish up here," she insisted.

I can take a hint when asked or told twice, so I headed to the house for breakfast. It was kind of odd as I was going in the back door, Mom was heading out the front door with a small box. She seemed in a hurry and didn't want to talk. While I ate breakfast all I could think of was what Becky and Mom were up to. I ate quickly, brushed my teeth, and did my daily devotion before heading back out to harness the colts. Much to my surprise, as I stepped out the back door there were the colts standing under the Burr oak tree in the side yard with Becky and Mom. The closer I got the more Becky smiled. It took me a little while to see what this was all about. While I had eaten breakfast, they were braiding the manes and tails of the colts. They were beautiful! They had royal blue ribbons braided in their manes and royal blue bows on their tails, and their tails were up in a bun. I stood there just admiring how nice it looked, then walked around them slowly. I couldn't believe how much it changed their look.

"Jude, when you're done gawking I'll take some pictures of you and Becky and the colts," Mom said.

"Becky, this is awesome! When did you think of this idea?"

Becky was just a-smiling and waving her hand as she spoke. "Last year at the fair some of the drafts were braided up like this, so Mom and I made the ribbons and bows and looked on the net to see how to do it. Do you like it?"

"They are beautiful! Thank you for doing this. Wait till Mr. Olson sees them."

Mom took pictures from all angles: front, back, sides. We took pictures of each colt without us in the pictures. I harnessed while Becky ate breakfast, and then it was off to Mr. Olson's. Becky and I each had a distinguished strut as we led Pete and Joe over to Mr. Olson's place.

"Would you take a look at that?" Mr. Olson chuckled as he rubbed his chin. "Becky you've got them colts looking pretty sharp. Are you sure you want to hitch them when they look that fancy? My, my, I have to admit ribbons and bows can sure make them look like a pair of fancy hitch geldings."

Becky asked, "Did we do it the right way?"

As Mr. Olson pulled on their manes he said, "Well, the braiding is a little loose. With time, you'll learn to keep the braid tighter, but for a first time I would say you did a very good job. I should probably go in and change my clothes otherwise you won't allow me to ride along."

"Why is your pickup truck behind the hay wagon?" I asked.

"Jude, you've heard of wagons with built in brakes. Well, this is my version of brakes. While Pete and Joe are hitched to the wagon, I'll be in the pickup applying the brakes if needed. We don't want these guys getting out of control on their first solo excursion. I will give them a little brake just for some extra pull at times and if they try to run, we'll see how they like pulling Mr. Ford."

We hitched the lines to the colts in the barn and I line drove them out as a team for the very first time. I was very proud. Becky was taking pictures as I drove them around the yard. I laughed when Becky would stop and fix their ribbons now and then so her pictures would look the best. I attempted to step them over the hay wagon pole a couple times. Mr. Olson helped guide them a little on the third attempt. All three of us checked all connections before we headed out. Mr. Olson was in the pickup with Becky and I on the wagon.

"Pete, Joe, step up." They seesawed a little at the start and then got us moving. They both seemed a little hesitant and I think each one was wondering where Ladd and his teeth were. They weren't perfect but they were doing okay. I could tell when Mr. Olson would add some brake and when he would let up. Becky got off and took pictures. We trotted and walked and drove around as many obstacles as we could fit by. Twice Mr. Olson locked up the brakes and let the tires skid on the truck. Pete and Joe dug in pretty hard when that happened. After awhile I stopped to give them a rest.

Mr. Olson got out of the truck and came up to us. "Jude, you and I are gonna switch places now. You really have to pay attention on this next maneuver. I'm going to let them go into a slow gallop just beyond a trot. You stay off the brakes unless Becky signals you from the back of the wagon. If she does signal you, don't lock them up, only give us partial braking. We are teaching Pete and Joe that they can run and stay in control. If Becky gives you the cutthroat signal, then lock 'em up. Any questions?"

"No, sir." As I went back to the truck, I checked the chain to make sure it was still hooked up at both ends. I gave Becky the thumbs up when I was ready and off we went. It didn't take long and Pete and Joe were in a slow gallop. It was kind of neat watching how Mr. Olson handled the reins. With his weathered hands he had them right where he wanted them. Becky would signal me for slight pressure on the brakes at times. Pete and Joe were in pretty good shape from all the hitching we had been doing, so they were moving along at a pretty good clip, nostrils flaring, hooves pounding, ribbons streaming, and lather foaming.

Then Mr. Olson hollered, "Whoa!" Joe and Pete didn't really stop like they should, so I locked up the brakes as quick as I thought to. That stopped them because Mr. Olson had put a bunch of extra weight in the back of the truck.

Mr. Olson was laughing. "Now wasn't that a pretty good ride, Becky? These boys need to stop better than what they did, but otherwise that went well."

We did that several more times and then it was my turn to drive them at a gallop with Mr. Olson back in the truck. We even headed down the road at a walk, trot, and gallop. We took our parade to our place for Mom and Dad to inspect. By the time we were done, Pete and Joe were stopping on a dime at any gait.

We pulled back to Mr. Olson's and stopped. "Jude, that was a very good session. Hitch them at home as much as possible and be sure to think each time about no mistakes. You're doing well and so are the colts, but it is easy to go backwards with one little mistake. Line drive them and back them a lot before hitching to anything. Hitch for now only with help from Becky or your Dad. And remember to think ahead and look ahead to predict what might set them off so you're ready. I'll check next Saturday to see how you're doing."

Dad, Becky, and I did what Mr. Olson suggested. We hitched to different things and drove to different places, up hills, down hills, and even buzzed them with four wheelers. Joe and Pete were doing great. They stepped over the pole well from both sides, they didn't seem to spook at traffic or when pulling into strange yards, and we did most of these with Pete and Joe hitched as both the left and right hand horse. It is very important to train them to be used to both sides of the pole.

Sure enough, Mr. Olson pulled in the yard that next Saturday just like he said. "I'm looking for a good team of broke hitch geldings." He laughed. "Jude and Becky, how did it go?"

"We think it went fine! They never tried to run, we went to all the neighbors, and traffic doesn't seem to bother them. They step over the pole and back up pretty good," I said.

As Mr. Olson smiled, he said, "Then it's time for a Sunday drive to town with them colts. Should we do that tomorrow?"

"Sure we can," I answered.

"Drive them over to my place after church and we'll drive them to town and have lunch at the Blue Banana. I'm buying."

As he was pulling out the driveway I asked Becky, "Do you think you could braid their manes and tails for our first run to town tomorrow?"

"Consider it done."

After church on Sunday, Becky braided manes and tails before we harnessed and headed to Mr. Olson's. Dad and Mom said they might meet us up there. We picked up Mr. Olson and we were on our way to Belgrade for Pete and Joe's debut in town. That required us to drive right beside state highway 71. The colts were doing fine with the traffic noise, even from the semi trucks. Motorcycles coming at them got their attention the most. We made it to town and headed for the Blue Banana for lunch. By this time Pete and Joe were pretty tired so they were ready to stand. Mr. Olson and Becky got off the wagon as I held the lines. Next thing I knew a super loud pickup truck came skidding to a halt right beside us. It was Greg Shants and Judy Clemons. Pete and Joe were going to have none of that! They side stepped instantly almost hitting Mr. Olson and then took off on a full run. I lost my balance and was laying on the floor of the wagon as they built up speed. I was just starting to get up when the back of the wagon scrapped up against a tree, down I went for the second time. I had no resistance on the lines as I tried to get up, Pete and Joe were frantically running down the paved streets out of control! It seemed like it took me forever but I finally stood up and started pulling back on the lines as I screamed whoa. Somehow I lost the left line and was pulling on the right one only and they jumped the curb and cut across a garden. I'm sure we caught air with the wagon on that stunt. I was finally pulling back on both lines with all my strength and was shocked to see it had no affect on slowing them. Being in town stopped me from turning them in a circle, that can help slow a team of horses down. We were headed north down Oswald Avenue as I started thinking of what to do with the US Highway 71 junction? I have to admit jumping off came to mind but the black pavement didn't look real inviting. Mr. Olson had told me you can always ride as fast as they can run during a runaway. The closer we got to 71 the bigger my eyes got, and my arms were starting to feel like rubber. Pete and Joe shot across 71 barely missing the back end of a semi. I screamed whoa many times as I pulled back with all my strength as my grip was getting weaker. As they approached Main Street they shot south with a hard left and Joe just about went down. We were now headed back towards Highway 71! I glanced behind me quick and noticed Mom and Dad following. Pete and Joe were starting to tire and were slowing down a little as they approached 71 again. The muscles in my arms were screaming for relief as we crossed 71 with cars screeching to a halt. The squealing tires put

Pete and Joe at full speed again in the wrong lane. My confidence was long gone by now, as I wondered how and when this would end? All of a sudden Dad went flying past me on the side barely missing the side of the wagon and stopped crossways in the street up by the school. Pete and Joe were all lathered up with sweat and gasping for air as we approached the school. Dad was standing in the street pointing towards the school parking lot, hoping he could turn them. Pete and Joe were starting to look for other places to go since Dad's pickup was blocking the street. I knew Dad's goal was to get them into the big parking lot so I could put them into a circle.

I turned Pete and Joe a little too soon which caused the back of the wagon to jump the curve. We drove into that parking lot at full speed ahead as Dad ran towards his pickup. I put what little strength I had into pulling on the right line to force them into a circle. It was working, we were going in a big circle and Pete and Joe were starting to slow down. I kept pulling to the right as our circle was getting tighter. Soon Dad was in the center of the circle getting ready to jump on as we passed. I hoped Dad would jump on soon because I didn't think I could hold on much longer. Dad made his move and grabbed the back of the hay rack as we passed beside him. I looked back as he tried to get his feet up on the rack kind of like the stunt men in the movies. Praise God, Dad made it the first try up and over and I was glad to hand him the lines. My fingers could barely straighten as I stood there trying to hang onto the front of the rack.

"Dad, you need to put them into a full run again!"

Not exactly what I wanted to do, but Pete and Joe needed to learn that running was not any fun. With new arms on the lines and a wide open parking lot we could have a controlled runaway! Soon Dad had one leg over the front of the rack and was slapping the geldings with the ends of the lines.

"Get up! Pete and Joe! Get up! We'll show you how to run!" Dad hollered.

We made left circles than right circles and every time they showed signs of slowing down Dad was right on them with the ends of the lines. Pete and Joe seemed to be begging to slow down but Dad wouldn't let them.

Dad drove as I rested my arms and hands, knowing I would have to drive soon to bring them down to a walk and to stop them. We had a few spectators watching every move we made.

"Dad, I need to finish this so I'll be grabbing the lines soon."

I have to admit I was a little gun shy at this time, I slowly grabbed the lines and held on. I turned them several times and started allowing them to slow down. Pete and Joe were more than happy to slow down.

"Easy boys, easy." As they slowed to a walk.

"Whoa!" I shouted firmly as they hesitantly came to a stop.

Pete and Joe were sucking for air as they pranced in place, not totally sure if they were doing the right thing.

"Easy boys, easy." I tried to reassure them.

The sweat was pouring onto the pavement. They had dirty white lather all over them as they were still nervous. They were exhausted and wondering what really just happened. Dad got down and stood in front of them just in case.

"Mom can you drive up to the Blue Banana and get Becky and Mr. Olson?" I asked.

"How did this happen and did you hit anybody or anything?"

"The back of the wagon scrapped up against a tree as they first got going and we also ended up cutting through someone's garden, the rest of the trip was on the streets."

"Okay, but that doesn't explain how this all started?"

It was then my anger started building. "Those jerks, Greg and Judy came sliding in beside us at the Red Onion with that loud pickup! Pete and Joe lunged and I lost my balance. I can't believe they are that dumb! They're going to get a piece of my mind when I get the chance!"

Dad stated as if he was talking to himself. "Romans talks something about do not take revenge, but leave room for God's wrath. It also states do not be overcome with evil, but overcome evil with good."

"But Dad!"

"It's up to you Jude. Here comes your mother with the rest of the gang."

Mr. Olson and Becky came up to us as the geldings were still fighting for enough air. I was curious what he would say.

"Jude are you okay?"

"Yes."

"And the geldings are they okay?" As he started to run his hands down their legs.

"I think so."

"Thank you Lord! That could have been really bad. Now what

do you think is next Jude?" Mr. Olson asked.

"I'm not sure what to do Mr. Olson."

As he rubbed his forehead, "I'm kind of hungry so I say we go back to the scene of the crime. I think it's best to take them right back to where they started to run, and teach them that there are no bugger men there. Why certainly."

"That doesn't sound real great to me, maybe we should go home and get the trailer and haul them home?" I spouted off with an edge to my voice.

Mr. Olson hesitated for a moment. "Jude, there are very few teams in this world that have not had a runaway somewhere during the training process. You can't blame Pete and Joe and you can't coop them up the rest of their lives. I'm sure your confidence is in the gutter but what is best for you and the geldings is to drive them right away like this never happened and go right back there. Hopefully that loud truck is still there."

I looked at Dad and he gave a quick nod, I looked at Mom and she gave me a quick nod, and so did Becky. I reluctantly got up on the wagon and grabbed the lines as Mr. Olson and Becky followed.

"Pete, Joe, Get up."

As we headed to the Blue Banana Mr. Olson gave me his thoughts. "When we get real close you watch their heads. They will probably get nervous as you pull into the same spot. Talk to them with your voice and don't give them any extra slack in the lines. If you need help I will grab the lines."

Pete and Joe were getting more antsy the closer we got to the Blue Banana. Was this a God thing or what? There was Greg's truck in the same spot with the space that we took off from still open. Joe whinnied as we got closer and they both started to prance and side step.

"Easy boys."

I had a firm grip on the lines with no slack as the geldings hesitantly drove beside Greg's truck. Joe was snorting as he does when he's nervous. We made it!

"Thank you, Lord."

I scanned the crowd and spotted Greg and Judy at a picnic table.

"Mr. Olson can you hold the geldings I have something to do?"

"Why certainly, why certainly."

As I walked towards their table they both took a quick glance at me and looked away. I think they were more surprised when I sat down across from them. As I sat there neither one of them would look my way.

"Greg and Judy look at me." I got no response so I took a French fry and dipped it in ketchup and ate it. That got their attention! I couldn't believe it, Judy sat there trying not to laugh at me!

"I owe you an apology. After you displayed how stupid you really are I had some real nasty thoughts about you that were ungodly, I want to apologize as those thoughts do not honor God, so I ask your forgiveness." With that said, I took another French fry and got up to leave.

"Greg and Judy I need to ask a favor. If you leave before me please leave as quiet as possible, thanks."

I knew they would not honor my request and that is why I said it. I wanted to have them leave as loud a possible so the geldings would get used to it.

When I got back to the wagon Ma had our lunch ready to go. Pete and Joe were standing there resting. They certainly drew a crowd, especially smaller kids. Many questions came from the crowd. "How old are they? Can we pet them? What are their names? How much do they weigh?"

Greg and Judy were getting ready to leave so I jumped up and grabbed the lines just in case. They were right beside me when I said. "Greg, Judy have a nice day."

They got in their truck and didn't even acknowledge that I said anything. When he started the truck Dad and I did a lot of talking to the colts to keep them calm. Greg backed out and gunned it as he left. The sound was deafening, but Pete and Joe handled it very well. They pranced in place just a little. We finished our lunch and made the rounds in town, and the colts were doing fine. We were even able to give them a passing grade when the train went through town.

On the way home Mr. Olson said, "Jude, I do believe you can call these colts broke at this time. You've done a fine job and you've got something to be proud of. Just remember, they are still just colts. Don't get them in a situation they can't handle. And I assume you will be sending praise God's way soon? That runaway could have been much worse! People could have been killed or horses disabled or both. Why certainly."

"Thanks Mr. Olson and thank you for all your help! Without

you none of this could have happened."

We dropped Mr. Olson off and headed home with a team of broke Percheron geldings.

Chapter 16
"God's Saving Grace"

We had a pretty nice fall so I was able to hitch Pete and Joe quite a bit. Much to my surprise, Granny and Gramps gave me a bobsled for my birthday, which would allow me to keep hitching Pete and Joe throughout the winter. I couldn't wait for snow and snuck in a few prayers to God to deliver some of his white stuff. Dad really didn't like snow all that much so I had to sneak them in when Dad wasn't listening.

Well, as the Bible states in Matthew 7:7-8: "Ask and it will be given to you, seek and you will find, knock and the door will be opened to you. For everyone who asks receives, he who seeks finds, and to him who knocks, the door will be opened." I took this verse as God's answer to my request for snow. Sure enough, Thanksgiving morning it started to snow with great big soft flakes!

Granny, Gramps, and Mr. Olson always came over for Thanksgiving dinner. Granny and Gramps got there pretty early so Granny could help Mom and Becky with dinner. Mr. Olson liked to see the draft horses that are in the parades, so he didn't come till the parades were over. By the time he arrived, we already had about four inches of snow. I was dreaming of hitching the colts after dinner and going for a sleigh ride. Dad was one step ahead of me as he met Mr. Olson at the door to let him in.

"Welcome, Quinn. Happy Thanksgiving! Let me take your coat." Dad continued, "Didn't I hear you state one time that you should wait a couple days after the first snow before hitching a young team of fine hitch geldings?" Becky and I were standing right there, taking in every word.

"Why certainly, why certainly, my granddad always said it would give them bad sores on their feet if you hitch in brand-new snow. It's too bad, otherwise after dinner one might think of going on a ride."

Gramps even chimed in, "It's funny how it only affects fine young hitch geldings. You can hitch young mares and even stallions, but those fine young hitch geldings will get sores on their feet every time."

Dad replied, "Quinn, maybe we could run to your place after dinner for that ride behind Molly and Ladd."

Mr. Olson was trying not to laugh. "Not only can young hitch geldings get sore feet in fresh snow, but if you think about it I'm not sure if that pair Jude has could pull a man's hat off, let alone pull anyone through fresh snow!" He started to laugh, but then he caught my eye.

"Oh, hi, Jude! Didn't see ya standing there!" He laughed all the harder.

Before I had a chance, Becky piped in, "Jude, you going to stand there and let them talk about Pete and Joe like that?"

"Don't worry, Becky. You, Mom, Granny and I will just leave these guys sitting at home while we hitch them fine young hitch geldings and take a spin through the fresh snow."

"Mr. Olson, is there enough snow already to carry the bobsled?" I asked.

"Why certainly, why certainly. I even brought my winter clothes just in case you were up to hitching those fine young hitch geldings."

Mom outdid herself with the help of Becky and Granny. We had an awesome Thanksgiving dinner with honey glazed ham, sweet potatoes, twice-baked potatoes, homemade gravy, fresh dinner rolls, and of course Granny followed up with her pecan and pumpkin pies. Another tradition was Mom's Christmas fudge early. It was her mother's recipe and no one made fudge like that! It was always my duty to do dishes after Thanksgiving dinner since the ladies did all the cooking. I was getting started and hurrying as fast as I could so we would have time to hitch Pete and Joe before chores.

"Jude, I'll take over for you so you can hitch Pete and Joe.

Otherwise chores will come before you know it," Becky said. "Just don't forget to pick me up to go along."

"Wow Becky! Are you sure you want to do this for me?"

"Get going before I change my mind! Make sure you curry and brush them so they look their best."

I hustled out of the kitchen and upstairs to change clothes as fast as I could. Dad, Gramps, and Mr. Olson were waiting by the back door when I came back downstairs. As we walked towards the barn I whistled for Pete and Joe. It was still snowing pretty hard so you couldn't see them in the pasture. We heard their thundering hooves before we saw them. I have to say they looked pretty sharp trotting towards us, cutting through the big white snowflakes. Gramps and I brushed and curried them while Dad harnessed them. I do believe Dad was just as proud as I was of Pete and Joe.

Gramps, almost complaining, said, "My goodness, Jude, a man needs a bale to stand on when working with these boys. And hey, take a look at those feet. You're doing an excellent job with your trimming."

"Thanks, Gramps. I try to trim them every four weeks."

It wasn't long and we had them hitched to the bobsled. We pulled up by the house and picked up the ladies and Fuzz. I had been dreaming of doing this, and what a perfect day for it! The temperature was just right, it was still snowing, we were just floating over the virgin snow, and there was hardly any wind. I cut though the back grove and headed to the trails Mr. Olson had in his woods. Pete and Joe seemed especially proud, They were high-stepping with heads up high all the way. The only thing missing was sleigh bells. Fuzz ended up on Becky's lap, all snuggled in. We stopped and took some pictures by the spring-fed stream cutting through the woods. I was having so much fun I almost forgot to offer the driving privileges to Gramps. After all, it was he and Granny who had bought the bobsled for me.

"Gramps, are you ready to drive this fine young team of hitch geldings?"

"Why, I was thinking you would never ask. Do you realize it has been probably sixty years since I drove a team of horses?"

Gramps came up right away and took the lines. He looked like an old pro and Pete and Joe didn't miss a beat under his guidance. He seemed to really enjoy driving them.

"Jude, I'll let you take them back home while I snuggle with your grandmother." Gramps winked as he handed the lines back. Becky even took a turn driving them before we got back to the barn, while I held Fuzz. We got back home safe and sound.

I do believe that was a Thanksgiving few of us would forget. The snow stayed even though the temps stayed mild, so I was able to do quite a few sleigh rides for hire. Pete and Joe were actually making me some money. The moon was full and the snow glistening as we glided over the trail. Life was pretty good for me and I thanked the Lord for what he had provided almost daily. There were not too many high school seniors that had a well broke team of Percheron geldings.

I would find any excuse to hitch Pete and Joe, haul wood, go to Mr. Olson's, haul hay to the young stock, and even haul a few loads of manure from the calf barn. Right after Christmas we had a big snow storm. We ended up with nine inches and it was blowing so hard it drifted a great deal. I had to take the old car hood out and groom the sleigh trails in places. The side roads had a layer of ice and patches of snow frozen to them. This made it very slippery when driving a car.

I will never forget that Saturday morning after the snow storm. I was over at Mr. Olson's with Pete and Joe on the bobsled. I helped him pitch a few loads of manure from the calf barn and spread it. Pete and Joe had to work pretty hard in the deep snow pulling the spreader. Molly and Ladd watched from a distance and I think they were glad it wasn't them pulling the load.

"Thanks, Jude. You get them colts home and let them cool down in the barn before you let them out."

"Yes, sir."

Usually I take the scenic route through the woods home, but since it was so cold I drove along the road. The wind was coming out of the northwest and it had quite a sharp bite to it. I hunkered down as I drove and was thinking about how God had blessed me and challenged me. I was very pleased and blessed with Pete and Joe's progress. My mind wandered some more and all of the sudden I was focused on Greg Shants and Judy Clemons. I have to assume God was not impressed with my attitude towards them. Many times I would catch myself scheming plans to get even with those two outlaws. Why did God seem to always put them in front of me and worse yet, he seemed to let them win every time! I was fixated on that thought process when I heard Fuzz whine at me.

"Fuzz, it will be nice to get home and out of this wind."

Suddenly a small car went past me going too fast for the road conditions. When it got to the curve I thought I could see it spin out and into the ditch. Sure enough, as I got closer I could see it was definitely stuck in the ditch with whoever was driving still in the driver's seat.

"Whoa, Pete and Joe." I tied the lines tight and jumped the fence to see if the driver was all right. I walked through knee deep snow to get there. The driver hadn't seen me. She had her head on the steering wheel and looked like she might be hurt. I knocked on the window and she slowly looked my way. I saw some blood running down her face and a swollen eye. I'm not sure if she knew who I was, but I certainly knew who she was. It was Judy Clemons!

I tried to open her door but it was wedged into the snow bank. She slowly lowered her window as she winced in pain.

"Are you okay?"

She answered back with a long groan, "Are you kidding me. My right ankle really hurts and so does my head. Can you help me get out of here?"

"Are you sure your neck is okay to move you?"

"Yep, it feels okay, and I'm moving it just fine. I think I turned my ankle bad when it slipped off the brake pedal, and I must have cut my forehead on the sun visor."

I tried the other door and it was also wedged in with snow. "You'll have to climb out the window."

I helped her get out and there we stood, Judy on one leg, knee deep in snow. I could wait for another car to show up or I could get her over to the bobsled. She wasn't getting any warmer standing there and neither was I.

"Can you walk?"

She tried and fell into the snow bank right away. I helped her get upright again and decided I would have to carry her to the sled. I swooped her up in my arms and started wading through the knee high snow. I have to admit, I consider myself a fairly strong farm kid but this was way harder than I thought. I was huffing and puffing pretty hard when I finally got to the fence. I set her over the fence, jumped over, picked her up, and got her to the bobsled. I took off my jacket and draped it over her, and of course Fuzz snuggled right in with her.

"Hang on! Pete, Joe, get up!" Pete and Joe were moving before I said "get up." I think they sensed something was wrong. We trotted home at a good clip. I pulled up in front of the house and hollered for help. Soon Mom and Becky were there. Pete and Joe were pretty wired from our trip home so Becky held them while I carried Judy into the house. Dad was heading across the yard from the barn. I went back out so Becky could help Mom.

Dad asked quickly, "What happened?"

"Judy Clemons spun out on the ice at the curve. Her car is stuck in the snow and she is banged up some. Mom is checking her out in the house."

I put the colts away and headed to the house to see how she was doing. When I got to the house Judy was talking with her parents on the phone. Mom was holding ice on her head and she had her foot in a tub of ice water. She looked pretty rough but seemed to be doing okay. I don't think Judy realized who I was until I came in from the barn. She was hesitant to make eye contact with me. I wondered if she was thinking of all the strange things she had done to me over the years. I just sat there while Mom and Becky tended to her and she spoke with her mom.

As Judy held the phone she asked Mom, "Mrs. Bonner, my mom can't get here for two hours. Is it okay to stay here till then?"

"No problem, young lady, unless you want me to take you home."

Very abruptly Judy said, "Oh no, Mom's at work and she thought if I could stay here till she's done, then I wouldn't be going home alone."

"Then I guess you're stuck with us for the next couple hours." Mom laughed.

"Yes, Mom, that is fine and I'm feeling much better now. I was just so scared when it first happened. I'll see ya in a couple hours."

Dad stepped toward Judy. "Hi, I'm Bud Bonner. Jude has talked of you but I don't believe we've ever met before. Glad to meet you. So, what is the prognosis?"

"Mrs. Bonner and Becky think I have a sprained ankle, and then there's this cut on my forehead. I was mainly just scared when it first happened, but I'm doing much better now."

"Jude, don't you think we should get out there and get her car out of the ditch?" Dad asked.

Dad startled me. I guess I was distracted thinking how ironic it was that Judy Clemons was in my house getting help from Mom.

It just seemed so strange. But as always, God has plans that we just don't understand at times.

Dad and I headed out the door. I took one last look back and Judy was watching us leave. That was only the second time she looked my way while I was in the house. Dad and I took the four-wheel drive pickup truck, shovels, and a log chain down to Judy's car.

"Jude, this probably won't work. The truck will never get a grip with the ice on the road. You'll probably have to get them colts and pull it out through the ditch."

I thought he was just kidding about the colts. The wind was cutting through us like a knife. We got the truck hooked up but all it did was spin like Dad thought it would.

Dad shouted against the wind, "Hustle home and get them colts, your good oak evener, and the clevis. I'll dig out in front and get the chain hooked up while you're gone."

I drove home as quickly as I dared with the ice. As I drove, all I could think about was how Pete and Joe would do pulling that car in the deep snow. Pete and Joe were still in the barn and harnessed. I put their bridles back on them, hooked up the lines, and grabbed the clevis and evener. I drove them back to Dad and, as usual he was all ready for us. I had to do a little coaxing to get them to go down the embankment in the knee deep snow, but they eventually eased in cautiously, snorting as they went. Dad hooked the log chain to the clevis and stepped away.

"Jude, when you get it going, head to that east approach. We can hopefully drive it home from there."

My mind was racing. This was both exciting and scary at the same time. Could they? Would they? Should they?

I finally got up the courage and gave them the signal. "Pete, Joe, step up!" I watched as the chain came tight. Much to my surprise, the car didn't budge! Pete and Joe danced side to side a little and quit pulling.

"Jude, you're probably going to have to get pretty aggressive with your voice to get it started. The car is really wedged in the snow. The colts have never pulled something this heavy before. You can't let them stop on their own or you'll end up with baulkers. Now let's get this done so we can get home!"

I laid the lines in the snow and went up front to have a talk with the boys. "Pete, Joe," I said as I looked them in the eye, "you can pull this load like it's nothing. I want you to show Dad what you're made of!"

I stepped back behind them and took the lines and collected the bits in their mouths.

"Pete, Joe, get up!" I hollered as loud as I could. They hit it pretty hard and it seemed to move a little. Next thing I knew, they were starting to let up.

"Get up there! Sheehaw! Come on Pete! Come on Joe!" I was screaming at them. You should have seen it. They hesitated and next thing I knew they were digging down with all fours, bellies barely off the ground. Joe was a-snorting. They were scratching for leverage, thigh muscles rippling, the chain was tight and the car started creaking. It slowly started rising out of its temporary grave. Pete and Joe fought for all they were worth, taking short stocky steps, nostrils flaring, as you could hear the leather stretching on the harness.

"Atta boy, Pete! Atta boy Joe! Keep her going!" It was great how Pete and Joe responded to the tone of my voice. I think they could have pulled a bulldozer out of that ditch once they got with the program! Once the car came totally out of the depression, they pulled it with a little more ease. We had to go quite a way to make the approach. There they were knee deep in snow with a car behind that was bulldozing its way through the same deep snow. About three quarters of the way there they showed signs of wanting to stop. I talked to them to keep them moving. If I had let them stop they might have an even harder time restarting since they were tired. We finally made the approach. Up the grade they went and soon the car had to do the same. My goodness, Pete and Joe were pulling with pure grit and determination. When that car started up that grade, they dug even lower than before and scratched and farted till it popped up to level ground. I stopped to rest them when the car was on the road. Pete and Joe just stood there taking a well deserved rest. They were sucking air like there was no tomorrow.

Dad and I both went up to them immediately and gave them some praise. We looked them in the eyes and hugged them, praised them with our voices and rubbed their necks. Steam rolled off their entire bodies as they stood there. Dad went back to try to start Judy's car and the engine slowly cranked over. It seemed like it was groaning in pain, but it finally started. Dad got out and unhooked the chain from underneath the car and headed for home.

"Pete, Joe, get up." The colts took a slow step forward, waiting for the tug chains to tighten, and I sensed a sigh of relief in them when they realized they had no load to pull. It was a long journey home, but I was very proud of my boys. Fuzz even cheated and rode with Dad. The geldings were awfully glad to walk in the barn door. I unharnessed them and brushed them out good. Dad had put Judy's car in the barn so some of the snow would melt off. I closed the barn up tight to keep the drafts off the geldings.

Dad was already in the house when I got there. Judy's mom was late, so I told myself to talk with Judy. It was awkward but I had to keep in mind Romans 7:12: "So in everything, do to others what you would have them do to you."

As I stepped into the dining room all I could hear were screams and laughs. Mom, Becky and Judy were playing a card game called Dutch Blitz. It was kind of surprising to see Judy Clemons acting in this fashion when I was used to seeing her at school in a whole different light.

In between games I asked, "Judy, how are you feeling?"

Without making much eye contact she replied, "Much better than before. I think I'll be on crutches for a while though."

"Dad and I and the geldings got your car out of the ditch. Dad put it in the barn to thaw out some. You might try to leave it in there overnight and by morning it should be free of snow."

Dad said, "You should have seen them geldings pull that car out of the ditch! Wow, it was a sight to behold."

Just then the doorbell rang. I answered it, and it was Mrs. Clemons coming to pick up Judy.

"Hi, come on in, Mrs. Clemons."

"Oh, thank you. Is that daughter of mine okay?" she replied as she stepped in. I noticed that Judy really didn't seem to look her way. Sadly I think I could smell alcohol on Mrs. Clemons' breath.

As she walked toward the dining room she said, "Judy I hope you're all right because we can't be chasing all over the country for you just because of a little slip on the road. Now let's get your things together so you're no longer a burden on these folks."

It was sad. Before Mrs. Clemons had gotten to our place Judy was laughing and enjoying herself. That ended when Mrs. Clemons entered our home. I looked at Mom and Becky as Judy, expressionless, tried to stand up slowly. She almost fell. Mom caught her and helped her get her coat on.

"Mrs. Clemons, I want you to know Judy was no trouble at all and we were glad to help," Mom said. "We had ice on her ankle most of the time, and make sure she keeps it elevated as much as possible."

Judy asked, "When would be a good time to get my car tomorrow?"

Mom replied, "We have church in the morning."

Mrs. Clemons laughed under her breath.

Mom caught the snicker and without skipping a beat said, "Well, yes, and you are more than welcome to come to church with us if you'd like, Mrs. Clemons. Sunday school starts at nine o'clock and God's word at ten o'clock sharp."

You could have heard a tick crawling across the floor. We all stood there for a moment in awkward silence.

"Judy, we should get back home around noon," Mom continued. "So anytime after that you can get the car. Now, Jude, don't just stand there, help the lady out to the car. She can't put any weight on that ankle."

Wow. First Mom sends that little zinger at Mrs. Clemons about church, then she has me help Judy Clemons out to the car. I was wondering if Mom really understood who Judy Clemons was. There I was, half carrying Judy Clemons back out of the house with Mrs. Clemons mumbling under her breath the whole way. As I lifted Judy up into their pickup, I swore I saw a little smirk on her face.

I helped Dad with chores and we let the geldings out of the barn just before we came in. A hot shower felt pretty good that night. I was chilled to the bone from yanking that car out of the ditch. Mom had a feast prepared for supper. Becky and I did dishes afterward and sang a few songs. Dad whisked Mom off her feet and danced in the living room. It was pretty neat to see that my parents were still in love.

"Jude, I know it was a little awkward for you helping Judy tonight, but I thought you handled it well. I thank you for that," Mom said. "And I think we might have seen why Judy acts like she does at times. I wonder if Mrs. Clemons has a problem with alcohol. We need to lift them up in prayer."

The next morning Dad and I got Judy's car out of the barn just in case she came for it while we were in church. After church Becky and I hitched the geldings and Judy's car was still there. Sure enough, though, we soon heard Greg Shants' loud exhaust pipes heading our way. It was a perfect time to see how Pete and Joe would respond to that noise again. I drove them right alongside the driveway as Greg and Judy came up from behind.

"Easy, boys, easy," I commanded as they were starting to get wound up. They weren't perfect but they did okay. I gave Greg the signal to go ahead of us, thinking to get them used to that too. All in all they did well with the loud exhaust pipes. It was good that we were able to expose them to that noise again.

While Judy, crutches and all, hobbled to her car, I had Becky sneak in the house for some cookies. As Judy and Greg left, I think they waved. Becky and I headed out on the trail. It was a beautiful afternoon. When Becky took a turn driving I picked a fight with Fuzz. I spun her around and roughed her up and she came back and latched onto my leather glove and started growling and pulling like crazy. I grabbed her and threw her off the rack into a deep snow bank. I had to laugh as she disappeared for a second in the snow. Ol' Fuzz scratched her way out of that bank of snow and headed as fast as she could towards the back of the rack. She wanted to get even with me for throwing her off the rack. Becky had never stopped the horses so Fuzz had some ground to make up. I got down on my hands and knees to get ready for her. As soon as she jumped back on the rack I buried my head in my hands. Ol' Fuzz dove into me with a vengeance. I was laughing, so that made her all the more determined to get me. She pried her little nose everywhere she could find an opening, growling and play-biting as she went. I would reach out and grab her lip and squeeze just to antagonize her. We went a couple more rounds and then we both eased up.

"Fuzz, you worthless piece of dog flesh, what would we ever do without you?" I said as I was trying to catch my breath. "Becky, are you ready for school to start again?"

"Oh, I guess so. It will be kind of interesting to see how Judy Clemons acts toward you and me after yesterday's episode."

"Yup, I've been wondering the same thing."

School started after the Christmas break, along with our regular church Wednesday night youth group with our youth minister, Carl. Each year right after the Christmas break Carl had a big retreat for senior high kids that included ice skating, snow tubing, and a night at a water park. Harold, Perry, and I always had a blast at these events. This would be Becky's first chance to go. Carl announced it on that Wednesday night and many kids signed up. Dad usually signed up as a senior high leader for that night so we could play "Kill the Carrier." This is the type of game that separates the men from the boys. You use a rubber football and whoever has the ball gets tackled and when their head goes under water they let go of the ball and the next guy grabs the ball and runs. Dad was usually the best player in that game, but Perry and I thought we might have a better chance this year.

At school the next morning, Perry asked, "Dude, is your Dad going to be there for the swim night?"

"I'm not sure. I'll mention it to him to see if he can make it."

"Well, you tell him to be there. I owe him from last year," he said and laughed. "Do you think you and I can handle him by now?"

As I turned to go to my next class the hallway seemed fairly empty, that is, except for Judy Clemons and her crutches. She was heading right towards me, which was odd. Usually she just ignores my very existence at school.

"Hi, Judy, how's the ankle doing?" I asked as I tried to get around her.

Judy seemed to be blocking my path. "Jude, can we talk?" she asked with a sober look on her face. "Mr. Kline's room is empty this hour and I need to explain a few things, please."

I looked her in the eye and she seemed to be serious. "I, I guess so."

Judy hobbled down to Mr. Kline's room and I followed. I closed the door and helped her get a chair.

As Judy gazed out the window she said, "I feel like such a fool! You and your parents really helped me last weekend, and I never even thanked you."

"That's okay, Judy. No big deal, we were glad to help you out."

"Jude, the more I think about Saturday, the more foolish I feel," she said as she doodled on some papers.

"Judy, we all have made driving mistakes. It was a blessing you weren't hurt more."

"I'm not talking about that, Jude. Don't you realize how many years I've hated you, and then you show up like a knight in shining armor and save my butt? That's why I feel so foolish!"

I laughed a little. "Knight in shining armor is quite a stretch. Besides, I did what anyone would have done in that situation."

Judy continued, "I have to admit, I'm jealous of your family. I sat there playing cards with your mother and Becky and had a great time. I just don't understand how that can be," she said as she rubbed her forehead. "It just seemed like there was something very different about your mother, and how she treated me and even Becky."

"God has blessed my mother with a very caring heart. Becky and I are so lucky to have a mother like her."

"That's what I was afraid you would do is throw 'God' in," Judy said in a sarcastic tone of voice. "Why does everything have to come back to God for people like you? Can't you keep God to yourself and have a normal conversation?"

I stood up as I was thinking. "I heard you say you hated me. The next thing you said was that there seemed to be something very different about my mother's treatment of you. And lastly, you seemed to be asking for some type of answers about your thoughts and it all has to do with God."

Judy sat there in silence.

"Judy, this God I talk about can also be your God if you allow him into your heart. I remember accepting Jesus into my heart when I was eight years old at Lake Beauty Bible Camp."

"You religious people think you always have the right answers!" she blurted out, then shrank back. "I'm sorry I said that, Jude. But can't we just keep God out of it for now?"

I was thinking to myself what to say next. I was not going to deny God. "If you want to talk school, the weather, or about your pet dog, yes, we can keep God out of it. But, if you're asking me why you felt foolish and why my mother seems different, then it is impossible to keep God out of it."

Judy had a blank look on her face. "You can stand there and tell me that some god is in charge of all my questions? I suppose the next thing you'll say is only Christians go to heaven." She laughed a little.

"Please listen, there is only one God, not some god, and it isn't important what I say about who goes to heaven because I don't know. For many years mankind has tried to fabricate ways of getting to heaven. People need to read God's word about what he says about entering heaven."

"Fine, fine, I just don't understand why I need a book to tell me how to live," she said hesitantly. "But I can tell you're very serious about this God thing. I guess I should respect you for sticking to your first answer."

"Roman's 3:23, 'For all have sinned and fall short of the glory of God." I quoted. "Think about that verse and if you think my mother is better than you or anyone else, then you're wrong."

I think Judy was in the early stages of searching for God. She seemed very frustrated and angry as she shook her head back and forth. I said a few silent prayers as I stood there waiting for Judy's next question. It was very quiet in the room for several minutes.

I broke the silence. "Earlier, you said that you hated me. Well, it's not like all these years I have not returned that hate! I owe you an apology. Please forgive me for having hateful thoughts about you over the years. That hate does not honor God and I need to ask your forgiveness."

"Are you kidding me? Jude, I'm not sure what to think right now, my head is just spinning."

The class bell was ringing, Judy and I were running out of time. "Judy, I'm writing down a Bible verse for you to look up if you wish. Luke 10:27 might help you understand what Jesus wants for his people. I hope your ankle continues to heal and if you need to talk more, give me a call or something. If you'd like we can pray right now, Judy."

"No, Jude, no disrespect but I'm not ready for that," she blew air out her lips.

"I have to get to my next class, Judy. God Bless and I will try to remember to pray for you. Bye."

I figured I'd better stop at Mrs. Norman's room to explain. Mrs. Norman was waiting at her door in the hallway. "How did it go with Judy?"

I was confused. "How did you know what I was doing?"

"She came to me first, and if I talk 'Jesus' to a student they will haul me off for a life sentence. But if a fellow student happens to bring the gospel to another student, then praise God." She winked at me and headed into her room.

That Friday night, Harold, Perry, and I went to the movies. After the movie we went to the local dairy treat place and saw Carl Toney with his family. Carl had three little kids, two boys and a girl. Watching the little ones with ice cream was better than the movie. We play fought with the kids and, of course, we had to let them win.

Saturday morning came in a hurry. Much to my surprise, the temp was above zero when I awoke. The wind wasn't blowing hard, so I figured it should be a perfect day to drag home a couple loads of wood with the geldings. Mom had our regular Saturday morning waffles waiting as Dad and I came in from chores.

"Mother, Jude and I are going to snag a couple loads of wood with the geldings. What are you and Becky going to do on this fine day?" Dad asked.

"Cookies. What is your preference?

Dad replied, "Warm soft molasses cookies are hard to beat after a day in the woods."

As I headed to the barn I called for Pete and Joe. They came a-running through the snow looking as beautiful as ever. That's something I'll never get tired of watching. They came to the gate kicking and play-fighting with each other. I opened the gate and they trotted in to the barn, heads up and proud. I harnessed while Dad got the chain saws ready. Dad and I quickly measured them when they were on the flat concrete. They each measured 17-3 hands now as coming three-year-olds. That is a pretty good height for three-year-olds.

Fetching wood with Pete and Joe was one of my favorite things to do. It was good for them too because they learned to stand while we loaded the rack and while the chain saw was running. It was pretty as a picture coming home through the snow with a full jag of wood on the rack.

As we pulled in the yard we noticed a car in the driveway. "I wonder who the visitor is," Dad said. "I better check, especially since it gives me a chance to get a warm cookie while I'm in there."

Fuzz and I unloaded the wood while Dad went in the house. Of course we had just finished when Dad came back out. He did bring me a few cookies so I let him drive while I shared them with old Fuzz. Mom would skin me if she knew Fuzz was eating her warm molasses cookies. When we got back with the second load of wood Mom still had her visitor.

"Dad, whose car is that anyway?"

Dad rubbed his chin in thought. "I reckon it's your turn to go in. I'll unload the wood and you can see for yourself."

As I stepped in the back door all I could hear was ladies talking a mile a minute. I got my boots off and was very curious who came to visit Mom. I took a peek through the crack of the door, and much to my surprise there sat Judy Clemons helping Mom clean up after the cookies. I wasn't quite sure what to do. What would I say to Judy this time?

I decided to keep it simple. As I stepped into the kitchen, I said, "Hi, Judy."

"Hi Jude." she replied like we'd been the best of buds all these years.

"Did you get a different car?"

"Nope, I borrowed my mother's car. The heater works much better."

Mom said, "Jude, take a look at that three layer cake on the dining room table. Judy brought that over to us for helping her out two weeks ago. Pretty nice!"

I walked over to inspect the cake. "I'll say it's pretty nice. Cream cheese frosting, that's my favorite."

"Now, young man, you keep your muggy mitts off that till after supper," Mom scolded.

Judy asked, "How are Pete and Joe doing? Your mother and Becky told me all about them as we made the cookies."

I have to admit I was a little flustered being in this situation. One day Judy and I are not on speaking terms, then she talks to me in Mr. Kline's room, and the next thing she's in my house asking about Pete and Joe like she cares?

I finally stammered out, "Pretty good."

As Mom was scrubbing dishes she said, "Jude, if you are done hauling wood for the day then you might consider giving Judy a ride. She claims she's never been on a sleigh until two weeks ago and that one wasn't for fun." What could I say to that? Ma kind of put me on the spot, I had to say something.

"Judy, is your ankle up for it?"

"Oh, it's a little stiff but I've been off crutches for the last two days. I really didn't bring any warm clothes to wear though."

"Judy, it's up to you. Becky could borrow you a few things if you'd like to go. Jude would be glad to take you for a ride," Mom declared.

"Jude, I would like that, if you have time!"

I laughed. "Judy, it doesn't take much to give me a reason to drive Pete and Joe. I'll go out and clean the rack off."

When I got out to Dad he had all the wood put away and had even swept off the rack. Did Dad know something I didn't?

Dad asked, "Are you pulling up by the house to pick her up?"

"Now how did you know Judy was coming out for a ride?" I asked. "I hope you and Mom didn't invite her out here today. Judy is someone that can't be trusted. I'll take her for a ride but that doesn't mean I trust her."

"You're right, son, she can't be trusted, but she can be forgiven. Matthew 6:14: 'For if you forgive men when they sin against you, your heavenly Father will also forgive you.' " He looked me in the eye. "I wonder if Judy has Jesus knocking on her door?"

Just then the back door opened. "Dad. I better get going."

Judy was limping slightly on her ankle as she walked our way. It was kind of funny to see her in Becky's work clothes. Judy was usually dressed to kill with the latest fashions. I pulled the geldings her way and stopped twenty feet in front of her. I was surprised when she stopped and rubbed their necks as she went past. Pete and Joe surprised me even more when they whinnied and nuzzled her.

Dad helped Judy step up on the rack and off we went. It was mid afternoon and the sun was out full so the temperature was really pretty warm. Judy stood beside me just watching every step they took. I was still thinking about what Dad said about forgiveness and searching for words to say that would be appropriate without sounding stupid.

"Jude, this is awesome! They are so graceful and strong. All those times going past you these last couple summers when you were training them, I just thought, 'what a waste of time'. Now I can see why your ma encouraged me to tag along, the runners just slice right through the snow."

"I'm glad you appreciate this. Do you hear that, Pete, Joe? Judy thinks you guys are awesome," I laughed.

"Can I ask you more questions about religion? I did read Luke 10:27, and I tried other verses but the Bible really seems hard to understand."

"Sure, I'll try to answer them," I said. The geldings were walking slowly. "Judy, you have to keep in mind that many things said or read when first learning about Jesus will not make any sense to you. The Bible talks about that very subject in the book of John."

"Is your mother always that nice? And she really seems to love your dad. Or is that just a show when I'm around?"

"Mom is a very special lady, and no, she is not one to put on a show. I'm blessed to have parents like them."

"She seems so calm and in control. It makes me want to be like her."

"Those things you like about Mom are simply God working in

her life."

"How do you know that there is a God?" I thought for awhile before I answered her.

"First, because the Bible states that clearly, and second, take a look around you. See how beautiful the things around you are. Do you think the trees, streams, snow, clouds, the stars, birds, and Pete and Joe just happened from two gigantic rocks hitting each other? This is God's creation and to top it off he even made us humans in his likeness."

Judy stared at me for a while. "Why would God send me or anyone to hell? I'm a good person."

"Have you ever told a lie?

"Yes, but who hasn't"

"Have you ever stolen something?"

"I guess, but what does that have to do with it?"

"So you're a liar and a thief just like me. A good person doesn't lie or steal. God created a perfect world. Since God created this world, that gives him ownership and the right to have rules. Imagine if no one ever lied, cheated or stole."

"You really don't follow the Bible as much as you say, do you?"

"Judy, I try to. But the sin in my life doesn't allow me to follow it perfectly."

With a bit of frustration she said, "I never really looked at the Bible until the other day, but it has to be so out of date with today's world."

I thought for a moment. "That's the beauty of the Bible. It is one of the oldest books in the world yet it is the best-selling book each year. The Bible is very up to date if you know how to use it. It's God's Word to man while we are on earth."

She blurted out, "But it's so full of rules. How can a person have any fun with a Bible holding them back?"

"Oh, Judy, if you would read God's word you would experience a whole new meaning to life. Those so-called rules are God's protection for us. The Bible gives believers so much freedom, starting with freedom from sin. God's word is full of his promises of peace, joy, and grace. God helps you with troubles, shows you how to live a full life, and shows you how to handle spiritual warfare. All that God says through his Word is still relevant to this age just as it was two thousand years ago."

I stopped Pete and Joe. "Whoa, boys."

Judy sat on the hay bale and looked up with a tear in her eye. "You said before that you did not want to be called religious, but would rather be called a follower of Jesus Christ. I don't understand." She put her head in her hands and seemed to be crying.

I guess I'm a softy because I found myself tearing up right along with her. It was so special. The power and presence of the Holy Spirit was upon Judy that afternoon!

As I was wiping tears from my eyes I said, "Judy, the power you are feeling right now is the Holy Spirit. Please don't ever forget this time with him."

Dear Lord, did that ever set Judy off. She just wept and wept as she sat there. Sobbing like a child, her mittens were soon soaked. She was trying to stop but Jesus wouldn't let her. I sat beside her and put my arm around her. That set off another round of uncontrolled sobbing. The Holy Spirit, Judy, and I just sat there.

Judy was starting to settle down. Half talking, half sobbing she mumbled, "Oh, I feel like such a fool, crying like a baby in front of you."

I didn't tell Judy this, but her makeup was smeared all over her face.

"Jude, does your whole family follow Jesus Christ?"

"Yes, they do. And to answer your earlier question, there are many religious people that aren't followers of Jesus Christ. In fact many churches are religious but not Christian."

"Then that means you guys never do anything wrong?"

I jumped down off the rack so I could look her right in the eye. "Judy, we all do things wrong every day, Mom, Dad, Becky, and of course me. That wrong is called sin. So as Bible believing Christians we are forgiven of our sins and no longer judged by God for them. Remember when I said there is none righteous, not one. That includes the Bonner family. It all comes down to the cross. Jesus died on that cross by taking responsibility for your's and my sins. God's gift of salvation, to those who accept it, was Jesus taking on the sins of all mankind that day."

The tears were starting to come again. "Judy, you have to listen carefully to this next point. Neither you, nor I, nor anyone can earn this salvation. We can't buy it, we can't work our way to it, we can't be good enough to earn it, and we can't create our own individual special way to get to heaven! It is truly a gift of grace that we can choose to accept or ignore. The Bible teaches that we are saved by grace, not by works."

As Judy started weeping again she blurted out, "But I've done so many rotten things. How could God ever accept me?" Judy was wailing as she fell to her knees and shouted, "Oh, God, please help me!"

I couldn't take it anymore. I fell to my knees in the snow and was bawling just as hard as Judy. If you have never felt the Holy Spirit at work, I pray someday you will. The power was taking my strength away. I looked and saw a shadow moving swiftly across the ground, I looked up towards Judy and saw an eagle fly right over us, screaming as it passed. Judy looked up with tears in her eyes at the sound and watched as it flew out of sight.

I asked, "Judy, did you hear what you just said? You just asked God for help! Praise God!"

She paused for a moment. "Yes, yes I did!" She reached out and hugged me.

"I Timothy 1:15: 'Here is a trustworthy saying that deserves full acceptance: Christ Jesus came into the world to save sinners of whom I'm the worst,' " I quoted. "In other words, Jesus takes all sinners, no matter how bad you think the sin is. The Bible states that everyone is a sinner, and if you accept the gift of grace you can be released from your sins."

Judy sat there silently wiping tears and looking around. Fuzz was staring at her like she was hurt or something.

"Now if you are ready, you can go through the salvation prayer."

"What is that?"

"Remember, you decide if you're ready, but it is a prayer that you can repeat after me that confirms you accept Jesus Christ as your personal Lord and Savior."

Judy laughed as she said, "Well, I think I ran out of tears, so if it requires them I'm out of luck. Jude, yes, I think I do want the salvation prayer." She had a look of joy on her face.

"Please repeat after me." I held my hand up to the heavens.

"Heavenly Father, you are the one and only true God." Judy repeated the same. I continued,

"You are the I am."

"Jesus I am a sinner."

"Jesus, I ask you to take away my sins."

"Jesus, you died on the cross for my sins."

"Jesus, it was your blood on that cross that set me free."

"Jesus, I accept your gift of salvation and I realize this is a gift and I cannot earn it."

"Jesus, surround me with the Holy Spirit." Judy was repeating every step of the way, The tears were coming back full force. Judy was shaking and having a hard time talking.

"By the POWER of Jesus Christ I rebuke Satan and kill any of his powers over me." Judy fell to the ground, shaking and weeping uncontrollably. The devil didn't want to let her go!

Come on, Judy, stay with us! "By the POWER of Jesus I rebuke Satan and kill any of his powers over me."

Judy reached to the sky and looked to the heavens and shouted, "By the power of JESUS I rebuke Satan and kill any of his powers over me!" She started to rise from the ground and stood with both hands held up to the sky.

"Jesus, I accept you as my personal Lord and Savior from this day forward. Amen!" Judy repeated the final part with a look of determination in her blood shot eyes.

Judy looked at me and smiled bigger than I had ever seen her smile before. In fact, I'm not sure if I ever saw her really smile all those years.

"Congratulations, Judy, you are now a child of God. Pete, Joe, did you hear that the devil lost one today? Praise God." Pete and Joe whinnied in unison.

As we headed back to the house, Judy asked a few more questions. Pete and Joe seemed to understand because they were right up into the bits, heads up, high tailing it home. Judy actually started softly singing "Amazing Grace" with a huge grin as we went. I had to smile a little as God did not gift her with a singing voice. As I drove home I was counting my blessings for being allowed to witness God's saving grace.

As we pulled into the yard, I helped Judy off the rack. "Judy, I would like to give you two more suggestions."

"Sure, go ahead."

"One is, remember this was real and that you are saved by God's grace. The Devil will tell you over and over that this didn't really happen. And two, you need to tell someone of your new salvation, preferably your parents."

Judy and I unharnessed the geldings and headed into the house. Mom was standing by the table when we got to the kitchen.

"Judy, how was your first sleigh ride?"

Judy looked at me like I was supposed to answer Mom's

questions and she started crying again. Mom headed her way and I stepped off to the side. I've seen ladies before when they get together about Jesus stuff and they need room.

Mom took Judy's hands in hers and asked, "My goodness, Jude, what did you do with this poor girl on that ride?" Mom had that certain tone in her voice that meant business.

"It wasn't what I did, Mom, it's what the Holy Spirit did!"

"Land sakes, Jude, why didn't you tell me sooner?" Mom hollered in excitement.

Mom looked Judy in the eyes and Judy lost it even more. Mom just stood there holding her hand, not saying a word. The Lord sure has different plans than we do at times. Judy Clemons was my worst enemy all those years and now she was born again and crying with Mom in our kitchen. I quietly went upstairs to get some fresh socks.

While I was upstairs I could overhear Judy and Mom talking. Mom said, "Judy, I'm so glad you're one of God's children now. But I must say you look a little silly with that mascara smeared all over your face." They both laughed.

Mom continued, "This calls for a celebration. How about we take you out for dinner tonight and then come back here for some of that cake you brought?"

"Mrs. Bonner, I would like that. Can I use your phone to call my mother and tell her what I just experienced with God?"

"Yes, you sure can. It's right over there. Maybe they want to go with us tonight."

I headed back down for chores. "Jude, tell your Dad to hustle through chores if he can because we're going out for dinner with Judy."

"Okay, Mom."

As I put my boots back on I could hear Judy talking on the phone. It wasn't sounding very good.

"Hi, Mother. I'm still over at the Bonner's," Judy seemed to be a little shaky as she spoke. "No I'm not being a bother." I was praying for strength for Judy when I heard, "Mother are you sober?" I couldn't imagine having to ask Mom that question. "You'll never guess what I did today. I gave my life to Jesus Christ." Judy hesitated, "Mother," she sighed in exasperation, "You can call it what you want, I call it being a follower of Jesus Christ. Mother I'm sorry if that offends you, but I've never been happier. Are you and Dad able to go out to dinner with us tonight to celebrate?" She waited for an answer. "Hello Mother, hello," Judy hung up the phone, turned to Mom and said, "My mother hung up on me."

Mom replied, "Judy, I'm sorry to hear that. Would it be better if we didn't go out tonight?"

"Oh, no, Mrs. Bonner. I really need to go out with your family, if it's okay with you."

Judy headed home to get cleaned up and Dad and I hustled through chores. We picked up Judy by 8:15 and headed to Willmar. Judy wanted to go to Pizza Barn, they have a Saturday night buffet. She sat by Becky and Mom and had other 'Jude says he's not religious questions' now and then. I overheard Mom warn Judy that her decision to follow Jesus would be tested soon, and when she would least expect it. Becky and Judy seemed to be getting along very well. Dad and I weren't saying much, but it was kind of neat to just sit back and watch the ladies mingle.

Judy asked for our attention and said, "I would like to thank the whole Bonner family for these last couple of weeks, especially for today. I thank you for dinner tonight and remember we have cake..." Judy trailed off and fell silent.

Mom was right that Judy would be tested early and when she least expected it. In the middle of her sentence, Greg Shants walked right past our table. He was so shocked when he saw Judy that he ran into the wall with his food. We all looked at Judy to see how she would respond to this.

Judy sat there awhile in silence with her head down. She looked in Mom's direction and said, "As I was saying, leave room for cake. Now I must ask one more question, Mrs. Bonner. Would it make sense for me to go over to Greg's table and tell him of my decision today? You said I would be tested and I'm not going to let Greg Shants give me a failing grade here. The sooner the better for both of us."

Mom replied, "Judy, be respectful and you will do fine. God only knows, maybe Greg will come to Jesus."

We kept our eyes averted as Judy headed over to Greg's table. She was back before we knew it and we could see the stress in her eyes from the encounter. She seemed to be struggling with what to say next. Ma reached out and put her hand on Judy's shoulder and said. "You did fine Judy." Dad and I made one last run through the chow line while the ladies talked, and then we headed home for some of Judy's cake.

As we sat around the table at home Judy explained, "Guys, I hope this cake tastes okay because it's the first cake I've ever made."

Mom replied, "I'm sure you did just fine, but if you don't put that knife to work we will never find out." We all laughed.

Judy started cutting healthy slabs of cake, while Dad scooped ice cream. Each of us started in on the cake with enthusiasm. Most of us had our first bite going and you could see the chewing motions gradually slow down. Dad was soon reaching for the milk and so was I. Wow, I had never had cake that bad in my life! Judy hadn't yet taken a bite and we watched as she started in. Dad was on his second full glass of milk for just one bite of cake as Judy started chewing on her first bite. We were all watching to see how Judy would react. I was trying to kill the taste with a combo of milk and ice cream. I was shoveling it in so fast I even ended up with an ice cream headache. Sure enough, Judy's jaws came to a grinding halt. She looked around, saw that all of us were watching her, and turned twelve shades of red. She spit cake out of her mouth onto her plate.

"Yuk! That's horrible!" Everyone was scanning everyone else to see who was going to make the next move. Sure enough, it was Judy heading towards the milk jug. She poured a full glass and chugged it without stopping. When she finished the milk all eyes again were on her. She looked back at us and I thought she was going to cry.

She hesitated. "Aren't you glad you all saved room for cake?" she said and burst out laughing. That's all it took. I was just taking a drink when I started laughing and I sprayed everyone with milk. Judy and Mom were laughing so hard they had tears flowing. Becky was just about on the floor. I laughed so hard my cheeks started to hurt. We would start to get our composure back, then Becky would lose it again and send us all back to the funny farm.

While Judy was both laughing and crying she asked, "What went wrong?" That was it. Becky lost it again as tears ran down Judy's checks.

Mom got up and tried to console Judy, but even Mom was having a hard time from laughing again and Judy knew it. So there was Judy doing one of those laugh-cry combos. Each time she'd look at Mom she would interrupt her cry with a laugh, back and forth.

As the hysteria finally slowed down, Mom asked, "Judy, do you think you maybe switched the quantities on salt and sugar?" Becky went off again laughing uncontrollably. Once Becky gets going it's hard to stop her. She even had to leave church once because she started to laugh during the sermon.

"Oh my, I think you're right, Mrs. Bonner. That explains the instant urge to consume large amounts of milk after just one bite." We all lost it again.

By this time it was getting pretty late. Needless to say, no one finished their cake. Mom broke out the cookies, and Judy apologized several times for the mistake. Dad thanked Judy for the good old-fashion laugh session and warned Mom not to throw the cake in the garden or it would kill all plant life next spring. Dad led us in a collective prayer and the party was over.

Becky and I had to run Judy home. We told her about youth group and Carl, our youth minister. We told her of the winter retreat Carl had coming up and gave her Carl's phone number. She thanked us over and over.

"God Bless, Judy."

"God bless, Becky and Jude." Becky and I watched to make sure she could get in the house and then headed home. I was one tired boy. It had been a very emotional day for me. The old bed was going to feel pretty good that night.

Chapter 17
"Senior Prom"

It was interesting at school to watch how kids and teachers reacted to the new Judy Clemons. Her old friends wanted nothing to do with her and new friends were hard to come by because most people didn't understand why Judy had changed. With Judy's permission I told Harold and Perry. Even though she was a senior, Judy was able to hang out with Becky and her friends most of the time. Judy did very well at showing people she was serious about her faith, without looking like a snob. She would say, "hi" and acknowledge her old friends as she passed them in the hallways, but she refused to stay with that lifestyle. Most of her old friends seemed to despise her.

We woke up the morning of our youth group's big winter retreat to find three inches of new snow. Carl, our youth minister was in his glory. It was great to see him use his God-given talents. We started off with skating, then tubing, and lastly swimming at the water park. We had enough guys and girls to get in a good game of hockey. Hockey was one game that Harold, Perry, and I were better at than Carl. Carl just couldn't stop very well and he continually used his stick for balance. Carl picked the teams and let Perry, Harold, and me be together. Carl left himself with Will and several girls that played high school hockey. We had half the ice for our hockey and the other half was for those that chose to free skate.

We huddled up before we started and Perry said, "Okay, guys, let's show them who's boss, especially Carl. Anyone want to take a stab at how many sticks he'll break tonight?" Carl was a pretty big guy so when he would lean on a stick for balance it would often crack.

We played best of three games and Carl didn't even break one stick. In fact, Carl's skating skills seemed much improved from last year. Our team worked hard but just couldn't get over the hump, and Carl's team took all three games. Boy, Perry, Harold and I would never live that down.

Carl laughed as he said, "Gentlemen, you will need to mark this day down in your journals. This was your last hockey game as seniors in youth group. It's just a shame that an old youth minister and some girls had to put you in your place. Now don't go home and go crying to your mamas!"

"Yes, sir," Perry said. "Since when did you acquire skating skills?"

"You see, this kid named Will and I spent the last three weeks getting ready for this very afternoon." Carl snickered.

Next we went to the tubing hill, and with the new snow that morning it was looking pretty good. Judy even showed up. This was her first time in any type of youth group function. She hung out with Becky and her friends. Dad and Mom served hot chocolate at the bottom of the hill. The old legs felt pretty weak after skating and climbing that hill. Carl set up relay-type races, seniors against juniors. One race required going down the hill and carrying a person back up the hill. We were soon looking for the lightest person we could find. The juniors grabbed Becky before we had a chance. The next lightest was Judy.

The race rules were that the team had to go down together on one toboggan and carry the person up the hill without that person touching the ground. The first team back to the top won free milk shakes. Perry, Judy, Harold, and I represented the seniors. As we sat on the toboggan, we looked to see who was against us. Sitting in the back of the junior's toboggan was none other than Carl Toney, Mr. Ex-College Football Powerhouse.

Harold and I started to complain. "Carl, what's this? You ain't no junior! This ain't fair."

Carl shouted as he started pushing his toboggan downhill, "Boys, God never promised life would be fair. See ya later!" He laughed as his toboggan slid away.

Not only did they have Carl with them, but they also left us eating their dust! "Harold, push!" we all screamed.

Harold pushed for all he was worth and we were on our way. We must have been on a slightly better path because we were gaining ground on them. Perry was in the front and when we caught up with them he reached out and pushed one of their middle people. It was awesome. The person he pushed lost her balance and fell to the side. This caused their whole sled to change directions, which allowed us to get to the bottom of the hill first and start carrying Judy back up. We took turns, with two guys forming a chair and Judy sitting in between. Even though we had a good jump on the juniors, this was way harder than we thought it would be. Our chair-type carry was not real fast. Carl and his crew were gaining ground.

As Perry was sucking wind, he shouted, "Let's do a log carry, dudes!"

That was a great idea. It allowed three guys to carry instead of two at a time. Perry and I were on one side and Harold was on the other side. We shouted out numbers and got in the same step. The juniors had gained some ground in our transition. Judy was screaming at us to hurry, but we were losing strength with each step. Between being totally exhausted and half laughing, the top of the hill looked a long way away. We almost dropped Judy a couple times, which would just add more laughs to the equation. It's pretty hard to lift stuff when you're laughing. Carl and his juniors were gaining on us.

The next thing we knew, Judy yelled out, "You bunch of wimps, now are you going to get going or what?" Her tone was that old familiar voice from the past.

That's all it took. We all picked it up a notch and got her to the top, ten feet ahead of the juniors. We collapsed in an exhausted heap when we crossed the finish line. Next thing we knew, Carl was attacking us. I have to say he did get the best of us. All we could do was laugh and it's hard to wrestle and laugh at the same time.

When we were done sledding, Carl got us all together at the bottom of the hill for instructions for the water park.

"Okay, kids, load up on the bus if you're going to the water park. Remember, gals, no two-piece swimsuits allowed," Carl said.

I noticed Judy asking Becky something and figured out that

Judy didn't have a one-piece suit. Becky talked to Mom and they decided to take Judy to Willmar to quickly find one. The rest of us headed to the water park. Harold, Perry, Dad, and I jumped in the hot tub first. Dad was ribbing Perry about Kill the Carrier. Mom, Becky and Judy got there and in short order. The ninety-foot water slide was the biggest attraction for most of us. We ended up playing other games like freeze tag and blind man's• bluff. Those games usually turned into Kill the Carrier. Dad and Carl set themselves up against Perry, Harold, and me. This game got pretty rough and separated the men from the boys. Dad loved this game, You'd think he was a kid again. He'd grab the ball and start heading straight at one of us with a look of determination on his face. We did well against Carl and Dad, but they were still stronger than us.

I tell you, after skating, sledding, climbing the stairs to the water slide, and then a strong game of Kill the Carrier, I was one tired and hungry boy. Carl ordered pizza after swimming and that was a welcome sight. Everyone chowed pizza and told stories of the evening. Judy fit in pretty well from what I could see. The pizza was getting scarce and it was time to head home.

Carl gathered us together and said, "Hey, did everyone have fun?"

"Yes, sir!"

"How 'bout we go back to the sledding hill?"

"No, sir!"

"Guys, I want to thank Judy for coming tonight, and Judy, we hope to see you on Wednesday nights. You know you are more than welcome. Okay, let's close in prayer and we'll get everyone home. Lord, we thank you for the safety tonight. We thank you for the laughs tonight. We thank you for the food. Lord, we thank you for exercise. We ask for a safe trip home and a good night's rest. Amen."

Winter in Minnesota can get long. This winter was certainly showing us that. In March we still had a couple days of twenty below zero. I didn't hitch Pete and Joe much in February or March; between cold and wind it was hard to get motivated to hitch. Many days it seemed all we got done was move snow, haul manure, and thaw water troughs. Mom and Dad took a couple of weekends off, so that left chores for Becky and me.

By the end of March, spring was finally starting to come around. Pete and Joe would lay their black bodies down in the white snow and absorb as much heat as possible. As the days got warmer, they got friskier. Even the cows got frisky as the days warmed up. The annual frost heaves on the roads showed up and made driving tough on some roads. The frost can go down six feet in our part of the country. As soon as the frost is out, our friendly pocket gophers start digging. This is the best time to catch them so Fuzz and I would make the rounds.

We were trapping at Mr. Olson's one day and went into the barn to say hello. "Did you see the mound on the east side of the grainary, Jude?" he asked.

"Yes, sir."

"Jude, take a look at the auction bill in the milk house. I think there's a few things I might bid on. If you'd like to go with, I'd appreciate it."

Fuzz and I grabbed the sale bill and brought it back out by Mr. Olson. One of the main pictures was a fancy hitch wagon. There were a lot of draft horse items on the bill so it was hard to tell what Mr. Olson might be after. "I give up," I said. "Which items are you looking at?"

He stood there with a grin. "Jude, I've always dreamed of owning a nice hitch wagon. And if you'll notice I'm not getting any younger, so I'm going to be looking hard at that and the patent leather show harness to go along with. Now are you going or not?"

"Wow, that is pretty neat, Mr. Olson. Sure I'll go, if it's okay with Dad."

"Why certainly, why certainly." He hesitated as he took off his hat and scratched his head. "You never know when my neighbor kid will need that wagon for his wedding day." He laughed.

"Now don't go getting me hitched too soon, even if you do have a fancy hitch wagon! Fuzz and I got to go. I'll check with Dad on that auction and let you know."

As we walked home all I could think about was that auction coming up. It was funny to see how excited Mr. Olson was as he talked about it. We set a few more gopher traps on the way home. As soon as I got home I showed Dad the auction bill and asked if I could go. He said the only way I could go is if he went with.

That next Saturday we all did chores a little early and headed for the auction. It was about two hours from home so we took a flatbed trailer just in case Mr. Olson bought the wagon. The auction site was buzzing with people. Dad and I followed as Mr.

Olson made his way to the wagon. He went over it with a fine tooth comb, checking the wheels and bearings, the fifth wheel gear, looking for dry rot. The wagon was in very good shape. It was white with maroon trim and the leaf springs were extremely heavy duty. The front and back axles each had forge welds in them so that meant it was very old.

Mr. Olson rubbed his chin. "Why certainly."

Yes, Mr. Olson seemed to like what he saw. We looked at it for awhile, then we searched for the show harness. The show harness was on a team of Belgians in the barn. The harness was like brand new. It was patent leather with wheat hames, full Scotch collar housings and chrome hardware. I just stood back and watched as Mr. Olson studied the harness.

As he looked he mumbled, "Looks very sharp."

Dad, Mr. Olson, and I got some bidding numbers and looked at the other equipment for sale. Dad bought us lunch at the chow wagon and the sale got started. The auctioneer announced the sequence of the sale. Like we figured, the harness and wagon were to be one of the last things to go. I bought an evener and neck yoke, and Dad got a couple good hay forks.

Mr. Olson was very calm as the day went on. Soon the owners were hitching the Belgians to the hitch wagon to bring them into a round pen. It didn't take long and that round pen was surrounded by people. Mr. Olson stood on a hay rack so he could see above the crowd. They started with the Belgians, then the harness, and at last the wagon. Dad and I stood by Mr. Olson to help keep track of the bids.

There seemed to be lots of bidders on the Belgians. They were well-broke and well- matched, just the wrong color for a Percheron guy. The auctioneer started on the harness right after the horses sold. Mr. Olson stood there motionless for the longest time, and I was wondering what he was waiting for. I thought he had changed his mind about the harness. I was wrong. He soon entered a bid and stayed right with it.

The auctioneer shouted, "Going, going, gone, to the gentleman on the hay rack. Your number please!"

I watched Mr. Olson closely after he got the final bid. I thought he would react with excitement or something. He just stood there, expressionless while I was about to do cart-wheels in excitement.

The auctioneer continued, "Folks, take a look at this fine hitch wagon! Wagons like this are hard to come by, so don't let this one get away. The paperwork shows all the cost of the restoration that was done three years ago. Now who's going to be the proud owner of this fine showpiece?"

The bidding started and it was a frenzy. I bet there were eight bidders going and Mr. Olson wasn't one of them. He stood there stoic as can be, then he looked in his pocket at a slip of paper. Right after that he sent his first bid in. One of the spotters came his way and watched his every move after that. Several bidders were bowing out and soon it was Mr. Olson and a gentleman in a gray jacket left bidding. The auctioneer would go back and forth between Mr. Olson and the guy in the gray coat. The other bidder would take his time but Mr. Olson would counter his bid immediately. When it was over, Mr. Olson was the new owner of that hitch wagon!

I heard him murmur to himself, "Why certainly, why certainly." Dad and I shook his hand as he stood there. "Jude, Bud, that's over with! If you don't mind, I'll go and pay my debts if you guys would start rounding up the harness and the wagon."

Dad and I helped them unhitch from the wagon and pull harnesses. We brought the truck and trailer closer to load the wagon. We put the ramps down and asked for some help and pushed the wagon on by hand. Dad started to strap it down while I loaded eveners, harness parts, and the pole to the wagon.

We were just finishing when Mr. Olson got back. "Boys, looks like I missed all the fun." Mr. Olson double-checked the straps and inventory to make sure we had all the items we needed. We loaded up in the truck and down the road we headed. Mr. Olson was pretty chipper as we drove along. "Ya know, tomorrow I just might have to hitch Molly and Ladd and see if they can pull this here wagon. Why certainly."

We stopped a couple times and checked straps to make sure things were tight and soon we pulled into his driveway. We got things unloaded and Dad and I headed home for chores. Sure enough, after church the next day Mr. Olson pulled up our drive with Molly and Ladd in the patent leather show harness pulling the hitch wagon. He was all smiles. Becky took many pictures of him and we all took a quick ride. It was great, sitting up that high and looking down on the horses, turning on a dime and hearing the sound of the heavy wheels crushing little stones under all the weight. Mr. Olson showed us the brakes in action and backed it up like he was backing up to a loading dock, which is what the hitch wagons were used for years ago. They were Dray wagons, hauling freight around town and backing into tight spaces. I followed him home and helped him put his prize hitch wagon and harness away.

We had some nice spring rains in mid April. This was good for the hay crops and for getting the last of the frost out of the ground. Pete and Joe hauled many loads of manure that spring. I would pitch loads by hand just for exercise. Pete and Joe were muscled out very well, now that they were three years old and working almost daily.

Every once in a while I talked Becky into pitching a load with me. Becky was on one side of the manure spreader pitching and I on the other side. She took a little break and looked my way. "Jude, this is your last year of high school."

"Yeah, I guess so."

"What are you doing for prom?"

"Now, Becky, what makes you ask that? Nothing, I guess, unless you want to go with me," I laughed. "Besides you're looking at the world's worst dancer!"

"It's not all about dancing! I just hope you don't regret not going, there are a lot of nice girls that would love to go with you."

"I really haven't thought much about it, I kind of told God I wouldn't date till I was older and out of high school."

"In one month you'll be out of high school. Going to your senior prom is not dating, think about it." She shook her head. "Men!"

A couple days later I was at Wednesday night youth group. Becky had stayed home with a sore throat. Judy was attending most of the time, ever since she came to the Lord. It was kind of ironic that Carl spoke of dating that night and how young kids can go too far and dishonor God. He even mentioned prom night as being very dangerous for young kids. Youth group ended and Perry, Harold, and I talked awhile, then we headed to our cars to go home. As I reached for the door handle of my car, I heard someone call my name. It was Judy. "Do you think you could drop me off on your way home?"

"Sure, hop in."

As I drove, Judy brought up the theme that Carl had spoken of, dating and proms. "Last year I went to prom for all the wrong reasons. I got drunk and oh my, I don't even want to think of it again." She stumbled for more words. "Jude, I hope you don't think of this as brash and I'll understand if you say no, but I would really like to go to the prom with you."

There was a long silence from both of us. I was running many things through my mind. The main thought was I really had no intention of going to prom. I searched for the right words to give back to Judy. We were just pulling into her drive as I spoke. "Thanks for asking me to go, Judy. I need a couple days to think about this. I want you to know that I had no intention of going to prom this year, so I haven't given it much thought."

"I'm sorry, Jude, I shouldn't have asked you. I feel like such an imbecile."

"Judy, that's okay! I'm glad you asked. Let me get back to you by Friday at school, okay?"

With that, Judy headed into her house and I headed home. My mind was going back and forth about prom. I tried to picture Judy and me as prom dates and just couldn't get that in my head. I have to admit that Judy's past came to mind again.

The next morning as Becky and I ate breakfast with Mom, prom was the center of their conversation. "So did ya say yes?" was Becky's question.

"How did you know she was going to ask me?"

"It's a girl thing. You'll never understand. So what did you tell her?"

"Okay, kids," Mom said with a smile on her face, "who is asking who to what?"

"Judy asked very nicely if I would consider taking her to senior prom."

"And what did you tell her?" Mom asked.

"That I really had no intention of going this year, but I would give her an answer by Friday."

Becky put in her two cents' worth. "I think you should say yes."

Mom said, "Jude, it is your last opportunity for prom, but it's up to you. You're a big boy now so pray about it and let her know. Now you two better get off to school before you're late. Skedaddle."

As Becky and I drove to school we talked more about prom. She was pretty good friends with Judy now, so she explained that Judy's heart was pure in asking me. It was a little awkward in school when I saw Judy. She didn't want to look me in the eye much and I rehashed it in my mind each time we passed. Harold and Perry encouraged me to go to prom. Much to my surprise, Perry was taking Becky.

That evening I prayed about it and soon, I was dialing Judy's phone number.

"Hello?"

"Is Judy there?"

"This is me."

"Judy, this is Jude. How are you doing?"

"Fine, and you?"

"I have decided to go to prom this year, but I'm asking this new girl at our school."

There was a silent pause at the other end. "I understand, that's fine. But I can't think of any new girls at school."

"You haven't noticed the new Christian girl in school? She's taller than average, blond hair, and very pretty. The only problem is she kind of owes me a cake." I was biting my lip to stop from laughing.

There was even a longer pause at the other end. "Jude, are talking about me? Are you accepting my invite to the prom?"

"It depends on the cake."

"Remember what the Bible states about forgiveness," She laughed.

"Judy, if your offer is still valid I would like to take you to prom. Now can I speak with your dad to get his permission?"

She quickly said, "Oh, ah, he's not home right now."

I could sense some tension in her voice. "Are you okay, Judy?"

"Oh, yes, I'm fine and I do thank you for calling, and I look forward to prom. I've got some homework so I better go. See ya in school."

As soon as I hung up the phone Mom and Becky were waiting for an answer, so I sidestepped them without making eye contact and went on my way. Next thing I knew they each had a hold of my ears. Boy, if that doesn't make a guy stop in his tracks!

I went on my knees. "Okay, okay, I'll tell you anything you need to know!" They increased the pressure. "Promise!" "Ouch, I promise." Wow, God didn't intend ears to be bent in those directions. "Yes, I'm going to prom."

"Is that all you've got to say about it?" Becky hollered.

"Remember I promised to tell you everything you Need to know. You don't need to know the rest." I covered up my ears.

With her motherly voice, Mom said, "Maybe you don't NEED

supper tonight, young man." There she was not playing fair again. Why do mothers always barter with food? I was a growing boy.

"I'm really not hungry tonight. I'll probably go to bed early and pray for you and Becky."

Before I knew it, they each had one of my thumbs in their grips. Now that's dangerous territory, let me tell you. I was screaming uncle within seconds. We sat there and I told them every detail of Judy's and my conversation. They each sat there starry-eyed. It's amazing how God wires ladies different from men. They asked what I was going to wear, where I would buy flowers, what restaurant we would go to, and then Becky asked the most profound question of all. "What color ribbons do you want in the geldings?"

"What color what?"

"Duh! Jude, you are taking the geldings to prom aren't you? If you don't, I will!"

"It never crossed my mind to take the geldings. I'm glad I thought of it! The ribbons will have to match her dress, Becky."

"Okay, Jude, since I have to figure out your prom night for you, here is the rest of the story. You will use Mr. Olson's new harness and wagon. Navy blue ribbons in their manes and tails will match her dress and your suit. Dad will have the geldings and wagon at the elevator in town for you and Judy to climb aboard for the Grand March. Do you have any questions?"

I sheepishly asked, "What color undies will I have on?"

"Knowing you, pink." Becky laughed.

I soon found out Becky really had thought all this stuff out beforehand. She had asked Judy if she would mind the horse ride and what color dress she would wear. Judy and Becky were in agreement on all issues, they just needed me to ask Judy to prom. I was fine with what they had planned. I know Becky was only helping me out, and she had become good friends with Judy.

That weekend I headed to Mr. Olson's to check on the harness and hitch wagon. "Mr. Olson, I'm almost afraid to ask because it's not right, but would you consider renting your hitch wagon to me for prom night?" As I asked, I decided not to mention the harness.

His answer came very abruptly. "Nope."

Wow! I didn't know what to say next.

"Jude, do you have to rent your dad's tractor or car?"

"No, sir."

"Why do you think you would have to rent my new harness and wagon then? I never had a wife or kids and I consider you and Becky as my own kin. Don't take the joy away from me by offering payment for something I consider a privilege. When I bought that old wagon and harness I had you in mind just as much as me. Now I expect you to use that wagon for prom and someday I want to see you and your bride perched on that seat! The only thing I ask of you is this," he slowly looked away. "If Molly and Ladd are still alive, please use them with the wagon for my funeral. If not, use Pete and Joe." He looked me straight in the eye for an answer.

"I promise, Mr. Olson. Yes, sir, I promise. Who says you are going first though? Maybe I'll need that wagon for my funeral first."

"Now if we're not careful we will be crying like a couple little school girls!" He laughed. I double-thanked him for all his kindness and headed home. Soon it was the day of prom. I got up early and washed the hitch wagon and helped load it on the trailer. I came home and washed Pete and Joe. After washing I tied them in the barn so they wouldn't roll in the dirt.

"Boys, you have to be looking pretty sharp tonight. We are going to be watched by many people. Let's give them a show!" I hugged each of them for a long time and left the barn. I hooked the pickup truck to the horse trailer and checked the tire pressure in all the tires. I checked the list I made for things to take with and realized I had forgotten my top hat that Mom bought me.

I was soon on my way to pick up Judy for early dinner. I was very nervous as this was really my first date with anyone. When I was younger, Dad talked of being very careful of dating in high school. I was curious which restaurant Judy had picked. This was her surprise to me that evening. My palms were all sweaty as I drove down Judy's driveway. This would be the first time I would meet her Dad. There I was ringing the front doorbell of Judy Clemon's house on prom night.

Her mother answered the door. "Mrs. Clemons, I'm Jude Bonner. I'm glad to see you again."

"Oh yes, and nice to see you, step in." She turned and yelled upstairs. "Judy your date is here, Hurry up! You don't want to keep him waiting."

"Were in no hurry, Mrs. Clemons."

Just then a man who I assumed was Judy's dad came around

the corner. "Chuck, this is Jude Bonner, Judy's prom date."
He slowly staggered his way to me and shook my hand.
The smell of alcohol was overwhelming. He was drunk, slurred
speech and all. I tried to make small talk as we three stood there.
Chuck would start on some story that seemed inappropriate for
the setting and Mrs. Clemons would nervously interrupt him and
change the subject.

"Mrs. says you're one of those religious people."

"Mr. Clemons, I'm a follower of Jesus Christ."

I knew I didn't want to ignore that type of question from him.
That would be denying God and the Bible warns against that. My
statement seemed to sober him up some.

"So you think I'm going to hell."

Just then Judy started her descent down the stairs. As I looked
up, I thought, "Wow! She is beautiful." Her dress was just
right and her hair was all up and wavy. I just stood there shell-
shocked. All my attention was on her. She smiled at me and I
think I just gave a blank stare back. I was just dazed. I finally
came to my senses and gave her my hand for the last couple
steps. We locked eyes for what seemed an eternity. Our gaze was
broken by Mr. Clemons statement.

"You religious ----"

Judy cut him off right there. "Dad, shut your mouth. This is my
prom night and you aren't going to ruin it." Yes, sir, Judy put him
in his place and I actually saw hints of the old Judy in that attack.
Mr. Clemons staggered to his chair and sat motionless. Mrs.
Clemons took us to the front yard and got some pictures. We said
our goodbyes and headed down the driveway. I could tell Judy
was on edge so I stopped at the end of the driveway.

"Judy, please know that I understand and don't let this ruin our
evening. Now let's pray and give it to God and let him deal with
it." Judy and I prayed and she seemed much better afterward. "I
want you to know how nice you look in that dress and your hair,
I've never seen it like that before."

"Your mother and Becky helped me pick out the dress two
weeks before you asked me to prom. We had so much fun that
day. Becky is so lucky to have a mother like your mom. If it
wasn't for them and you, I'd probably be going to this prom
drunk again."

I didn't want to think about that, so I changed the subject.
"Okay Judy what restaurant did you choose?"

"First we need to go over to Harold's place and meet up with them."

"Yes, ma'am. And by the way, did I mention how nice you look this evening?"

We pulled into Harold's and it seemed like everyone was meeting at Harold's place. Perry was there with Becky, along with Will and his date. And there was Mom with Harold's mother and dad fixing on a big outdoor barbecue. Come to find out we were all eating there instead of going to a fancy restaurant. The food was great! Watermelon balls, vegetable dip, hot wings, baked beans, wild rice, brats, burgers with big slabs of onion, potato salad, and chips. Mom and Harold's mother served us as we sat around two picnic tables in a screened in tent. The finishing touch was added when they brought out the pies; lemon, pecan, banana, and coconut cream.

After dinner we had some group pictures taken, along with couple's pictures. So far the evening was going great. Judy seemed to have put her father's episode behind her, the weather was perfect, and we all had full bellies. We soon split up to head in for the grand march. Harold and Becky were driving a 1957 Black Chevy Nomad. Perry had a '69 Mustang, and Will had a 1975 Corvette. For the moment Judy and I had our minivan.

"Jude, I want you to know that I thank you for taking me tonight, and I hope you're having a good time because I certainly am."

"Yes, this is awesome so far."

We pulled into the driveway where Dad and Mr. Olson were waiting with Pete and Joe. Mr. Olson had them braided to the tee. They were just leading the geldings up to the wagon as we came to a stop. In my excitement I got out and started to help them.

Dad gave me a look. "Jude, you let us do this! I believe you have a door to open for a very pretty young lady!"

"My goodness," I thought, "what kind of gentleman am I?" I hurried back to the car and slowly opened Judy's door and reached out my hand. She elegantly took my hand and stood facing me. "Judy, I'm truly sorry."

Judy said nothing. We stood there gazing into each other's eyes, her blue eyes mesmerized me in my tracks. As I stood there I spoke with God and thanked him for creating the opposite sex! The beauty of a woman is so intriguing. I was studying every angle of her face, eyes, nose, and cheek bones. I thought of kissing her but knew I shouldn't.

We were both in a trance when it hit me, so soft and so silent, bird poop on the lapel of my suit! That certainly put an end to the staring match. Judy laughed hysterically as I looked for the bird. It was a filthy starling. When Judy finally stopped laughing she helped me clean the lapel off with a paper towel. We got most of it off.

Dad and Mr. Olson were waiting for us. Dad held the geldings as I helped Judy up to the wagon seat. This is quite an ordeal for someone in a prom dress. I got her settled and came back down to go to my side. I stopped and talked with Pete and Joe a little. I made my way up my side and sat by my prom date. Dad took several more pictures and then we headed up town. We had a little extra time so we traveled down several streets before heading to school. Many street rods were among us, and people would come out of their homes and clap as we went past. Pete and Joe were in their glory! They knew this was a special event and they high stepped their way, heads up and proud as can be. Judy held my arm as I drove. I would look her way and smile as she was taking it all in. I whistled at Pete and Joe and they whinnied back.

We got into line right behind Greg Shants' truck with the loud pipes. This wasn't ideal but we were in a tunnel of people and couldn't turn around. I kept my distance so the noise wouldn't bother us too much. We sat back as Greg unloaded with his date, which gave us some extra room so I could trot the geldings into the unloading zone. I collected the bits in their mouths and whistled to them and off we went. Pete and Joe were in perfect stride with each other at a full trot, and the crowd erupted with applause. They whinnied and tucked their heads into the bits, mane ribbons flowing in the breeze. Cameras went off like the fourth of July! Pete and Joe were stealing the show. Dad was waiting at the unloading zone standing right in front of where we were to stop. I kept them geldings at a full trot and at the last second brought them to a stop with a hearty, "Whoa!"

Pete and Joe stopped within three inches of Dad's face and Dad didn't even blink. This sent the crowd into another round of applause. Pete and Joe snorted a little and stood there dancing ever so slightly as I helped Judy down from the wagon. We stood for a few more pictures and then we headed in to the school. As I looked back, the crowd was still clapping as Dad headed the geldings out of the parking lot.

The prom committee had the school gym looking very nice. We sat at a table with Perry and Becky, Harold, Will and their dates. The band was doing a fine job mixing slow dances with faster dances. The only problem was, several times as I danced with Judy, Greg Shants bumped into me. I think he was drunk. Ever since Judy came to Christ he seemed even more bent on hatred. I asked Harold, off to the side, "Have you had any run-ins with Greg on the dance floor?"

"Yes, sir, and my patience is wearing thin. I think the loser is drunk again."

The king and queen of prom were elected and seated on their thrones and then it was time for the dance contest. Perry and Becky had actually practiced for the event at home. Our whole table entered and we were dancing our hearts out. If Mrs. Norman tapped you on the shoulder you were out, and Greg Shants and his date were one of the first to go. I watched out of the corner of my eye and he seemed pretty upset. Judy and I were tapped out pretty early too. Becky and Harold were still going strong. Judy and I were cheering them on as they cut the rug.

I could smell the beer before I saw him. Greg came from behind me and purposefully bumped into me as I stood along the dance floor. I almost fell over from the hit. "What's the matter, Bible Boy? Can't stand up?" It was hard but I ignored him. The dance contest was getting stronger and louder. "Judy, how about coming home with me tonight? I could teach you how to break several of those Bible commandments!"

That was it. I grabbed him by his sport coat and got in his face. I was irate. "You watch your mouth around my date!"

"Now boys, what's going on here? My, my, Greg, Jude, do we need to call your parents?" Mrs. Norman broke it up.

Greg slowly walked away, but that didn't mean it was over. Judy and I brought our attention back to the dance contest. The dancers were on their last dance of the contest, a swing- style dance. Perry and Becky ramped it up. They fed off the crowd as they flew around the dance floor. Yes, sir, when it was over they were number one. Judy ran up and gave Becky a big hug.

As they celebrated the win, I headed to the back restroom. As I rounded the dark corner something hit me right in the stomach. I bent over in pain.

"Bible Boy, what do you think of that? Where is your Jesus now?"

As Greg stood there laughing I rammed my right shoulder into his gut and drove him back into the lockers with a loud crash. He clenched his fists together and slammed them into my kidneys. That hit forced me to the floor, as I withered in pain. I was struggling to get back up as Greg kicked me hard in the stomach. Wow! I went back down sucking for air.

Greg stood over me. "You Jesus Freak. From now on keep your Jesus to yourself." As he wound up to kick me again. "If you think God is so strong, take this!"

I was able to duck his kick and scurried to my feet as Greg lost his balance after missing me. I was heading his way to give him more when somebody grabbed both my arms, it was Nick Grudden and Bill Masters. I struggled to get free as Greg slowly approached me and drove his fist into my gut again. I doubled over in pain as Greg's punches were powerful. I was defenseless as Nick and Bill held me up like a human punching bag. I tried to tighten my stomach muscles before each blow. Greg had a smirk on his face as he planned each hit. I decided the only way I could somewhat win this battle is through Jesus Christ. I started reciting the Lord's Prayer with all my mental energy. After the Lord's Prayer I went into other scriptures, yes I could still feel the punches but it didn't matter anymore, I was talking with my Jesus!

Bill and Nick started to tell Greg I had enough, I really think the word of God was bothering them.

Greg paced in front of me. "You think you're so high and mighty you holy roller!" The strong smell of alcohol spewed from his mouth when he bent down and whispered in my ear as I hung there face down. "Bible boy, I'm gonna make sure you remember this prom, yes sir!"

He grabbed my hair and wrenched my head back as he swung hard with a left into my mouth. It was finished. Nick and Bill dropped me to the floor.

I lay there as my lip bled onto the hard floor while my stomach was in knots. I quietly prayed. "Lord Jesus, help me." I crawled to the bathroom and pulled myself up by the sink. I turned on the cold water and buried my face in it over and over. I straightened up and looked in the mirror at my swollen lip, it wasn't as bad as I thought. I gradually tucked my shirt in and fixed my tie. I arched my back to stretch my stomach muscles and tried walking a little. My gut was super tight and sore but actually I was doing

God's plans for you?"

"Could be true, I guess. Get up Pete, Joe."

"Have you ever thought about all the times Judy has been in your life, both good and bad? Do you really think it is just a coincidence that she was your bitter enemy, and the next thing you're doing is carrying her into our house after the accident, and then you're the vessel that helped lead her to Christ!" She shook her head as I stopped the horses. "She baked a cake for you. She almost had to beg you to go to prom! This has God written all over it!"

I sat there trying to think of some type of answer. I felt myself getting mad, confused, and humbled all at the same time. Was Becky right? Had I been blinded to God's work? Had I been disrespectful to Judy? I didn't know what to say, I sat there starring out into nothing.

"Jude, I love you as my big brother, but I think you need to wake up before God takes her away."

I tied the reins back and wrung my hands together, looking for the right words. "Maybe you're right Becky. I'm not sure what to do? I know this much, horses are a whole lot easier to deal with than girls."

"We're not that bad."

I sat there trying to talk but words were not there to be spoken. I swallowed hard a couple times and stood up. "Becky, I'm afraid. So maybe it would be better if God did take Judy away. Ya see, I've had the same dream a couple times, a nightmare would be a better word."

Becky had a concerned look on her face. "Can you tell me about it?"

"I don't know, it's so creepy. Each time it is the same and I'm trying to figure out the meaning. Pete and Joe are there, Judy, Mom, Dad, Mr. Olson, even Greg Shants. Pete and Joe are acting real nervous like something is bothering them. Judy and Mom are crying, and nothing I say helps them. Greg Shants is there but I don't know why? Each morning after waking from that nightmare, it's the only thing I can focus on."

"Wow Jude that does seem strange! I'm sure glad I don't remember my dreams."

"At the end of the dream God is there and He seems to be talking me into 'Surrendering the Reins.' "

We sat there in silence. Becky broke the silence. "At least God is in the dream!"

That got me thinking! "How can I call it a nightmare if God is in it? God has been with me all these years. Without Him I fail every time. Look at all God has done for me, His saving grace, Pete and Joe, He kept them alive for me, gave me the strength to deal with Greg and Judy." I started to laugh a little. "I almost forgot Mom, Dad, a great sister named Becky, and Mr. Olson."

"Don't forget Fuzz!"

"Yes ma'am! Fuzz is pretty special. But you're probably right, God kept sticking Judy in my life until I learned to forgive her and show love instead of hate. God is perfect and has a reason for everything, so I guess we'll see what God has in mind for Judy and me."

About Pete and Joe

Pete was born on March 20th and Joe on March 13th of 2006 on the Art Eller farm near Pierz, Minnesota. Their first six months were spent with their moms and other mares and colts in a beautiful pasture with a fresh water stream running through it. Pete and Joe are half – brothers, with the same sire.

In August of 2006, Les Graham came to inspect Pete and Joe. After Pete and Joe were weaned off their mothers in September of 2006, they were bought by Les Graham of New London, Minnesota and were loaded into a horse trailer for the 80 mile ride home. At home, Pete and Joe shared a pasture with Ladd, a 21 year old Percheron gelding. They did their best to make Ladd's life miserable with their playful antics.

Training started a couple weeks after Pete and Joe were settled in their new home. Pete was fairly easy to train and learned quickly. Joe had his own ideas, so Les spent double the time in training Joe. Training involved learning to lead, feet work, sacking out, backing, honoring a human's space, and eventually hitching with Ladd for pulling. Pete and Joe tried to run away the first couple of times of being hitched, but Ladd kept them in line. Pete and Joe do sleigh rides, cutting and raking hay, some funerals, weddings, and a few parades.

Both Pete and Joe grew up to be around 2100 pounds and close to 18 hands high. Both horses are black with very uncharacteristic white blazes on their faces. Pete has a wide white blaze and a little white on both back feet, while Joe has a narrow white blaze and a little white on one back foot. Pete is as steady as a rock when hitched or ridden and has a very smooth trot. Joe is not as trustworthy as Pete when hitched and requires an experienced driver to keep him in line. Pete loves to be scratched and curried and Joe loves to put his muzzle in your face so you can blow air into his nostrils.

Did You Find the Cross?

Mike Bregel the illustrator has drawn a cross into each illustration. Some are fairly obvious, others are somewhat hidden. Did you see them the first time or do you need to go back and find them?

Thank you so much for your time in reading my novel. Most of my test readers assumed this was a story of Les Graham as a child. The unfortunate answer is kind-of yes. The problem is I was way more like Greg Shants than Jude Bonner.

It's easy to look back and say I wasn't quite as bad as Greg Shants, but I was probably worse! No I didn't do drugs and drink, but I was a secret agent in the world of hate, prejudice, judgment, and pride!

Praise God I had people praying for me for many years. One of those was college roommate Jim Klier. Thank you Jim for not giving up on me!

I accepted God's saving grace on January 18th, 1993. God has blessed me with so many things, one of them is this story He allowed me to write.

Are you spending eternity in heaven or hell? The only way that can be truly answered is to read God's Word. God is VERY clear in His written word on HIS way to heaven, not man's way to heaven.

John 14:6 "I am the way and the truth and the life. No one comes to the Father except through me."

God Bless,

Les Graham

Excerpt from *Surrendering the Reins* by Les Grahm

Copyright © 2014 by Les Graham

Published by:

BRITCHIN BOOKS from Colfax Publishing
616 270th Ave NW Suite G
New London, MN 56273

Chapter 1

"Who Gets Revenge"

In more ways than one Greg Shants was right when he said I would remember prom night. Not only did I go to Prom with a girl that I once despised, but Pete and Joe, my very own Percheron geldings, drove us there. And last but not least, Greg Shants and his boys punched my lights out.

I woke next morning with my stomach killing me. It hurt to breathe, to bend over and to walk. I thought I was going to die as I pitched manure. You never think about your torso muscles until they are screaming for relief from every little thing you do. Chores took longer than normal that morning. I was moving like I was 80 years old. With each shot of pain, I found anger building towards Greg Shants.

I was having a hard time with God for allowing Greg and his boys to have their way with me. I found myself scheming ways to get even, which of course involved me pounding on them in several different scenarios. As always, just like in the movies, I was untouched by the bad guys and they lay there wishing they were never born. I was leaning over the pitch fork in a trance as I pictured myself standing over them victorious!

"Jude, are you alright?" Dad asked as I was startled out of my trance.

I tried to stand upright without Dad seeing I was hurting. "Yeah, I'm fine! I guess I was just day dreaming."

"Son, I thought I would never have to ask you this. Are you hung over?"

I started to laugh but that only made my stomach muscles hurt more! I bent over in pain but I couldn't stop laughing. I'm sure Dad was wondering how I could laugh about his question. I slowly straightened up with the help of the fork handle and looked Dad in the eye.

"Dad, I'm sorry, but no I'm not hung over. Greg and his boys beat the snot out of me last night! My stomach muscles are killing me this morning. You caught me thinking of how I was going to get even."

"Is that all that's wrong?" Dad laughed a little. "I was worried there for a second."

"Is that all! You make it sound like those jerks beating the crap out of me is okay! Whose side are you on?"

Dad scratched his forehead as he thought. "I'm on God's side, and you know what the Bible says about pride and how it comes before the fall." Dad walked away and left me standing there dumbfounded! How could dad blame me? What did I do wrong? What pride do I have? All these questions came to mind as I followed dad in for breakfast. With each step my anger was building. I slammed the back door as I stepped into the utility room.

"Dad, we need to talk. How can you stand there and tell me this is my fault?"

"Jude, after breakfast you need to use the concordance in the back of your Bible and look up pride, revenge, and forgiveness. Talk with God as you look up all the verses related to those words. Let God tell you where you're at!" He started laughing softly while stirring his coffee. "Oh how I remember when I got my bell rung back in third grade by Sam Turnquist. I came home looking for sympathy from my mother, thinking she would fix everything. She gave me a little hug, looked me in the eye and said I would be fine. Jude, you're putting a lot of energy into this fight you had and rightly so, but this is how God builds you and teaches you. Someday you'll look back on this and chuckle at how small it is compared to other mountains God wants you to climb."

"But Dad, it was three against one!"

"Jude, read those Bible verses and pray about it! Romans 12:19 talks about not seeking revenge and allowing God's wrath to work! Satan is telling you to get revenge, God is telling you that He will do it. Who are you going to listen to? Now if I was a young man in this situation I would be doing pull ups, pushups and building some strength just in case God uses you to bring His wrath to Mr. Greg Shants."

About the Illustrator

Mike Bregel was born in 1987 in the frozen tundra of Willmar, Minnesota. He studied graphic design at the University of Minnesota Duluth. He has shown work at the Tweed Museum of Art and won the Howard W. Lyons/ Alice Tweed Tuohy Award at the U of M Duluth Annual Juried Student Show. Since then Mike has been on a creative roller coaster that has included freelance illustration, commissioned paintings and professional web & print design. He co-owns and designs for Horizon Clothing Company and currently works as a creative marketing specialist at Life-Science Innovations.

You can find more of his work at bregelart.com